Dr. Edith Vane and the Hares of Crawley Hall

Suzette Mayr

Coach House Books, Toronto

first edition

Conseil des Arts
du Canada

Published with the generous assistance of the Canada Council for the Arts and the Ontario Arts Council. Coach House Books also acknowledges the support of the Government of Canada through the Canada Book Fund and the Government of Ontario through the Ontario Book Publishing Tax Credit.

This book is a work of fiction. Names, characters, places, and incidents are products of the author's imagination or are used fictitiously. Any resemblance to actual events or locales or persons, living or dead, is entirely coincidental.

LIBRARY AND ARCHIVES CANADA CATALOGUING IN PUBLICATION

Mayr, Suzette, author
Dr. Edith Vane and the hares of Crawley Hall / by Suzette Mayr.

Issued in print and electronic formats.
ISBN 978-1-55245-349-0 (softcover)

I. Title.

PS8576.A9D72 2017 C813'.54 C2017-900547-2

Dr. Edith Vane and the Hares of Crawley Hall is available as an ebook: ISBN 978 1 77056 504 3 (EPUB), ISBN 978 1 77056 505 0 (PDF), ISBN 978 1 77056 506 7 (Kindle).

Purchase of the print version of this book entitles you to a free digital copy. To claim your ebook of this title, please email sales@chbooks.com with proof of purchase. (Coach House Books reserves the right to terminate the free digital download offer at any time.)

For Robyn Read and Jonathan Ball
There from the beginning(s)

‘Imagine the iron rebar skeleton inside,
the bones for this rugged flesh.’
– Mark Kingwell, *Concrete Reveries*

‘ ... college and university professors,
those lepidopterists of literature ... ’
– Stephen King, *Danse Macabre*

August

The washing machine dings in its tiny closet.

The washing machine dings a second time, clunks, sounds out three half spurts, then clunks one more time. Edith pushes herself away from her desk, slings open the washing machine door. Her clothes slump into a soggy pile, scattered with chunks of undissolved laundry soap.

She needs a new washing machine. She has no time to buy a new washing machine. She wonders how anyone ever finds the time to make a major purchase like a washing machine, and how she can become one of these people. So serene, so capable. She has so much work to do: her Academic Achievement Overview, course outlines, a unit assessment report, emails. She slams closed the washing machine, wedges herself back into her desk chair. The washing machine simmers, clicks. Sick and resentful. She hoists herself up from her nest of books and papers and presses every single button one after the other on the control panel. She clicks every button exactly ten more times. The machine pings, clinks, thumps, but the clothes refuse to move, the water refuses to gush.

She pads back to her office. A crooked stack of papers on her desk slides, fans, flutters to the floor.

Screw it.

She scoops up her car keys and screeches off in her cracked-up red Ford Taurus to Bull Head Shopping Centre to buy a new machine. Her car buzzes past the University of Inivea campus, but she refuses to look in that direction, Crawley Hall crouched near the edge of the highway, its boxy presence chiding her like an unfun aunt.

Fifteen minutes later, Edith bypasses the endless escalator chain that leads to the household appliances floor, seduced instead by the starburst of perfumes and jewellery on the main floor. The perfume sample on her left wrist smells like vanilla pudding, her right wrist wooden petunias. She adores them both but cannot make up her mind. A pearl bracelet burbles at her in its blue velvet bowl. So refined. So Jackie O. So much money.

She jams her purse into her armpit, bullets for the escalator and the washing machines.

At the very last microsecond, she swerves.

Eighty-nine minutes later, Edith's feet whine in their strapped loafers. Her shoulders slump. She stands, sixth in line, at the glass-and-white-quartz counter in P. T. Madden, the new women's clothing store to the left of the caramel popcorn stand at the south end of the shopping mall. To the right of the faux-Victorian lotion shop that sells hand lotion for $125 a tube. A part of the mall she never visits, but her mother's birthday looms. Edith wants to buy hand lotion made from avocado, goat's milk, and Bali sea foam to spoil her mother, her mother's hands rough as Brillo pads from so many years as a hairdresser, and her mother agrees once a year at her birthday to indulge in a bucket of caramel corn even though she has to take out her three false teeth to do so. Edith noticed a professor from the School of Drama and Philosophy in Edith's university was browsing in P. T. Madden, so she zoomed in, sorted through hangers and geometrically folded stacks of clothing, then settled on three new blouses and a stiff cardigan. She knows the patterns are wrong; her mother's always reminding her she doesn't have the body type for patterns. – Your boobs turn patterns into porridge, Edith Lynn, her mother reminds her. Frequently.

When she was a teenager and she'd show off her new clothes to her father, he would tsk and down another cognac. – I'm not sure why, he'd say, – you gravitate to clothes that make you look like ... a dining room table.

His daughter a porridgy, furniture-shaped disappointment.

Her parents' wardrobes always so natty, so on point and properly symmetrical.

She shouldn't be spilling money on clothes. She should be planted in front of her desk at home. Or in her Crawley Hall office, burrowing into her books and papers for her next conference, her next peer-reviewed article, like a proper professor. Or at the very least filling out her Academic Achievement Overview.

But Vivianne said she could shop. Said Edith *should* shop, as a reward to herself. One blouse has tiny navy-blue flowers clustered all over, like in a rock garden in a murder mystery where someone is about to get smacked from behind with a rusty, dirt-crusted shovel. But you can't tell they're flowers unless you're extremely close. She loves their tediousness, the repetitiveness of their petals, stamens, leaves. She strokes the collar. The dry, textile fragrance. She deserves these clothes. For she is finally the author of a bona fide *book*.

Her heart flutters, like the pages of a discarded paperback. It took her nineteen years to write *Taber Corn Follies: The Western Canadian Life Story of Beulah Crump-Withers*, soon to be published by University of Okotoks Press, a William Kurelek prairie painting reproduction on the cover. Twelve years as a PhD student, seven as a professor, and just in time for this year's Academic Achievement Overview. The giant diamond that will sit in the platinum, Times New Roman setting of her AAO. The pages being folded and glued likely at this very second on a massive printing press. She can't wait for the buzz of the intercom in her condominium lobby, the mail carrier in his or her smart uniform asking her to sign for the cardboard package, her slicing open the package to copies of her very own book with her very own name on it, the pages smelling of coastal forest and binding glue, the covers shiny and perfect, then moistened with her tears of elation and success. Her discovery and revival of the lost work of Beulah Crump-Withers, former sporting girl, then housewife, prairie poet, maven memoirist, and all-round African-Canadian *literary genius*, finally complete.

She hugs the new clothes to her chest. *Beulah*.

The cardigan will drape long, like a cape with sleeves. An *author's* cardigan.

Edith wonders if maybe she could somehow reboot her washing machine by unplugging it, then plugging it back in? If she runs a cycle without detergent or clothes, just hot water, maybe the machine will resurrect and return to her? She strokes the new clothes in her arms, their uncomplicated cleanness. It's too bad she can't phone Coral for washing machine repair advice. Coral would know.

The professor from Drama and Philosophy left the store almost forty-eight minutes ago, and Edith has no idea what she bought, but she estimates that all the other female professors who have published books wear long cardigans like this, or unstructured blazers that drop past the hips, or skirts that fall below the knee. Patterned blouses. She has never managed to dress au courant. She imagines she would be happier in the 1920s housewife clothes Beulah wore. Dresses recycled from sturdy, sprightly patterned flour sacks. A single, Sunday-best dress for special occasions. Her outfits always morph into ill-fitting costumes once she rolls her car up to the university campus, sits through meetings, pontificates in classrooms. But this year will be different. This year she will look like everyone else. With a book, she will *be* like everyone else. And finally Beulah will get her due and eventually settle into her place in the Canadian literary canon. This year will be perfect.

She tugs a credit card from her wallet, deposits the ironed folds on the counter, their buttons ticking on the glass. Her watch bangs the glass too: 3:03 p.m. This afternoon is drifting away from her.

A pair of fake pearl earrings, each pearl the size of a knuckle, perches on an oily faux-satin ball under the glass of the counter.

– I'll need those too, she says. She taps her credit card on the glass. – And this scarf. Please.

She twitches a scarf from a stand on the counter, it waterfalls into her hands. She smiles at the clerk. The clerk shows Edith her teeth.

She could perhaps wear the scarf, an airy tulle thing with harlequin diamonds, around her neck. The pattern moves her, the cloudiness. But she never wears scarves. At best she might twirl around with it exactly once in her bedroom, pretending she's Josephine Baker. But then it will likely just go in a drawer. Or she'll tie it around the handle of the small suitcase she takes to conferences.

She needs the proper clothes to start the academic new year right. Her new psychologist told her to try it. – They don't call it *retail therapy* for nothing, said Vivianne. – Back-to-school shopping isn't just beneficial for children, she said, her voice rich and nutritious as an avocado on the other end of the line.

Edith has never met Vivianne in person, but she imagines her as an older black woman, with elaborate grey braids, round and wise as a fir tree. An older version of Beulah, but contemporary. Silver drop earrings. Or old Roman coins. A stuffed owl on a perch in the background.

Edith will continue filling out her Academic Achievement Overview and finish her third course outline tonight. Also write the first draft of an abstract for a conference she should attend next year.

Next Edith will buy shoes from Hangaku even though they don't look that comfortable, verging on too architectural for human feet. All the fashionable female professors wear Hangakus. The distinctive hourglass-shaped heels. Edith learned about them last year when she finally broke down and asked a history professor in line at the IT help desk what they were. She scribbled the name down on the edge of a student's essay, ripped the corner off the paper, and stuck it with a magnet to the fridge.

– Clothing is how you want the world to see you, said Vivianne.
– See *me*, your clothes say. Look at who *I* am.

Edith will tighten up her marshmallow body too; she's signed up for a Wednesday night Ballet for Beginners class at a ballet studio near her house, and she will do some kind of exercise at least once a week. Vivianne suggested she try a scheduled, regular fitness class to encourage her to balance her work and life. When Edith told Vivianne she enrolled in a hatha yoga class some years ago, bought a mat and everything, but thought it made her too twitchy and worried about inadvertently farting, Vivianne told her to try a class that didn't seem like exercise and didn't happen in a gym. Like a ballet class with the Inivea City Ballet Company. Or scuba diving.

Edith said, – I like watching ballet. I like to swim.

Vivianne said, – Excellent! So swim your heart out. The negative ions in the water will stimulate your happiness centre. The University of Inivea has an Olympic-calibre swimming pool, so you could slip in a swim before or after your day.

– But there's never any time.

Vivianne cleared her throat, turned pages. No doubt in a notebook she uses to write down assessments of her patients. No doubt Vivianne's fingers starred with silver rings and turquoise rectangles. A hippie earth goddess with multiple PhDs who begins each morning with a hundred fervent sun salutations.

– There's time for anything if you *make* time, said Vivianne. – Time is an illusion. Think about the metaphors. Time spent, lost, wasted, behind the times, passing, keeping time. Time being made. What's something you like to make, Edith?

– I like to ... when I was a teenager I used to like making ... matrimonial squares.

– Make your time the way you would make matrimonial squares. Time is your tool. Delicious.

– Time is my tool, Edith repeated. – Delicious.

– Time doesn't own you. You own time.

– I own time.

– Yes!

– Yes.

– Make the time. Eat the time.

– Make the time. Eat the time ... like matrimonial squares.

– You own yourself.

– I own myself.

Once upon a time, Edith's PhD supervisor, Lesley Hughes, said, *I own you*. But that was a long time ago. And of course Lesley lied. Edith blots out the thought.

Vivianne always told Edith to forget about Lesley. Edith would fret about Lesley becoming an Endowed Chair at the university, worrying about how she would cope with being in the same room, the same building, as Lesley, day after day.

– That's a history best left interred, Vivianne's voice would cluck from the phone. – Move on with your life. Let Lesley move on with hers. You are a *Philosophiae Doctor*. You have tenure. You are not her puppet. She is not your puppet master. Bulldoze away that room. There. We've bulldozed it.

In her brand-new Hangakus with their hourglass heels, Edith stilt-walks past the Victorian lotion and the caramel corn shops without stopping, wobbles past the escalator leading up to the rows and boring rows of white and stainless steel refrigerators, dishwashers, washing machines, and dryers, her hand swinging a cloth bag with its P. T. Madden logo, another bag with the Hangaku brand swirl holding her old loafers, her wrists smelling like imaginary gardens. She bought a bottle of the perfume that smells like vanilla pudding too, so her neck smells new. She attempts to stride, swinging her bags, like a proud professor, about to swing into a new academic year. Bold, brilliant, and fresh as a girl in a tampon commercial.

The shoes still stiff, she admits, the odd heels like walking with spurs. But all shoes need some breaking in, right?

She piles her bags into the Taurus.

Riding a wave of self-congratulation, she tops up the gas tank at the Novacrest station at the east end of the mall parking lot, the clicks of the litre indicator matching the clicks of happy retail-therapy self-righteousness. Her credit card bloats just a little bit.

She revs around the concrete silos of the shopping centre parking lot to the ramp leading onto the highway, her right Hangaku heel digging in, her car bullying its way into belligerent traffic. She motors past the campus, past Crawley Hall, barely registering its brutalist gloom. She drives five more minutes, then clicks to turn left toward the thicket of brand-new condominiums where she lives.

On her quilted bedspread at home, the P. T. Madden bag crinkles as she slides out the clothes in their tissue paper envelopes. She unfolds the first envelope. She holds the navy-blue flowers up to the fading afternoon light through the window.

Sweet william. Or ... lobelias.

She peels off the P. T. Madden sticker on the second envelope. Black sweet williams or lobelias.

The third envelope. Olive-green lobelias or sweet williams.

She slides her hands into the armholes of the navy-blue blouse. Buttons it closed one by one from her throat to her lower belly.

The mirrored closet door reflects the petals back at her. She smooths her hands down the sides. Strange little florets. No one will pierce this armour.

Not Lesley, her old supervisor.

Not even Coral. Her former, now returning, colleague. Her sometime ex-inamorata. Her *friend*.

Whom Vivianne told her to stay away from. – Sometimes, Vivianne told her, her earrings tinkling, – sometimes too much passion is not good for a person. Occasionally, said Vivianne, – in certain circumstances, a person's unchecked imagination, her misdirected intelligence as it were, can lead her on a journey into an unhealthy place.

– But then maybe I should try to help her?

– Or you could just stay away from her, said Vivianne, sounding like she was smacking her lips. – Not let her speculations and imaginings splash onto you and distract you, jeopardize your reputation as a scholar heading into mid-career under a newer, more energized headship. This next round of your Academic Achievement Overview. You're not ... ah ... the most prolific academic, Edith.

Edith's right eyelid had twitched so hard she'd clapped her hand to her eye. The eyelid bucked twice again under her fingers. Vivianne paused.

– You have a book coming out soon, and kudos for that. But you can't afford distractions. So that means you have to excel at many things, which you certainly do, I assure you. You just have to excel at a few other things too.

Edith could hear Vivianne's likely Madeira Wine lipstick smile on the other end of the phone. Why was Vivianne being so cruel?

– But if you watch your p's and q's, maintain your work-life balance, stay out of the company of troublemakers like Coral, well, that definitely helps in the long run. Avoid negativity. Correction: *flee* negativity. I've witnessed the positive effects with other clients from the university.

– You really think so?

– I *know* so. Say this with me: *I am the architect of my life; I build its foundation and select its furniture.*

Edith had closed her eyes. She would do this right. She would make Vivianne proud of her.

– I am the architect of my own life, Edith said. – I build its foundations and select its fixtures.

– Furniture, said Vivianne.

– Furniture, repeated Edith.

– You, said Vivianne, – you, Edith, are the architect of *your* life. You don't have to invite anyone into your house if you don't want her there.

– You're right. Thanks, Vivianne.

– You're welcome, Edith. We're at the end of our time now. Goodbye.

The phone clicked before Edith had the chance to say goodbye. Her appointments with Vivianne always end like this. The only disappointing thing about Vivianne.

She sits alone in her shiny condo. New clothes, new shoes, new smell, new tank of gas, but barricaded on every side by paper stacks, reports and reviews and letters she doesn't want to write but should. Must.

She empties crusted clothes from inside the washing machine. Slams the door closed. Unplugs the washing machine cord, then plugs it back in. She programs an extrahot, extralong cycle on the control panel.

Water rushes into the empty machine, and Edith shoots her fists into the air in triumph.

She rustles back into sitting behind her desk. Clicks on the Academic Achievement Overview webpage button.

Oops! This page does not exist, the computer barfs.

Her email pings. An email from Coral. She remembers how bumpily they kissed that one time, their lips refusing to match.

Edith needs to find a new friend.

She unbuttons the top button of her new blouse.

The very next morning, the sun still stretching itself awake, Edith pulls her car into the parking lot by Crawley Hall, refusing to let the frowny building guilt her for working from home yesterday. She'd like to park by the Kinesiology building, but her expensive university parking pass applies only to her assigned space next to Crawley Hall. Unless she wants to pay the parking fee at the Kinesiology parking lot. Ten dollars and fifty-five cents when she's already paid for a pass! Forget it. She would rather take the seven-minute shortcut through Crawley Hall to get to the pool.

She'll scoot through Crawley Hall and be side-stroking through invigorating waters in no time. She shuts her eyes and, clutching her duffle bag of swim gear, dashes through the tight hallways, dives past empty classrooms with gaping, vacant student desks, turns corner after corner in the mini-labyrinth, doors groaning as she tugs them open, hissing as they ooze closed behind her. Left, left, right, then left, then left again, then a short flight of stairs, then a final right, then straight through. No direct routes in this building ever, but she's memorized them all. She avoids the main lobby, determined that the building will not entice her up to her office, to the piles of unopened envelopes and the unread stack of journals she left on her desk two days ago, and the phony satisfaction that comes with shuffling through paper in her office so early in the morning. She's not teaching yet; she doesn't *have* to be here.

She wipes her nose with a disintegrating Kleenex as she run-walks, her nose suddenly dripping for no reason. She dumps the tissue in one of the overflowing garbage bins lined up in an already tight hallway and climbs the last short set of stairs to a tiny landing.

But this door's stuck or locked, even though it has no keyhole. She tugs and heaves, pushes, and tugs again at the door, slaps it, huffs. Like the door resents her wanting to exercise and improve her life. She has psychic *furnishings* to buy for her psychic *foundation*. She contemplates the door, trying to ignore the odour emanating from the walls, the ceiling: dust, mould, or fossilized compost in a recycling bin. She sneezes. Pulls out a nearly fresh Kleenex from her bag. Maybe a mouse got trapped in a nearby vent and expired. She wonders if she should call Security to unlock the door. If she circles back out the building and takes the long way, she'll miss the first ten minutes of lane swimming. If she phones Security, she'll also miss the first ten minutes of lane swimming. She can't let Vivianne down this way, this very first real day of being the architect of her life. She kicks the door with her runner.

Edith jumps when the door thuds open. Shoot! Maybe she broke the door. She hesitates in the doorway. The ceiling lights appear spotty with dust, as though they haven't been cleaned in years, the insides of the light panels clotted with grime.

And in front of her a matchbox-sized landing, and yet *another* set of stairs, this time three steps leading down. She doesn't recognize the landing. Or remember these stairs.

She's travelled through every part of Crawley Hall since she started her job seven years ago, but this hallway looks unfamiliar, the stairs redundant – what kind of pointless architecture is this? Three steps leading up to a doorway with a tiny nothing of a landing, just to go three steps down again? She's sure this design must violate some kind of building code. The lights grim, the corridor even narrower, if possible. Maybe it's the eerily early hour? No matter, she's late for swimming, and as she steps through the doorway, the door bangs closed *hard* into her shoulder.

She yelps in alarm, in pain. She rubs her shoulder as she steps carefully down the stairs. At the bottom, empty study carrels line the walls to the right and left of her, a single chair neatly tucked into each cubicle. She registers a flicker of movement at the end of the line of carrels, hears skittering, the far-off scrape of a chair. Probably students necking in the dark. But so early in the morning? Probably the same dorkmeisters who jammed the door closed so they could have their sex; she knows how sex ruins logic.

She starts to swing her bag to work the ache out of her shoulder as she walks, but swings too high once and almost slips, catches herself before she falls on the sparkly clean floor. The janitorial staff always polishes Crawley Hall's floors until they glisten at the beginning of the school year. They must have already started for the fall semester. Last time she checked, the floor in her office still held last year's scuffs and leftover grit from snow, now evaporated.

No one's emptied her office garbage can all summer, not since the spring Liberal Arts budget cut announcement, and her wastebasket brims with used bubble envelopes, old Cup-a-Soup containers, cellophane wrappers from journals, and cardboard coffee cups. But soon her wastebasket will be fresh and empty, perhaps it already is. The overcast light notwithstanding, this hallway gleams.

Silence has dropped like snowfall. She hears none of the white noise that insinuates itself everywhere else in the building: air vents, buzzy fluorescent lights, the distant ding of an elevator, the hum of a photocopy machine. Her sneaker squeaks violate the silence, as though she's accidentally trespassed into a medieval chapel. Or a dungeon. The shiny silence makes her want to tiptoe. She peers every so often under the cubicles to see if she can unearth the student lovers.

Nothing but skinny metal chair legs. No sound but the *memory* of sound.

She jogs toward the dawning sunlight slanting through the window in the exit door. It says *Push*.

But the door pushes back. Locked.

Through the wire-meshed glass in the door, a jackrabbit on the lawn pulls at grass tufts with its teeth. Crawley Hall's dawn shadow lies thick on the quad. The Kinesiology building twinkles only a hundred metres away.

She piles herself into the door, pushes and grunts, her bag clumping to the floor. She refuses to acknowledge this door's refusal.

She spins and rams her back into the door, but this door is so locked it's really just wall. She wipes her nose on the back of her hand. Rests her back on the door.

The hallway unspools ahead of her; her earlier rubber-soled footsteps are matte splotches dotting the floor's oily and unrelenting cleanness.

She slings her bag over her shoulder and walks slowly back down the hallway, her sneaker soles squelching.

Her sneakers stop squeaking in the gloomy light. She stops. Hairs prickle awake on the back of her neck, her shoulders, her forearms.

Where is she?

The tidy carrels with their neat, tucked chairs are no longer neat. The chairs scatter themselves in her way, every one pulled askew and turned around willy-nilly from their cubicles.

Who moved the chairs? Without making a single sound?

She just wants to go for a damn *swim*. Why is exercising always so damn *complicated*? Now she has to deal with supernatural bullshit too? She's always suspected something was off about this building. Coral used to say so too.

Time to leave, shortcut or no.

She wades between the parallel lines of study cubicles and their disordered chairs. She pushes and scrapes the flimsy chairs out of her way, rams herself through them. She refuses to register misplaced clusters of shadows under the cubicles, shadows that weren't there earlier, shadows too small and numerous to be a single pair of mischievous or desperate lovers. A shining red eye – she swears it's an eye – mirrors at her from a shadow under a cubicle.

She barrels toward the very first door – the door with the needless steps leading up only to stairs down the other side. But the steps on this side of the door, those steps that shouldn't have been there in the first place, have disappeared. The floor all the way to the door gleams clear and flat and wide and shining.

She pushes away a cold drip of fear.

Fed up, she violently shoves herself into the door, ready for it to stick. The door whooshes open and she stumbles forward, panicked that she'll tumble down the other set of stairs and snap her skull in half, shatter her knees. She stretches out her hands, lands on her palms – her hands and feet staggered on the steps – her bag thumping as it rolls down the steps. Excellent save. Her knees intact.

She stays crouched, panting, then gathers up her bag in her arms.

She scurries away toward a side door she knows leads to some outdoor nowheresville, but that hopefully will take her *out*. She turns a perfectly oiled handle, and the door bursts open.

A jackrabbit abruptly leaps away.

She gasps in fresh air.

A rush of dusty, dead-mousey air billows around her, announcing her to the outside world.

The door lolls open behind her.

The door yawns, moist air from inside the building soughing out the doorway. An inappropriately human sound.

She sways a little, her wrists still shocked, her shoulder bruised and aching, a new crick in the small of her back. Her synapses frizzled.

She has a feral desire to flee – hightail it for her Taurus, hurtle home, and collapse into bed wrapped inside two comforters. But she hasn't swum for three years. Vivianne told her to choose her furnishings. She will not let anyone or anything else, some grumpy, sticky-doored building with a half-assed paranormal hallway, choose her furnishings.

Illogical. Irritating. Time-consuming. Her time *consumed*. A small black marble sticks to her left palm. A jackrabbit turd. She flicks at it until it unsticks, bounces, thocks into the grass. She looks back at the Crawley Hall door swinging listlessly, like a tooth, in the dim, grim doorway. She needs to call Vivianne.

No. She needs to make Vivianne proud.

She plods heavily, warily, the long way around Crawley Hall's giant, protruding concreteness, past normal pine trees, along normal sidewalks past the library, past the students' union building to the Novacrest School of Kinesiology building. The electronic front doors slide open and wait for her, like gentle, non-racist butlers. She enters the glamorous, state-of-the-art building, its brand-new, open-concept loveliness, and pool-chlorine and squash-ball smells enfold and embrace her.

Edith curls her toes on the pool's edge, thirty-one minutes late for lane swimming. She snaps on her goggles and eases herself into the freezing chlorine soup. She thrashes out a single lap in the pool, then halts midway through the next lap, panting, choking for air. She paddles her arms and legs, floating in place, water sloshing in her earholes, waiting for her lungs to pump less frantically. Is she traumatizing her lungs by leaping into exercise so quickly? Shouldn't she go home and rest after being gaslit by Crawley Hall and nearly assaulted by rows of chairs? She is not frightened, but so many jammed and locked doors certainly rattled her; obviously, witnessing possible paranormal phenomena is a distressing way to start the day. She doesn't like having to believe in the supernatural, especially so early in the school year, and so early in the morning. She is a scholar, an intellectual. There has been no peer-reviewed, conclusive article published about the existence of the supernatural, but she also understands that some things can be unknown, some explanations still percolating and awaiting discovery. The first European scientists to examine a platypus thought it was fake, for goodness' sake. Edith ducks her mouth under the water and blows bubbles.

The teenaged lifeguard busily texts, grimacing at something on her phone. The clock at the far end of the pool reads 7:01 a.m.

I am the architect of my life; I build its foundation and select its fixtures.

She bobs in the water, remembers her back-to-school shopping from the day before. So what if there's a supernaturally contaminated hallway. The building's old and contaminated with all sorts of things. Maybe she's special and that's why the hallway rearranged itself for her. She should have tried to communicate with whatever mysterious entity it was instead of running away like a goose. The tiny balloon of elation still hasn't popped from the three new blouses hung side by side in her closet, the new cardigan tucked back into its tissue paper, and the new pair of Hangakus yin-and-yanged back into their cardboard box. She's launching into a new academic year.

Edith inhales a giant breath and plops her face into the pool water, begins side-stroking slowly, softly bumping up and down in the ripples and waves of the swimmers in the adjoining lanes. An old man's pale belly and spaghetti arms dipping in and out of the water with the breast stroke, his swimming trunks obscenely red and tiny. She thinks it's Angus Fella, her colleague, but she's not

100 percent sure. A woman in black with the body of a 1940s pin-up girl shoots past like a penguin. Pimple-like protuberances nestle in the mint-coloured concrete of the pool floor. An acned landscape for the floating scraps of Band-Aids, an errant pair of swim goggles. Dark jellyfish made of hair.

Edith makes time. She bakes metaphorical matrimonial squares. She wraps them in metaphorical gold-and-silver paper and sends them as a metaphorical *Just Because* gift to her parents, to Vivianne, to Beulah.

She lurches her face through the water. Seven-thirteen a.m. Her goggles starting to fog.

She has no time for swimming. The semester starts in one week, September 4. She has course outlines and syllabi to prepare, essay questions and lecture notes to write and insert into PPT slides, monographs to decipher, a graduate student's thesis chapter to red-pen, articles to cobble together, a conference presentation 6,000 words too long to jury-rig as best she can, a forty-three-page agenda and appendix about the CASC strategy to absorb for the next faculty meeting. Her next book to start drafting. Her AAO to fill out so she can prove her relevance for the next two years and avoid that awful circumstance of being *refreshed* by the dean.

When the jolly previous dean, with his waxed moustache and cowboy hat, awarded her tenure two years and seventy-five days ago, she believed that finally every day at her job would be Christmas Day, with spontaneously carolling students and her professor colleagues smiling at her and bestowing upon her bouquets of red and white flowers and pearly-bowed presents for no reason at all as she sailed down the halls, her healthy new self-possession shining a crystal-ball light. She wouldn't have to worry about job security anymore, she could intellectually and even literally wear pyjamas to work every day and no one would care: she would be free! But post-tenure Elysium was a rabbit on a greyhound racetrack. This new dean, Dr. Phillip Vermeulen, with his extraordinarily hairy fingers and origami-crisp silk ties, brought in one and a half years ago, is part of the new EnhanceUs university plan. He was brought in to *refresh* the Faculty of Liberal Arts. He wanted to refresh Edith the moment he met with her for the first time and opened her file on his desk. Refresh the heck out of her, just like he refreshed Coral and the tinier departments, the same way he refreshed sections of Crawley Hall's operational budget. He is white South African, which makes her nervous. What if he hates her because, well, *because she's a brown woman* with prematurely drooping body and face parts? Although her roommate in graduate school was a white South African girl, and they regularly guzzled too many zombie cocktails together, holding each other's hair back when they puked three times a weekend, every weekend. Misty sure could hold her booze. Really, the dean with his small, catlike head and fancy clothes just reminds Edith a bit too much of her father. Whom she loves, of course. You can't not love your dad.

– I see here, Edith, Dean Vermeulen had said in their first meeting, his hairy fingers slithering through her file, his elbows on his desk and his cuffs rucked up so she could see his thick hairy wrists too, – that for two cycles in a row you've received only four Value Increments on your AAO.

She nodded. Her right eyelid spasmed. She pretended to scratch her eyebrow but really gave her twitching eyelid a poke. Edith had thought his accent was English the first time she heard him; he did not immediately correct people who mistook him for British.

– One more AAO cycle with a four VI would confirm your eligibility for the EnhanceUs Refreshment Strategy, said the dean, his index fingers parked in the middle of a page.

His back was to the window. The sun bleated from behind a knot of clouds, and the leather of the punching bag planted in the corner of his office glistened.

– I've been writing my book, she said, jamming her finger into her eyelid. – I've been trying to complete my book, and that's why my publication record has appeared to slow down the past few years ...

– You're going to have to write that book and future books a lot harder, I'm afraid. This university is on track to be in the top 1 percent in the country in terms of excellence and globalization, but to do that we're going to have to shed those who diverge from the EnhanceUs strategic plan. You understand, eh, Edith?

He cocked his head.

She spilled out of his office, her head a tumbleweed, her eyelid dancing a tarantella no matter how insistently she pressed it with the palm of her hand. How could she explain to him, explain *properly*, that her book, her tribute, her temple erected to Beulah Crump-Withers, had to be flawless? No one could rush this book. Not even her. Tears dribbled out from under her palm.

On her way out of the dean's office she whammed her shoulder into Angus Fella, with his vodka-and-Vegemite breath. His hat jumped off his head and rolled partway down the hall. Combed-over strands of grey hair flopped in the wrong direction. She chased after his hat while he smoothed his hair. He resettled his fedora on his head.

– I'm sorry, she blubbered, her fingers over her nose, trying to stem the tears.

– Looks like you need a tissue, he said, and began patting the pockets of his blazer. – Aha! Found one!

He brandished a mangled shred of Kleenex. – I only blew my nose in it once, he said. – In this corner. You can use any of the other three corners. Go ahead. Looks like you need it.

She dabbed her eyes and wiped her nose. Handed the tissue back. She took a deep breath.

– I don't want to hear about your problems, he said. – Sorry, but I must be frank.

He scuttled away through the door leading to the stairs.

Edith claws through the chlorinated water in the university's Olympic-sized swimming pool. She squints though her goggles. Seven-thirty-five a.m. Soon it will be 8 a.m. and her day basically gone. Wasted!

Because her book will come out just in time to list it on this year's AAO, a published book the holy grail for a high VI, at least ten VI, or maybe even eleven VI, and Dean Vermeulen and his punching bag will *not* refresh her. Her book will unfresh her.

She pushes silver bubbles out of her nose. Her hands droop toward the pool floor.

She wishes she could drunk dial and weep and rave on the phone to Coral like she used to. But that would be dysfunctional. And Vivianne says no. And Coral's been away.

Coral's coming back. Coral might already be back. Coral is a passionate person. Edith worries that Coral's returning passion might affect Edith's AAO score. The dean grades on a curve.

That murky, bumping sound of water spilling into Edith's ears.

She should be catching up on her critical theory, not frolicking in pools in the middle of the day. Like she's a Lady Who Lunches. A Lady Who Laps.

She pulls herself up the metal stairs from the water up onto the pool deck, water streaming from her ears, her goggled eyes foggy.

She raises her arms like she's just won a race. She exercised!

September

An email from Coral has plopped into Edith's inbox. No subject heading. Edith hovers her cursor over it nervously, afraid to click it open.

Coral was refreshed a year ago, but now she has clearly returned. She evaporated following a faculty meeting in which the dean bawled them all out because, as he phrased it, a CERTAIN POLTROON employed in the Faculty of Liberal Arts blabbed to the media about new budget cuts and allegedly unsound asbestos-abatement procedures in Crawley Hall, and this unauthorized complaint to the media by a U of I faculty member DID NOT FOLLOW ESTABLISHED PROTOCOL.

– Complaints are supposed to be submitted to the GARG committee first, he raged, stabbing his index finger upward. – Then vetted by the HGA working group. Steps will be TAKEN, he pronounced, stabbing the other index finger at the ceiling too.

Coral and Edith's colleagues focused on their computer screens or on half-erased algebra formulas rococo-ing the whiteboard behind the dean. Leroy Hoffman the Victorianist cleared his throat, while Ian Bell the Medieval Historian crinkled a Werther's candy wrapper, while his wife, Iris Bell the Linguist, picked a staple out of some sheets of paper. The only other sounds were the remote buzz of a saw one floor up, a student's shrill laugh outside the room as she likely headed, carefree and sexual, to the student pub for zombie cocktails. Coral hunched with her arms crossed in the lecture theatre's bottom tier of seats.

– Dickhead, she muttered sideways to Edith.

Edith had slowly tried to shift her chair away from Coral's.

Immediately following the meeting, Coral ordered Edith to drink a coffee with her. Coral knotted her reddened fingers around her ceramic *Male Tears* mug. Edith clutched her paper coffee cup. Coral would be happy to leave, Coral said, this *factory masquerading as a place of learning.*

– Because the dean hates women, said Coral, her lips thinning into a clench, – and he really hates *me*, and what a convenient excuse to refresh me. If I was a man ... well, I just have to say, it's great to own a penis and be invited to drink Bellinis with the dean just because you have the same old boy and young boy boyfriends from the same alma mater. Like a certain Digital Humanities expert.

Coral slurped her coffee, the bitter smell exhaling every time she spoke.

– This coffee's shit, she said. – Everything's always shit.

Coral always complained that the coffee from the machine tasted like tree bark, but proper organic, fair-trade coffee was only sold in the Bull Head School of Engineering tower, of course. Edith secretly revelled in Coral's complaining. They were drinking coffee in the Jungle, surrounded by oversized potted plants, a small stone fountain dribbling in the centre of the overheated room. The Jungle remains the only place in Crawley Hall with real air, according to Coral, because the plants filter out the toxins. Coral held her smaller classes in the Jungle or outside in the grassy quad before the snow drove her and her students inside.

A staghorn fern trumpeted its antlers above Coral's left shoulder. Edith angled her bum deeper into her chair's coffee-stained seat, the glare of early autumn snow crusted in the skylights above them transforming Coral's face into an angry collection of angles and shadows. Edith tried not to remember how her nose had started bleeding after only a few seconds of kissing Coral, and how Coral had left a sad, almost perfectly round pink smear of lipstick around one of Edith's areolae. Their relationship lasted thirty-three minutes before they gave up, Edith still too heartbroken over her ex, Beryl, and Coral on to lovers who didn't bleed out the nose when she put her tongue in their mouths.

Coral told the *Inivea Tribune* and a local television station that the University of Inivea's Liberal Arts building, Crawley Hall, was stuffed with toxic chemicals to the point of bursting and that U of I administration was covering it up. That there had been nine cases of testicular cancer among teachers and staff in the past five years, but the men were all too embarrassed to talk about it.

On television the tendons in Coral's neck stood out as she answered the interviewer's questions, puppet lines etching around her mouth. Edith didn't have time to watch television, but she had it playing in the background as she microwaved a single-serving vegan shepherd's pie dinner she bought at the Kaffee Klatsch.

– The rate of stress and illness in this building is reaching exceptional levels, Coral was saying, her carroty hair stringy around her face, her freckled forehead shiny with acne. – The number of cases of advanced testicular cancer is unnaturally high. I also have anecdotal stories of chronic headaches among workers, colleagues in their thirties developing cataracts. Students losing their hair. I have been suffering from fatigue and migraines that my doctor cannot find the source of. I believe it's because of the piecemeal asbestos removal started years ago, the age of the building, and cheap, toxic materials. And this new dean is bringing in even more radical budget cuts to building upkeep and maintenance. Why can't they just move us into a healthy building that's up to code? There's a ribbon-cutting ceremony somewhere on campus every second week for some new energy-efficient learning centre dedicated to medicine, engineering, business. But not for the humanities. This building is sick. It's dangerous, and it's already started hurting people. And another thing: the women who work here are not being treated –

The newscaster's head cut in, a frowny wrinkle between her eyebrows as she switched to a report on a female karate black belt from Wollongong, Australia, who successfully fought off a grizzly bear with a single punch while hiking at Bow Falls.

Edith had kept on forking shepherd's pie into her mouth. The occasional bean burning hot, a few chunks of hard turnip still lukewarm. The mashed potatoes slimed and stuck to the roof of her mouth. It had never occurred to her that she could work in a building that didn't always have the ceilings ripped open. She remembered drywall powder dusting the trouser cuffs of her job interview suit. She guessed she knew some people who had fallen sick, like Leroy Hoffman, whom she saw once with a portable IV stuck in his arm while he was photocopying essay questions in the mailroom. Was the portable IV from testicular cancer? She'd heard it was because of a clot in his jugular developed from sitting too long.

And Otis the sessional instructor, who couldn't go on sick leave because he was on contract and so dragged himself coughing and wheezing into work, his skin glassy from sweat and hands shaking from fever, so he wouldn't forfeit his teaching seniority next year. Arnold Nash seemed to just dematerialize. Olivia Tootoo had an operation on her left eye last year for the single cataract she developed while serving as the department's union rep, but how could the building be to blame?

Elise Thurman went on stress leave, but that was because of that student who stalked her all the way through her sabbatical, wasn't it? Or was it because of the wrist braces she always wore? Edith attributed the braces to carpal tunnel syndrome or something normal like that. But Coral was always passionately ranting about something. She'd left a petition in the mailroom asking faculty members to sign: *This is a 'sick' building,* the paragraph at the top of the petition read. *A building this old needs proper maintenance that the administration refuses to do in order to save money. Sign here to force an investigation into how these new budget cuts are continuing to compromise the health of the faculty and staff who work here ...*

Only Coral's signature was on the petition. And Angus Fella's. But he's a queer fish.

The other reason Dean Vermeulen pushed Coral out was because she told him she wanted more money. As much as that new Digital Humanities hire, Leonardo Baudone, was making as his starting salary. How did she know how much the new hire was making? Because he *told* everyone how much he was making, he told anyone who happened to pass by his office when he first started, his kookaburra laugh, his flinty inflections ruining that hallway. First he reminded them about his breakthrough, crossover book, cited 1,232 times on Google Scholar and also listed as one of the Best Books of the Year in the *New York Times*; how he was one of the top thirty-five under thirty-five in *Boulevard* magazine. Then he told them how many job offers he got before he agreed to this job, how the dean begged him to take this job, then he told them how much he made, then he asked them how much they made. Coral nearly spat out her own tongue when she overheard that Leonardo, that adult-sized rumpled baby, was making more than her. Considerably more.

– I've been offered a position at the University of Bath, Coral lied to the dean. – So how much is this university willing to pay me to stay?

Edith could imagine Coral planted on the other side of the dean's wide wooden desk. Her tiny freckled biceps probably flexed, her demands in bullet-point form on an iPad scorching the desk surface. The dean with his spiky accent, his hairy thumbs, his furry lobes. His lips curling in a Grinchy smile.

– Were you wearing a power suit? Edith had asked afterward. – I wore a blazer last time I had to meet with him, and that didn't help with my confidence at all.

Coral had twisted her mouth unhappily. – So he says to me, she nearly shouted as she flicked the chipped rim of her coffee cup with her pointy fingertips, – Phil the Pill says to me, 'Why don't you just go, then? Have a lovely time in Bath, among the Baths! No point in staying where you're unhappy.'

Then his administrative assistant, Lisa Ives, coincidentally knocked on the door right then to let him know his meeting with the president had started five minutes ago.

– Yeah, because the president has so little to do that she needs to fill up her time meeting with *Phil*, the dipso dean of *Liberal Arts*, Coral sneered to Edith. – Red Alert! There's a poetry emergency! Caesura malfunction in room 12!

And he snapped his hairy old boy fingers and swivelled his chair away from Coral so he faced his view of the vast compound of concrete university buildings that Coral could *refresh* herself away from, muddy yellow backhoes mulching up the grass in the quad for the new exclusively solar-powered Sandersams Supermarkets School of Business scheduled to be fully erected in 2.3 years.

Coral was refreshed because after her plan to earn the same salary as faculty members with penises failed, she contacted the newspapers and the TV stations and ratted out the university, ratted out the dean of Liberal Arts, exposed the dean for being a maggoty little nabob, a fascist skinflint just like every other administrator at this university, willing to cut corners and sacrifice their employees to the asbestos-ridden, sick building Moloch of Crawley Hall in order to hire more managerial clones, splash money at their boozy dinners and catered meetings for university funders, and first-class trips to admin conferences in New York and Europe. Because the dean's directed the funds meant for repairs and finishing up the renovations to buying more expensive wine for the millions of receptions he likes to throw. Crawley Hall is falling apart and everyone knows it but no one's willing to say so on the record, and no Brown Bag Lunches and Town Halls moderated by absent-minded professors seduced into administration are going to stop the building from being sick. The asbestos-abatement work in their building has already killed one administrative assistant: that sweet guy Andrew with the animal-themed sweaters died of scarring of the lungs, everyone knew it; his husband did an interview with the paper too, and Coral was not prepared to be the next casualty. She noted the mysterious curdles of brown in the mucus she coughed up regularly, the migraines.

Coral had packed her complaints, petitions, and grievances into boxes with her books and computer, and begun teleporting into academic limbo.

The day after she was refreshed, Coral sneaked her head into Edith's office, her nose red and sharp. Edith swivelled from her computer, ready to hop up and hug Coral. Coral was wearing a 1950s-style housedress that looked like it belonged to a housewife who'd axed her husband to death in his sleep. A tangled ivy pattern.

Coral pushed her whole body into the office, the ivy cascading down the crinolined skirt too physically close to Edith, too too close.

– I'm not supposed to be here, said Coral. – But I left a file in my office.

– They took away your keys, said Edith.

– They don't know anything.

– Won't someone see you?

– I took the back stairs. Plus, who cares. By the time they find the right form for throwing me out, I'll be halfway to the Arctic Circle.

That day, Edith had chased paperwork in her office all day. An ache clutched the crown of her head. That gravelly headache that always descended at the end of the day from too much reading on the computer screen, breathing the stale, recirculated air. Coral shut the door behind her. The air suddenly close.

– Edith. I have a plan.

– Okay?

– And I need your help. All of the professors should do a mass walkout to protest the building's conditions and get us moved to a better building. Will you organize the walkout? You can start a petition and convince people to sign it, let them know you're not safe here. I've found out some things about this building, Edith. You can't stay in Crawley Hall. It's not healthy, it's getting worse, and I've agitated the wrong people, I've uncovered some things. I have to lie low and get a lawyer to help me get my job back. I'm going to launch a major grievance and if I have to I'm going to sue the university and Phil the Pill's asses off for wrongful dismissal. Legal suits always scare the pants off them.

An ivy tendril uncoiled from the elbow of Coral's dress sleeve and slowly licked the wall.

Coral swatted at her elbow distractedly, as though a fly had landed on her arm. The tendril retracted back into the dress.

– Edith?

Coral pinched her face into a frown.

Edith whirled back to her computer, concentrating on the winking cursor on the screen, assuring herself that her headache was making her eyesight fuzzy. That was it.

– I'm not brave like you, Coral, she said.

She pecked her fingers at her computer keyboard.

– You can be if you try, said Coral. – It's life or death, Edith.

– But ... , said Edith, her hands digging into her keyboard, – I don't *want* to.

Coral crushed her file to her chest.

– Edith? she asked. – Edith?

The dress brushed the edge of the desk right next to Edith's hand. Edith pulled her hands into her lap, curled the fingers closed like a sea anemone.

– I have a lot of work to do, said Edith, leaning forward, pretending to read small print on her screen. – Bye, Coral. I wish you every success, I really do. Email me. We can go for fair-trade coffee before you fly off.

She began tapping at her keyboard, embarrassed, ashamed. She was a traitor, a coward, a lousy friend, and she was having hallucinations.

She focused on her screen, refusing to look in Coral's direction, in the direction of the dress, because she knew if she did she might start to cry.

Coral clasped her hands in front of the skirt, the file crumpling.

– Goodbye, then, she said, tugging open the door. – Don't work too hard, eh? Open a window or something in here.

The skirt's bulk rustling as it brushed out the doorway. Her footsteps tapping off into the hallway, waning until they completely disappeared.

Edith sat on her lumpy beige office chair and peered out the sealed window while Coral slammed her car door in the parking lot, her car a dirty white blot on the asphalt, and spun off.

Edith ponders this brand-new email message from Coral. They haven't emailed in the whole twelve months Coral's been gone. Does this new email mean Coral has forgiven her? Edith clicks.

An e-card unfolds on the screen to the sounds of chirping violins: a cartoon of a piece of chalk scribbles *Back to School!* on a green chalkboard. An apple and a ruler dance the tango. The violins end. The apple and ruler separate. *Play again?* asks the e-card.

Vivianne is right. Coral is a distraction.

How she wishes she could call Coral.

She could call Vivianne instead. But her U of I benefits plan allows only twenty-five free sessions per year with a psychologist, and she's already down to five and it's only September and she's about to begin one of the hardest parts of the year. Should she use up a precious session on this? On worrying about Coral just because she exists? On feeling guilty because she let down her friend?

She clicks Delete. Opens up the next email.

Price tags snipped off her new blouse and new cardigan, new Hangakus posed by the front door.

Tomorrow is the first day of the new school year. Edith's bag by the front door sits packed with printer-warm paper copies of course outlines, syllabi, her memory stick with her first-day presentation slides, calendar, pens, books. The olive-green flowered blouse she'll wear tomorrow hangs neatly on a coat hanger hooked on the back of her bedroom door, along with a wool skirt, leotards, and twice-washed underpants because the washing machine is still being stubborn. And a bra. The coffee machine filled with water and ground coffee, ready to click on at 5:55 a.m. so that at 6 a.m. she can pour a hot cup right out of the pot and into herself.

The ceiling smooth and clear and white as the belly of a spaceship. The lights from the condo towers across the street punching into the room through the sheer curtains.

Ten p.m. She lies like a salami slice between clean, smoke-grey sheets. Not too early for bed. Not too late.

This will be her year, she repeats to herself. Her AAO year of triumph. Her year of finally becoming an author, the person she has always wanted to be. *I am the architect of my life; I build its foundation and select the wallpaper and window coverings.*

Ten-oh-three p.m. Her fingers paddle the sheets, her legs swish irritably. She snags a ragged toenail on the blanket.

She fumbles out of bed. She pulls on jeans, the pouchy wool sweater her oma knitted for her when she was a teenager. She grabs her wallet, unbolts the door, sneaks to the elevators in bare feet. She forgets her shoes. Her brown toes gleaming against the hallway carpet. She'll grab her flip-flops.

The elevator chings.

She buys a medium-sized cup of valerian-laced coffee from the newish barista in the Kaffee Klatsch. The barista's name tag says *Hi! I'm Beverly*. They have spoken briefly before. Bev usually works the 5 p.m. to 1 a.m. shift and recently graduated with a master's degree in ethnomusicology. She'd been doing the degree part-time for fifteen years, – But you know … with kids and everything, says Bev, while pulling another espresso shot, – and masquerading as a loving wife to the U of I Dean of Medicine as my other full-time profession for thirty-five years. Turns out I was his beard. Arthur, one of my twins, he told me that's the word for it.

The only reason she was able to do the master's degree was because those years she was high on uppers her doctor-professor husband gave her to help her juggle all the teenagers. One set of twins, one set of triplets.

Bev knocks used espresso grounds out of a portafilter.

– I said to him, you take the house and give me the sexy fuckpad condo where you took your little twinks for your phony meetings and sleepover conferences. That's what I told him. I was done with being the dummy. I was done with the house, all the dusty stairs, the perpetual cleaning. Laundry. Weeding, god I hate gardening, it's just all plants, bugs, and dirt. Never liked it. My job was never done. I could never go home after my shift. I was on the brink of pulling a Sylvia Plath.

Bev tucks a strand of grey curl behind an ear. Licks her lips.

Edith and Beverly fuck their brains out upstairs in Bev's condo from precisely 1:16 a.m. to 4:23 a.m. A pleasant, unscheduled surprise.

– Do you always have your eye on the time? asks Bev.

– I don't know what you mean, says Edith. – What an odd metaphor.

Bev so adorable with her questions.

The first day of the school semester. Edith shoots out of bed. Seven-fifteen a.m. Late. She tosses on the beautiful new blouse hanging off the door, the regal cardigan. She slides the Hangaku marvels on her feet. She smiles idiotically as her car wrestles traffic. First day of school! First day of the fresh-baked new year, fragrant, toasty, and just pulled out of the dog-days-of-summer oven. New students, new fixtures, new foundation.

She doesn't have time to fight the morning elevator crowds to get to her office and drop off her coat, so she hoists herself up one floor in the stale air of the northern stairwell, panting and wheezing, stumbling in her new shoes. No matter, her feet look magnificent as they trip over the concrete edges. She skips muddy shoeprints along the polished floor straight to her classroom, a surprise autumn snow-rainfall this morning on the very first day of school and her new Hangakus slippery with muck. Her heels leave long black stripes. She rubs a chilly raindrop from her eyelash. She tugs papers and books out of her bag as she lumbers down the corridors that turn and undulate toward her classroom, her Canadian Literature Before 1950 class. New furnishments for her foundation!

The first thing she hears is the shouts.

Identical red doors line the hallway on each side of her as she winds down this labyrinth so early in the morning the moon's still hanging in the sky. Her classroom is at the hallway's end, the outside of her classroom door clustered with students still bundled in their coats and bags, some of them thumbing their mobile phones, some of them shouting and shrieking. She steps more quickly, then starts to canter in her baroque heels.

Someone's shoved the desks up into a mountain beside the whiteboard, one boy on his stomach in his black puffy coat reaching his arm under the desks. The kicking and clatter of plastic chairs and tables; a mop handle someone found rattles among the metal legs.

A hare, surrounded in this spindly forest of metal and plastic, its ears greased back against its spine as it tries its hunched-low invisibility trick.

– Has someone called Security? Edith asks, thumping her papers and books on the long plastic table in front of the room. – Stand any closer than that, she warns the boy lying on the floor, his arm stretching out toward the hare, – and you'll likely catch rabies.

She yanks the Security phone receiver from the wall and jabs the button. Her books and papers have slid to the floor, students' mucky footprints crumpling the edges.

– Oh, please watch out for those papers, she says. – I need those papers, she says.

Students twisting and stamping on her papers, the edges tearing, the first page of her lecture notes ripping right down the muddy middle.

She hangs up the receiver.

She clambers down to the floor, trying not to get her coat dirty, her new scarf slithering in the grime. She guesses the janitorial staff hasn't had a chance to polish this classroom floor yet. Stretches out on her stomach so she can spot the hare, huddled in the corner next to the radiator, its yellow eyes clenched shut, trapped in its shadowy cage of table legs.

– I think it's dead, says the boy on the floor next to her. She remembers the boy from last year, Simon.

She peers more closely, the rabbit huddled next to the wall.

He is correct.

He is incorrect.

The jackrabbit abruptly rockets, streaks, and weaves through their legs, out the classroom door, students shrieking and stampeding.

Amidst the shrieks, the tangle and tumble of desks, the fears of rabies, Edith addresses her class.

– Good morning, class! she shouts, still panting a little from climbing that single flight of stairs.

After her very first class – she's not sure how it went, students can be so inscrutable sometimes – Edith crowds with the other bodies at the elevators in Crawley Hall. New, clean backpacks, stiff blue jeans on the students, pressed clothes and freshly trimmed hair on the professors on this first day, this brand-new semester. Today elevator #1 has a scribbled Out of Order sign taped to its silver door. Edith clusters with everyone else on the far side of the low-ceilinged lobby, waiting for elevator #2. Her colleagues Leroy Hoffman, Olivia Tootoo. She nods at them. They nod back gloomily. Leroy hoists himself more securely on his crutches, his foot in a plastic cast angled out in front of him. Olivia frowns at her watch; gauze covers her right eye this time.

– Your cataract operation was successful? asks Edith. – Did you have a good summer?

– Very successful, says Olivia. – Yes, good. Other eye's fixed too.

– I had a good summer too, says Leroy. – Cast'll be off in two weeks.

– Sweet, says Edith.

Crawley Hall stretches only five floors high, but everyone rides the elevators, the lobby packed with academics and their students tracking in dust and crud, or snow and mud. They carry themselves like prawns, standing like fiddleheads curled in fried butter. Walking up or down one of the stairwells would be more nutritious, but this morning nearly ate out her lungs because the air's so close in the stairwells. And she's so goddamn out of shape. And, truly, the staircases shrivel Edith's spirit with their angular, patchy concrete, the iron banisters curling around the corners of stairwells shadowed like abandoned wells. The fluorescent lights flattening out human features so anyone in a stairwell turns bloodless, looks like she is dying. Edith cannot hold her breath for long in the stale air of stairwells, and no view at all except concrete and pipes painted black. Plus, she doesn't want to sweat in her clean clothes before the year's even had a chance to begin.

Leroy pulls back his sleeve to check his watch too. Turns to Olivia.

– You going to the welcome reception for the new Endowed Chair? asks Leroy.

– Think so, says Olivia. – You? Edith?

– Not sure yet, says Edith.

Edith's eyelid tics. Lesley's reception.

– Lesley's a hoot, says Olivia. – I met her at a conference in Munich.

Edith's lips wobble into an approximation of a smile.

The welcome reception tomorrow – tomorrow! – means Lesley's likely landed somewhere on campus. Maybe even in the building. But Edith can't imagine Lesley doing anything as banal and mortal as waiting for a Crawley Hall elevator.

But that is all the brain space she allows Lesley. She must leave Lesley interred.

Elevator #2's door sleepily blinks open. They stuff themselves in, huddling under the flickering light. Edith can smell toothpaste breath, soap, dry cleaning, wine stains, shoe polish. She holds her breath.

I am the architect of my life, she recites to herself, *I build its foundation and choose the furniments.*

Once she's settled herself in her office, she will text Bev good morning and send her a rose emoji. Romantic. Then ask Bev if she wants to get married. Just joking. No. Edith shouldn't do that.

The lights above the elevator door wink.

In her office, Edith scrolls through the pounds and pounds of email accumulated inside her computer, each email a tiny loaded telegram reminding her of some thing she has to do, or some thing she hasn't done, or some thing she never did, a pinched nerve in her right index finger burning ember-red all the way to her elbow as she dully clicks her mouse, chasing after all the telegrams. Alice Z., the front office manager, warns that the drain in the staff room isn't working and that all the water in Crawley Hall will be shut off from Saturday, September 29, to Sunday, September 30.

A toilet across the hall flushes. Edith needs to pee. There's no time to pee. When she finally remembers to pee, it will probably be September 29.

Alice Q. in the front office has written that the lock on the back stairwell door is jammed, a locksmith's been called. Also all the photocopiers are broken but a technician's been called.

Sometimes Edith pees on the fifth floor even though her office is on the fourth floor. Edith's office, room C454, faces the fourth-floor bathroom. Between 8:30 a.m. and 4:30 p.m. the toilet flushes and gurgles while she prepares for lectures, while she's trying to read an article she's printed off, while a student complains about the price of the textbooks across from her at her fake wood desk, while she argues on the phone with Alice Z. or Alice Q. or with Suneeta in Human Resources about yet another office-supply reimbursement that hasn't come through, while Edith blows her nose, crying for no good reason at all, something she attributes to perimenopausal hormones. A cough, a flush, the grunting of the paper-towel dispenser as it wheels out rough brown sheets echo and resound in her office. Edith will squeeze her thighs and Kegel muscles tight, then plod up the vertiginous east staircase to try and urinate in the much-less-trafficked fifth-floor washroom. Or just to sit by herself momentarily in silent contemplation in a bathroom cubicle, the only space where it is culturally unacceptable for someone to bother her. But the stairwell is only for emergencies and escapes, the stale air unbearable, a boiled-egg smell, even more so between the fourth and fifth floors. And the jolt of tromping up and down so many stairs inflames the soft tissue behind Edith's kneecaps, and the flickering fluorescents hanging from the stairwell ceilings give her eye-spots. She tries to savour her toilet breaks, her silent alone breaks, regretfully heaving up from the toilet seat when she knows she's sat too long, flushing the toilet noisily whether she's used it or not, as she wipes the mucus from her nose, the tears slinking from her eyes. Bolting out of the bathroom before the person in the adjoining cubicle lets out her dainty farts and urine trickles.

An email from a student saying none of the books Edith ordered for the class are in the bookstore.

An email from the dean's assistant: *All faculty and graduate students are invited to a reception tomorrow welcoming the new Leung Endowed Chair. Mona A. Leung and representatives of the Leung Foundation, Novacrest Oil Sands, and Sandersams Supermarkets will also be present.*

Edith's office also sits kitty-corner to the faculty lounge: a chair and expired-coffee-machine graveyard, a small mouldy fridge with a grinding engine. A round table stacked with decades-old literary journals. Ketchup smears and cookie crumbs from the weird cookies

Angus Fella's sister sends him from Adelaide. Sometimes the microwave beeps, potent and radiated odours like plastic Beefaroni containers bubbling over. Once upon a time she had an office with sealed windows (not) opening onto a view of the white crackled mountains rimming the western edges of Inivea, a sky as blue and wide as a mouth, the only sounds the occasional footsteps of a colleague or disoriented student in the corridor. Her boxes of books and papers she still hasn't unpacked since she was relocated to this office a year and a half ago from her former, beautiful office, her teaching and meeting schedules always squeezed full, posters she needs to stick to the walls still curled in their cardboard tubes because she just had no time.

But she was *decanted* under the direction of the Building Resources sub-department; she had to move all her boxes and herself out of her office, which is what *decanting* really means, room B409, over a year ago because the bubbling brown stain on the white ceiling panels right above her desk one day matured and popped like a lanced blister, showering her head and her student papers and zigzag stacks of library books with chalky hunks and chunks of disintegrating ceiling tiles, grey scraps of fibreglass pink, little black marbles of who-knows-what. She tried to peer up into the cloudy maw of the ceiling, poked a swinging ceiling panel with her finger, but had to stop because the air and dust billowing out of the hole burned her eyes. Just a blur of shadow and dust. In the washroom mirror, her skin powdered in white disintegrated ceiling, her eyes bright red as her father's every New Year's Day. The dust mixing into a stubborn paste on her palms and beneath her fingernails under the tap, the brown paper towels she wetted pilling on her face as she tried to scrub the ceiling off her cheeks. Ceiling matted into her hair. Crusting onto her scalp.

Her old office, room B409, was for a long time a restricted construction zone mazed with ladders and women and men in construction hats, the ceiling split open and exposing its silver intestines, the floor peeled and raw. Once she was sure she saw a pair of workers dressed entirely in white, wearing white hoods and see-through plastic masks, white booties swaddling their feet. But she'd been xeroxing a lot that afternoon – the photocopy light made her brain brittle and her senses unreliable.

She stacked her ceiling-caked boxes of books and files against the walls in what she thought would be only her temporary office, room C454. A narrow and dank little cubby no professor or even graduate student had occupied in years, not since she'd started working there.

Edith does not know who was in C454 before the years it was outright abandoned. All she knows is when she opened the door with the key, she was washed over with the smell of metal bookshelves, of hidden dust, the harshness of old sweat. The desk drawers empty except for an old fortune-cookie fortune curled in the very bottom drawer: *If you don't burn out at the end of each day, you're a bum.*

The window in C454 faces out onto the parking lot, the dilapidated ribbon of highway. Two of the fluorescent lights in the ceiling are completely out. She pushed the other boxes into corners. Oh, how she planned to layer and layer the walls of B409 with pictures when she returned – posters of book covers, postcards of her favourite authors – finally unpack all her boxes properly, and fill those bookshelves to brimming. Maybe even buy a plant for the window. A philodendron or a hanging ivy. A small cactus with a merry pincushion top; they sometimes lasted up to ten months in her old office before they browned and withered away.

She never moved back into room B409. Malcolm in Facility Resources wrote her that Dr. Lesley Hughes would need an office when she arrived, and the Endowed Chair office was under construction as part of the new Sandersams Supermarkets School of Business building project, so they couldn't install her anywhere else. Dr. Hughes had also pointed out with fortunate foresight that the university president and the donor would not be too happy to see Dr. Hughes in an office just like every other professor's. Edith peeped into her old office shortly before Lesley moved in. Built-in, dark wood bookshelves lined one wall, and the remaining walls were each painted a different shade of mauve.

Edith remembers Lesley posed triumphantly in the doorway of her luxurious house on the south bank of the Edmonton River Valley back when Edith was still technically her student, back when Lesley could say *I own you* to Edith, and Edith would nod *yes*. One of Lesley's artsy-fartsy chandeliers, a bouquet of broken bottles crafted by a Venetian glass artisan, suspended above her head, its twin in the dining room, her marcelled and lacquered gold hair burning with the setting sun sticking its tongue out in the window behind her, her lips reciting familiar horror stories: that Edith's dissertation was an inferior piece of work not worthy of a first-year university student, that it had no chance of ever being published, only a desperate Canadian hack press would publish it. *You should drop out*, she scrawled in the margins of Edith's dissertation drafts. The book would be published only if the publisher were *paid*. Astronomical amounts of money. Six trillion dollars wouldn't even begin to cover it. That Edith was hare-brained and difficult, that Edith drove her, Lesley, to drink, and where was Edith's gratitude?

– All the things I've done for *you*, Edith, blared Lesley. – You have no idea how many bottles of antidepressants and wake-up pills and sedatives I've had to choke down to get through the tangled mess of paper you call your dissertation. Sometimes I take the pills all at once! Chased with a bottle of cheap whisky! Sometimes I lie in bed, weeping at the hopelessness. Your research questions are Byzantine. You, Edith, *have nothing to say.*

Lesley's past devotion to Edith had deflated like a lung poked with a pencil, suddenly and irrevocably. And all in the final year of her degree, just when Edith was on the verge of becoming a PhD, just when Edith made her major discovery about Beulah's past as a Vancouver sporting girl who dabbled in the fledgling movement for Black railway workers' rights. *A badass.* For years and years Edith was Lesley's cute and exotic-looking PhD student, her shy queer brown pet, and then when Edith was about to become a Doctor just like Lesley, when Beulah Crump-Withers suddenly became *complex and interesting*, Lesley curdled.

Edith had had to meet with the graduate coordinator in his office, sit with a Students' Union mediator, the university ombudsperson, to force Lesley to allow the dissertation to go through to defence, because in year eleven of Edith's degree, Lesley had instructed Edith to start all over again. With a new topic. New *everything*. And because if Edith insisted on continuing to study the memoir of Beulah Crump-Withers, whose second marriage was to a Ukrainian man, then Edith should learn *Ukrainian*.

– Supervising you is like turning the *Titanic*, said Lesley.

It was during the *Titanic* harangue that Edith's eyelid spasmed for the first time. Her eyelid jumped so hard it felt like Lesley had snapped an elastic band against her eyeball.

During the dissertation defence, at the long table of professors and Edith at the very end with her dissertation arranged in a neat, 583-page brick in front of her, Lesley typed on her laptop at the opposite end of the table, texted messages on her Blackberry, then when it was her turn to ask Edith a question, asked sweetly, her *s*'s sibilant in that charming way Lesley always used in front of strangers or the press, – I know this is an unfair question, Edith dear, she asked, – but does your dissertation topic even exist? I was in contact with the head archivist at the National Archives, and she told me that a letter uncovered just last month in the Canadian prairie section of the archives suggests that Beulah Crump-Withers was a pseudonym for an American, bootlegging, sleeping-car porter, a *man*, named Clarion Williams. This undermines the whole premise underlying your dissertation, doesn't it? If what we always thought was the hundred-year-old memoir of a queerly articulate farm wife from Amber Valley, Alberta, was just a fantasy written by an American man from Chicago in the 1930s? If the truth of her identity was disclosed in a letter written by the mother of her alleged second husband? A letter written in *Ukrainian*?

One of the other examiners, a woman with lime-rimmed cat's-eye glasses, choked, then gulped from her paper cup of water.

– This is what the most recent discovery is suggesting, offered Lesley to the room, her impossibly wide lips forming an impossibly small cherry-sized moue. – So what will you do if it turns out that Beulah Crump-Withers isn't even *real*? I suppose this dissertation is, by extension, moot.

Lesley rose to standing then, her fingertips tented on the table, the tallest building of them all. But she was lying. Edith knew Lesley was lying because Lesley was biologically incapable of telling the truth. In radio interviews she crowed that she wrote fifty pages a day. To colleagues she whispered that she had persistent migraines and often had to go home to bed, the migraines so bad they forced her to go home and ... post updates on Facebook about an upcoming symposium in Finland. Or Portugal.

Sweat dripped down the walls. Edith's eyelid danced the Cucaracha.

The external examiner, scraggly grey hair squirting out from under the brim of his fedora, his voice traced with an accent that sounded English but not, suddenly guffawed and slapped his flaking old-man hands on the table.

– *None* of it's *real*, Lesley! We're *literature* professors! We dedicate our lives to paper dolls and, bully for us, we get paid for it. Give this poor girl a reasonable question. Or a real criticism, one that can't be remedied with a simple footnote. Please.

Then he scrubbed his face with his hands as though he wanted to rub off his skin. He was wearing a watch with the Cheshire Cat on its face. Edith nearly puckered to kiss that watch face. Dr. Angus Fella.

Lesley simultaneously tapped all ten fingers on the tabletop. Exactly once. The tap ricocheted, the final sound of something small and precious keeling over dead.

The Examining Committee chair at the foot of the table murmured that members of the examining committee should remember to speak in turn, address the PhD candidate and not each other, etc., and flipped hopelessly among his papers, his sentence trailing off into ellipses. The professor with the cat's-eye glasses cleared her throat and began a question about Foucault's heterotopia and what gardening while looking in a mirror might suggest about the memoir form.

Edith's very own fedora-ed, paper-doll-playing, deus ex machina: Dr. Angus Fella. And when she was hired as his colleague in Crawley Hall, he didn't remember Edith one little bit, even though he was responsible for throwing her the wooden plank that saved her life. He just strolls past her day after day, his hands in his pockets, his trousers ballooning overtop his wool socks and Birkenstock sandals, his fedora jammed on his head, his Cheshire Cat watch looping his wrist. The ancient professor with the billy-goat beard who crumbles Anzac cookies all over the lunchroom and who refuses to take the elevator in Crawley Hall, gasping his way up and down the staircase. Dr. Fella, who leaves the photocopying room suffused with eau de vodka or rum at 8:55 in the morning and who puts out a 'revised' edition of the same anthology every third year. Edith assumes Dr. Fella tipples rum – is *tipple* even a verb? – which is supposed to be scentless, but that's a lie. When Edith drinks hard liquor, she also prefers rum. The jaunty labels featuring antique maps or fields of sugar cane, people with pooled brown eyes in hot places: Martinique, Island of Flowers; Cuba, origin of the Cuba Libre. She would like one day to share a glass of rum with Dr. Angus Fella and ask him more about the paper dolls that rule their lives.

Her left hip crackles as she stands up to go pee. She's been sitting at her desk for four hours. She knocks her knee on a stack of books heaped by the door. Sits down again. She forgot to email her PhD student, Helen Bedford. Just one more email. Then she'll pee.

Edith ponders sending Coral an email to thank her for the e-card, welcome her back, ask her out for coffee? Dinner? See you at the next faculty meeting?

She pushes away from her desk and grabs her keys. She'll try the fourth-floor bathrooms today because it's the first day.

Early Wednesday morning, Edith puts on her delightful new blouse with the navy blue flowers. She's hooked on a bra that harnesses her breasts in tight so the blouse won't gape in the buttons around her bosom. She tests the gape in the mirrored doors of her bedroom closet. Sits down on the edge of the bed. Raises her arms like she's flying. Stands up. Raises her arms again. Opens them wide. No gape. She scoops up her car keys, her papers. Lesley's reception is today. But in her new blouse, today will still be a great day.

At work, elevator #1 dings, and the doors crack open. She steps inside. She straightens the hem on her cardigan as the doors slide closed. On the second floor the doors sigh open again, and one of the building's cleaners in the university's blue smock uniform wheels a black plastic trolley heaped with swollen, bright orange garbage bags into the elevator. The elevator suddenly hot with the smell of damp coffee grounds, fermenting fruit juice. Old bloody tampons, vaginas, anuses, scrotums, leaking noses and mouths, and something else, something inexplicable and horrible. Edith presses the button for the next floor, scrambles out of the elevator as quickly as she can, away from the choking smell. The cleaner crosses her arms. Hovering in the elevator lobby, Edith pretends to dig for something in her bag as the doors close, then waits for the next elevator to take her up three floors to the fifth floor and Lesley's reception. She is starting to wish she'd stayed home, she knows it's a mistake, but Vivianne said she should go to the reception because making an effort to socialize with her university family might help when the dean evaluates her AAO this cycle.

Her stomach feels like she's eaten a bag of soil. It's only been two days, but she longs for Bev's earlobes.

Elevator #2 opens, empty, silent. Ready to sweep her up into the company of Dr. Lesley Hughes, the new Leung Endowed Chair.

Standing in line at the bar, Edith strokes the cuff of the right sleeve, the little pinprick flowers peeking out from under the cuffs of her cardigan. In front of her, Iris Bell bends forward to order her drink. She's wearing a grey cardigan that sweeps below her hips, just the way Edith's cardigan sweeps below hers. Edith blushes with conformist gratitude. At the bar she asks the bartender, a young woman with an artfully frayed braid tossed forward over her shoulder, for a glass of white wine.

She sips delicately from her wine, feigns interest in the Sandersams Supermarkets banner draping next to the bar as she surveys the room. Armoured.

Academics in twos and threes gesture at each other with drinks in one hand, little china plates of egg rolls and meatballs in the other, as they stand among white pillars in the brown-carpeted room, brown and downy like the fur of a dead animal. Or dead grass.

This year will be her *supernova* year. Even though the thought of seeing Lesley is like contemplating a dirty toilet she's just about to lick, Edith is ready. She will try to swim at least five times a week. She will only lick that toilet if she *chooses* to lick that toilet.

I am the architect of my life; I build its foundation and select the furniments. Even the toilets. And bidets.

Vivianne prepped her on how to do successful small talk, rehearsed with her lines about the weather, travel, work. Coached her on how to juggle a glass of wine and a plate of canapés at the same time by suggesting she just have wine first, then the canapés later. Don't pile the plate with canapés because that could be misinterpreted. Don't overindulge in the wine because that could be misinterpreted. But don't go and *not* eat or drink because that could also be misinterpreted. Choose canapés that are bite-sized, toothpicked, or dry to the touch rather than messy when you bite them. Toothpicked meatballs or small, compact slices of salmon roll are good; deep-fried spring rolls drizzled with plum sauce not good.

A glass of white wine firmly in hand like a roofer's hammer, Edith has built her own foundation and selected her roof shingles at this reception.

For she is an author. Of a book Lesley told her would never be. That's why she belongs here. With these people. These members of her university family.

She sips the wine from its genuine glass goblet, marvelling at the tink of the glass against her teeth. At receptions before this dean's reign and the EnhanceUs strategic plan, they always drank out of plastic, ate off paper plates. She piles every twig of courage inside her, strikes a match, and for the very first time on her very own decides to light up a conversation with the dean, the white man who wants to refresh her, who poses with his crystal wineglass, chatting casually to Ian Bell in his corduroy pants and hands loaded with a drink *and* a plate of spring rolls. She cups her wineglass with both hands, sips, says, – Well, this is a nice turnout, isn't it?

Ian Bell says through a mouthful of spring roll, – I have to find my wife.

– Go find the other Dr. Bell, Dr. Bell, says the dean, – heh heh heh.

This man is in charge of Edith. He is the central cog in this ravenous academic machine. Her *boss*. Although administration and faculty never use that kind of language. No words like *boss*. *Job*. *Employee*. *Teacher*. *Vacation*. *Money*. *Secretary*. Instead of *job*, it's *post* or *position*. Instead of ripping out old poisonous asbestos tiles, memos from the dean's *administrative assistant* bandy about phrases like *Asbestos abatement will commence next week on the second floor.*

The top of his head comes up only to her chin. But he is one of those men who make women taller than him feel like perversions.

Her father, a former CEO for an oil company, told her that schmoozing was how deals got done. – The more expensive the scotch, the better, he said.

– Isn't that part of the reason you were fired? she asked her father.

– The seventies were a great time, he replied.

The dean's face slides away in the direction of the other employees while she schmoozes. Did he travel to the south of France again this summer? she asks. How windy the weather has been! What a magnificent reception! This wine is really tasty, yes it is!

He murmurs monosyllables. Fingers his cufflink. Does she physically repel him? Marian Carson saunters up to the dean, a glass of red wine in her hand. Edith is schmoozing not only with the dean but also with the associate dean, Marian Carson!

Marian tells the dean, tapping him on the shoulder with the base of her drink, – You didn't make it to the HEC meeting last night, old buddy, old chum, old lifelong pal. Three prospective donors attended. The optics were not ideal.

Marian sips her drink, jauntily parks her other hand in her pocket. She wears a green carnation in her lapel, like a dashing gay man from the 1890s. Marian can talk to the dean about important things, she is his equal. They go to the same conferences. They are both Carberry alumni. Marian secretly makes Edith swoon.

The dean hoots a laugh. – Well, we never bothered to work that hard wooing only *prospective*, pissant donors at Carberry, he says. – Are you saying we did it wrong at Carberry?

Marian laughs. – Good one, Phil.

Edith has no idea what's going on so she also laughs, grabbing the pillar for support with a flowered arm. Coral would handle this so much more elegantly. Coral knows the codes, knows how to talk to higher-ups about dogs, children, hockey, movies. She knows the right boutique television shows to watch and chatter about. Where *is* Coral? The first day of school gone by, and no Coral in the elevator or the mailroom, not even an accidental hallway collision.

– I'd rather spend my time on the whales, not the guppies and the tadpoles, says the dean, sipping his wine, then grimacing.

– Yes, well, says Carson, – remember that as intimidating as they might appear in size, the biggest whales eat only plankton.

The dean reddens, purples, clenches the hairy fist not holding his drink as Carson turns her back to him and saunters over to the Novacrest representative, who hands her a stress ball with the Novacrest Oil Sands' eight-legged lion logo printed on it.

Edith studies the flowers in the textile garden on her chest. The dean rearranges his face, launches past her to the other side of the pillar, and assaults the two people there: – You two an item now, I see? Am I invited to the wedding? he asks shaggy Angus Fella, who is standing coincidentally next to the peppy new assistant office administrator from Facilities who ordered the catering and flower arrangements. Dr. Fella's pasty face blushes snooker-ball red, and Peppy rejigs a spiky chrysanthemum in the vase on the table. Edith pushes out a guffaw. The dean sips his white wine. – I prefer white, she once overheard him saying at a retirement reception for two faculty members. – Red stains the teeth.

Edith's face flushes. She slides after him.

– My first book's coming out month after next with the University of Okotoks Press, she blurts from behind his shoulder. She grips her wineglass, sticky and warm.

The dean pops his glittering eyes back up to the general area of her face. She cannot read his expression, his dry lips unsticking from his tombstone teeth and saying, – Oh, University of *Okotoks* Press.

Like, oh, University of *Okey Doke* Press.

– Well, harrumphs the dean. – You'll find a press that can give you a higher Impact Factor for the next book, yes? But that's a good effort for a new hire like yourself.

– I've been working here for seven years, she says.

– I'm going to find another glass of wine, he says.

– All right, she says.

She tries not to look down at her flowers.

The dean shoots for Mona Leung, the perogie heiress and philanthropist with her seventy-year-old yoga-and-golf body who's appeared in the doorway, her fingers and earlobes chunked with diamond, her hair a svelte white bob. Students and professors ooze up to her.

The dean is an old boy, and he likes his *hooch*, Coral used to call him and it. He likes to attend receptions and banquets where he can drink wine; he loves his hooch every Friday afternoon at 3 p.m. in the graduate student bar, where bolder employees who join him address him by his first name. *Phil.* He and his wife, Daphne, who also doesn't correct people when they assume she is English. She comes to many of these receptions in heels with red soles.

Daphne chatters with Mona Leung about English bulldog puppies.

The dean's large brown eyes, the colour of soil, nod at Mona Leung, and he sidles away, the back of his suit jacket flapping. Normally Edith feels reassured by brown-eyed people; normally brown eyes are cozy. Trustworthy. The dean's flat, receding buttocks, the specks of cork floating on the surface of her wine; the sad revelation that her new blouse and her new book burst triumphantly from her brain-uterus barely register with the dean. She is not networking properly. She draws a hair out of the bowl of green salsa on the table next to her. She obviously must write and publish another book post-haste, and publish at a more prestigious press, a press in England, Oxford or Cambridge, although why would a press in England be interested in any Canadian prairie literary reflections – growing up on the Alberta prairies, all she ever read were English children's books, with lots of *buck up*s and *hob*s and *shilling*s and *do let's do something!*s, in her parents' suburban duplex on London Road in a neighbourhood named Piccadilly Heights, but she doesn't think the Brits care about Canadian prairies. And she must learn to care about the differences between wines: take a sommelier course. She'll have to travel to France, then Italy, anywhere properly European where wine is produced. Her mother wanted to do a wine tour on a bus through the vineyards in British Columbia. Both Edith and her father agreed, for once, that a Canadian wine tour would be useless. And who has time? Even if she manages to write a second book, manages to find a British fool who'll publish it, she'll have to write another book right after that one, and another after that, for the punishing boulder of the AAO that she wrestles up that hill keeps bounding back down, aimed straight for her chin, and she will always be Sisyphus, until she dies of an aneurysm, probably sitting on a fifth-floor toilet, her skull literally deflated from lack of ideas. And then there'll be all that hope that someone other than the publisher might actually *read* her multiple books, might start regarding her as an expert in Canadian western landscape metaphors, in *something*. Publishing a book in England is the only path to strive for, everyone knows it, even the part-time catering staff presiding over the towers of glass wine goblets, the trays of peeled shrimp and mini meatballs, know it. She sips more wine. She asks the bartender for a refill.

The cinnamon musk of Lesley's perfume slugs her in the nose.

Edith ducks behind a concrete pillar. Lesley. Edith's graduate-school horror past tense resurrected in her present tense. She tries to summon Vivianne's warm, buttery voice, imagines Lesley bulldozed away, bulldozed away.

Lesley's voice chimes out behind her, – Mona, so good to see you ... I'm so pleased this didn't conflict with your golf game ...

Lesley paying her respects to Mona Leung, grasping Mona Leung's elbow, – Can I get you a drink, Mona?, then barking at a student in uniform holding a tray, – Ms. Leung needs a drink, stat! And I'll have a gin and tonic in a large, wide glass with a curl of mango peel instead of a lime wedge.

– But, ma'am, we're only serving wine and beer, says the server.

– Don't you know who I am? Don't you know who *she* is? asks Lesley, pointing at Mona.

The server skitters away, tray clasped against his chest like a shield.

– Terrible service, she murmurs sweetly to Mona Leung.

They sniff the blooms spilling from a giant vase.

Lesley turns to the dean. – Phil! The last time I saw you was at the PERP!

Other professors – the Bells, Leonardo the rumpled baby – cluster to Lesley and Mona Leung like horseflies.

A vomity burp rises in Edith's throat, so she gulps it down with a swig of wine that dribbles down the front of her brand-new blouse. She dabs at the dampness with her napkin. The flowers twist into tiny corkscrews where the wine has spilled.

Yes. Corkscrews. A strange optical illusion because of the fabric darkening under the transparent wine.

She recoils, tenting the blouse as best she can away from her skin.

She lifts her face to the ceiling, her eyes closed. The hum of the reception guests, the bing and clank of the elevator doors just two rooms away. A humming. Someone's humming. Her eyes pop open. She refocuses on the brown speckled broadloom stretching across the floor.

Edith's chest flaps. Her stomach flaps. She runs the greasy tip of her finger around the edge of her glass and drinks some more. She peers around the pillar toward the voice, the laboratory-generated cinnamon smell. Her new blouse is revolting, she needs to tear it off her body, burn it. Her feet spontaneously cramp, rejecting their new shoes. She can't leave. She promised Vivianne.

Dr. Hughes curls her arms around the dean and Mona Leung in a death grip, her hands squeezing their shoulders like stress-balls. This is the vivacious Lesley, the sunny, ever-networking Lesley. A photographer in a black leather jacket and boots corrals them with her giant black beetle of a camera, asks Olivia Tootoo to pose in the photo too.

– We need more diversity in these photos, says the photographer. – Say cheese!

– Cheeeeese! declares Lesley, shaking her Grace Kelly hair.

Olivia frowns. So does Mona Leung.

The camera clicks.

A tall young man with prematurely grey hair hovers in the background, a beer in one hand, carrying a woman's coat in the other.

Dr. Hughes's pearls are veneered, gleaming teeth, the elaborate gold clasp having slid toward her bosom. – You need to dress the part, she once told Edith in their distant, decapitated past. Lesley, her mother and father, Vivianne too, it occurs to her, everyone is always telling Edith to dress the part. Like life is a perpetual costume party she's always on the verge of being bounced from.

Edith concentrates on the pattern of Lesley's chemise. Little green balls encircled with tinier balls. Little Earths with orbiting multiple moons, the moons grinding their way slowly around every Earth. Edith should say hello before she leaves to rip off her own shirt, the corkscrews spiralling into her skin. The adult thing would be to say hello. Vivianne said so, – This university's motto is *Give Yourself to the Truth*. How would you interpret that in the context of your job at the University of Inivea?

Edith dodges among the professors, students, servers with trays, toward Lesley.

– Hello, Lesley, she says. Her smile stapled to her face. – My dissertation's going to be published as a book.

What a stupid way to start a conversation! What is Edith's *problem*?

Lesley glides around Edith, her perfume rippling out like nerve gas, cocking her head and smiling with her generous apple-red lips at someone behind Edith, as though Edith is just a cold spot. Or a splash of vomit in her way.

– You, says a voice behind another giant camera, – can you pose with the dean? Great.

The dean suddenly pops up at Edith's side, holding up his glass, his body so close to hers she can see skin flakes on his thinning scalp, he is so close he is almost pressing the top of his head into her chin.

The photographer points her camera at them, – Try to look like you're enjoying yourself, the photographer says. She frowns.

– Yesssss, says Phil, baring his teeth.

Edith tries not to blink. The camera's black mouth clicks, once, twice, then the photographer zips off. Edith turns to the dean, but he has teleported away. He is speechifying to the newest hire, Leonardo. Who is now schmoozing a suited man who must be from Sandersams Supermarkets because he's distributing gold Sandersams pens, and now Leonardo's schmoozing the dean.

She would like to hate the rumpled baby, but he always holds doors open for her. Always remarks, – Ladies first.

Which she finds insulting but also charmingly old-fashioned.

Rumpled baby in his blond cherub curls clanks out a laugh at a joke the dean's just made, no doubt eating up the dean's socially dysfunctional treatise on how listening to opera makes chimpanzees' brain cells multiply, and how the dean attended an intimate private dinner in honour of Prince Charles and his wife, the Duchess of Whatever. Monologues she's heard him deliver at every single university social event she's gone to since he was hired.

Much as she wishes Lesley would just die already, Edith should try to learn from Lesley. She needs to photocopy herself into a reproduction of Lesley, who publishes a book a year with her husband, Dino, who teaches at Carberry, gallivanting around the world in her oversized pearls and fancy dress suits and patterned blouses, cooking up institutes and hosting symposia in Morocco and Edinburgh, co-editing essay anthologies taught the world over, delivering standing-ovation-quality keynote lectures to throngs of paying strangers. Edith leans her back against the pillar, her nose in her drink; no one thought to set out chairs at this reception. Her book is at the printer's right now, she knows it, but her brain's gouged and bleeding in spite of her being an author in a proper author's cardigan. The strange corkscrews begin turning again. She tries not to touch the corkscrews with her fingers, curls her back and tries to concave her chest to stop the corkscrews from touching her breasts. She drags in a sigh that turns into a chiselled cough. The dean snaps his hairy fingers in a conversation with a pretty undergrad, but she is sure he is snapping his fingers disapprovingly at Edith's wrinkled wool skirt. She should have ironed the skirt too, but there was no time. She let the time own her instead of baking proper matrimonial squares. Why didn't she buy a new skirt too? Why didn't she properly wash and iron those pants still caught in an ongoing cycle in the washing machine and wear those? Everyone here wears pants or skirts that stop at the knee. Lesley's chemise breaks right at the knee. Edith's skirt wrinkles and droops down to mid-calf. She has the wrong foundations for her architecture.

– Oh, Staines-upon-Thames Press! exclaims the dean to Leonardo, then claps his congratulations on his back. – Bravo!

The cover of Edith's book in the University of Okotoks Press catalogue. Last February, when the catalogue slid out of her mailbox, Edith sliced out the page and taped it to her office door at work. Also a grainy thumbnail jpeg popped up on the faculty website, under *Upcoming Publications*, after Edith hounded Alice Q. to post it, bribing her with a box of expensive chocolates. Edith clicked on the faculty website 176 times in one day just so she could look at it. But the jpeg disappeared by the week's end, replaced with the announcement of Dr. Lesley Hughes's upcoming position as the Leung Endowed Chair, beside an image of the cover of Leonardo's new book from Staines-upon-Thames Press.

Yes, Edith has rolled up to the top of the publishing Ferris wheel, only to descend the other side and find out she's only made it to the University of Okey Doke.

Lesley lets out a showy yawp, and the dean puts a hairy hand on her sloping shoulder. The Earths and their little rotating moons on her chemise.

The Earths on Lesley's dress shoot out tentacles and devour all the moons. The chemise now covered in simple polka dots.

Edith tries not to moan out loud. She stumbles over the dead-grass carpet and out the door. Bends over.

A stranger's black suede Hangakus tick-tock up to beside Edith.

– Oh hi, Edie, says a woman's voice. – There you are.

Edith clasps her knees, perimenopausal heat pounding her in waves.

– Hot flash, she chokes, – Coral?

She tries to straighten to standing, but the heat enfolds her, sits on her like a fat man, the tentacles ate the moons, she saw them. *She saw them.* If she stands, her guts will drop out of her mouth.

Coral's upside-down face appears, ginger hair drooling to the floor. Coral seems to be unperturbed about the ends of her long hair twitching and coiling on the floor. Her hair so long since the last time Edith saw her.

– I looked for you at the reception, says Coral. – You really should go. They haven't even started the speeches yet. Bad form if you don't make an appearance. You don't want to get *refreshed.*

– I ... saw... moons, says Edith.

– I'd offer to drive you home but I don't want to miss the speeches. You never answered my Happy New School Year email. I thought we were friends, Edith. Friends answer friends' emails, Edith.

Coral's dainty black suede Hangakus clip away.

Edith curls into herself as she rides the elevator down with two blue-smocked cleaners. One holds a trolley heaped with garbage like a shopping cart. Edith tries hard not to be sick at the fermenting-food smell, the smell of dust, of dank; she turns away from the other who shepherds a murky bucket of mop water, the smell of carcinogenic, industrial-strength cleaners, the unfocussed and diluted decay. Only something rotting underneath needs to smell that clean. She flees the elevator, clutching her belly, as soon as the doors bing open, even though the elevator has only made it to the third floor. She clunks down the stairs, ignoring the stabbing in her knees, the thwack of concrete steps off her heels, the grime collecting on her right palm as she clutches the banister on her way down. She trails scuff marks on the shined floors behind her like ellipses, through the corridors between the dark concrete hulks of buildings, away from the reception, away from the meatballs, away from her university *family*, her humiliating cupboard of an office across from the bathroom on the fourth floor of Crawley Hall. She pushes a dirty glass door open and plunges into the stony fall air, that sub-zero chill of the new year letting her know the next horrible year is just beginning, just like the last one began before that and before that. No matter how much she tries new clothes, therapy, or a shiny new attitude, she's still herself. The clouds low, the leaves on the trees falling in soft, itinerant showers. The clenching of the nausea suddenly releases. She stumbles to a stop. She sucks in cold, clean, fresh air in gasps.

She crunches through scattered piles of fallen autumn leaves to her car in the parking lot by Crawley Hall.

Grazing jackrabbits the size of spaniels lope away when she makes as straight a line as she can to her car. Hares studding the dying green spaces of this campus, oversized and stringy. She should bring carrots for them. Lettuce. How much lettuce? Lettuce prices shoot up in winter, six dollars for a single clump of limp, blackening leaves. The jackrabbits gather in twos and threes, tucked around trees, bushes, feeding out in the unprotected grassy areas, and two hares swipe and jump at each other in a boxing match, clumps of hair drifting. She's looked it up: a *drove* of hares, or a *down* or *mute* or *husk* of hares. In the dusk she stays far enough away that they continue their grazing on the lawns or park themselves to contemplate hare matters on the gravel paths. In the half-dark they're just brown smudges against the brown gravel of the paths. She swears a hare is feeding on a dead squirrel splayed in the road. Do hares eat meat? That hare gnawing on red bone, snuffling through entrail. Edith sniffs. Okey Doke Press. A grainy, ephemeral jpeg. She stamps each foot one at a time, jabs the calcifying calf muscles with her fingers. Next to her old Ford gleams a silver Mercedes. HUGHES blares the licence plate.

She kicks one of Lesley's tires. Scuffs the leather toe of her new Hangaku. She scrubs at it with her finger, tries to rub the scuff away with a little spit on her thumb.

She yanks open the door to the Taurus. Shoves down the gas pedal.

Edith cruises the streets that twine and curlicue around the University of Inivea, hunting for where Lesley might live. Lesley favours big houses, ostentatious houses, even for short-time rentals when she's a Visiting Fellow, houses like the one in the River Valley in Edmonton all those years ago. Edith's Taurus slows down whenever her car approaches a house that's taller than the others on the block or an unusual colour, like periwinkle or lemon yellow. She's lowered the window, her nose alert for leftover whiffs of Lesley's musky cinnamon spoor.

Edith roars her car home to her condo, chewing her thumb.

She pulls into the low-ceilinged parking garage at the bottom of her building. The square concrete pillars. The spots scrapingly narrow. She eases the car forward. Taps the wall with her bumper.

In her tiny foyer she pulls off her coat, nervous about her blouse. So much money for a hideous blouse that will just end up in the garbage.

But as she begins unbuttoning the top buttons, she notices that the corkscrews have settled back into lobelias again. She brushes her chest twice with her hand just to be sure.

But this blouse is lovely! She clicks on the light in the foyer, shoves her arm toward the mirror where the light is brighter. The blouse is magnificent. Tasteful. Subtle. She must have just been overtired when she saw the corkscrews.

She unscrews a bottle of red wine. At home she doesn't have to worry about her teeth. She checks her phone to see if Bev has texted. Nothing.

She unbuttons her blouse, unhooks her bra, and her breasts swing loose. She throws the blouse and the bra in the dirty-clothes hamper and grabs her baggy sweater.

She slaps a slice of cold pizza into her mouth.

She slaps open the washing machine door to see how her clothes are doing. Powdered soap clumps splat to the floor as she tugs out a bath towel, a face cloth. She stuffs the cloth and towel back in. Slaps the door closed again. Sets the washer cycle back to the beginning. Sips her wine. Tops up her glass.

She slumps at her desk. She spiders her fingers across the desk's plane to the special section of her desk, draws toward her the Beulah Crump-Withers manuscript pages. The pages' delicious heft and angularity all stacked together, spiral-bound in a nearly book-like package. The glossy pages busy with writing and life. She traces the words on the title page, the sparkling jewellery of the font, the breaths of the paragraph breaks no matter what page she chooses.

This is what matters.

This.

She gently places the manuscript back on the corner of her desk. Her talisman.

She picks up and flips through several of the one-page essays she made the students write in class on the first day. She tries to read then grade the essays, the unruly pile spilling with her red scribbles. She shifts the essays to the edge of her desk and opens her laptop, dickers with a partial draft of her Academic Achievement Overview: the site's working today. Her AAO's not due until the second week of December, but Edith dreads that scrubbed-raw steel-wool feeling in her stomach and chest when she's filling it out at the last minute. She logs in to her MYUOFI, clicks again on the AAO button. Once she's finished finding and scanning them all, she'll upload her supporting documents. But right now, even though she's entered the portal and clicked on the button that opens her file, when she clicks the Revise Existing AAO button it just broods like a meatloaf no matter how many times or how forcefully she clicks. She'll have to contact IT and of course they'll roll their eyes at her through the phone. She doesn't have a PhD in computing science, for crying out loud.

She really should grade those essays instead. She tries to read a single paragraph. A single sentence of the third one-page essay. This essay by a Brooklyn Alonzo. Has Edith just dabbed pizza grease in the right margin of Brooklyn Alonzo's one-page essay?

The essay has no title. She told the students to include a title. She gave them a thoughtful speech about the importance of titles, and this essay has no title. She wrote on the whiteboard *PLEASE INCLUDE A TITLE.*

The essay is brief: *I have no idea what we taked about in class today. The pages you asked us too read in class were to confusing. it was boring to. was ther something about corn and a women. Sorry professor!!!!!! ((+_+))*

This essay was supposed to be a one-page essay on the garden as a metaphor in the first paragraph of Beulah Crump-Withers's *Taber Corn Follies* memoir.

Then she remembers she has to meet her graduate student, Helen Bedford, tomorrow. She extracts Helen Bedford's chapter from a stack on the floor, reads the last paragraph on page fourteen. Taps her teeth with her pen.

She turns back to her AAO. She hates doing her AAO so much she could brain it with a hammer. She punches the Revise Existing AAO button one more time. Nothing.

She clicks opens her email.

Coral's written.

Sad we didn't get to talk at the reception. Hope we can go for coffee soon. The dean refused to even look in my direction, now that I'm back and now that I've won the refreshment appeal. I hired a lawyer and scared them pissless. I've nailed that old turd to the wall good and hard. Hope you're feeling better.

Edith's fingertips hover over the keyboard, the warm smooth plastic of the alphabet, trying to compose an answer for Coral with whom she hasn't emailed for a whole twelve months. *I'm sorry, Coral. For everything. Thank you for the Back to School card.*

She deletes it.

I wish I'd seen you in the masses of people. No one normal was there. Lesley's dress ate itself before my very eyes. Why must we all wear such odd clothing?

Delete delete.

I hate you, Coral. You freak me out and my therapist says I should approach you with caution.

She pours herself another glass of wine. In vino veritas. She deletes the 'hate' so the email reads, *Coral. You freak me out. This is my truth. My therapist says I should approach you with caution.* She presses Send, her stomach thumping. They were close friends once. Friends tell the truth. Even friends with a complicated history. Friends shouldn't email their complicated friends after drinking so much, but the University of Inivea's motto is *Give Yourself to the Truth*, and she would like to think she is a good employee. She opens another email addressed to the entire faculty from the dean's office administrator about a 'FORT Research Opportunity Related to Business.' Because everything is related to business. Business has all the money. The new Sandersams Supermarkets School of Business building germinating right behind her own building, the jaywalking and trundling over lawns she has to do now to avoid the long cage fences around the construction site and the skeletal frame of the building-to-be on the south side of Crawley Hall. Buying a pita wrap in the food court in Leung Hall now takes twenty-three minutes because the shortcut from her office to Leung Hall is now a fenced-in construction site. Sometimes – well, too often – she'll just buy a terrible sandwich in a plastic container or an oversized starchy scone in the cafeteria in the basement of Crawley Hall and slither back to her office with that.

Maybe her next book will be about business and prairie poetry? If only she could find a memoir by a businessman's wife? A journal from the point of view of a cow on a dairy farm? Edith loves Beulah Crump-Withers for exactly who she is, her writing about the stewing and canning of rhubarb from her garden, and the sewing of dresses out of empty flour sacks. The wispy beauty of a cirrus cloud. Edith could write articles and books about Crump-Withers for the rest of her life. But Beulah Crump-Withers and Strategic Workforce Development? Flour sacks and Value Realization?

Edith scratches a budding pimple on her forehead.

Today is supposed to be a ballet exercise day. She paid for classes and she's only gone to one since she signed up last month, but she recently swam for the first time in years! She doesn't want to overstretch her joints, aggravate her lungs any further – that might make her sick. And her wrists still smart from her weird fall in Crawley Hall that day she swam. Really she should stay home because she's kind of drunk, the bottle of wine three-quarters gone already when she swears she only poured herself one glass. Is this the second bottle already? Plus she has too much grading to do. And she has to meet Helen Bedford tomorrow. And she hasn't read the book yet that she's supposed to teach tomorrow afternoon. Well, she's read it, she just can't remember it. She remembers opening the book and only seeing reams of tiny font in a language she once used to know. And her notes from the last time she taught it are only single-word cues: one page says *p. 81: Sloterdijk!*, another on a blue sticky note: *p. 243: motherhood??* She would like to travel back in time and kick herself in the neck for being so lazy and disorganized.

She twists open another bottle of wine.

The doctor at the university clinic said her blood pressure was a tad high. Then the doctor asked how many alcoholic drinks Edith consumed in a week. She frowned at Edith's answer.

– Do you smoke? asked the doctor, her eyes on her computer monitor.

– No.

– Well, that's something. Here's some literature I want you to read.

She handed Edith a pamphlet called *Rethinking Drinking* with a photo of a beer glass filled with icy, frothy beer on the front fold.

– But I just came in so you could diagnose this tic in my eye.

– Oh that's just stress, said the doctor, pecking at her keyboard.

Edith hadn't wanted to go to that clinic. Edith's mother told her a harrowing story about her own mother's massive heart attack, how her skin was the colour of clay the entire week before. Edith had no time to sit around waiting for teetotalling physicians in clinics, surrounded by frail, coughing people shuffling in and out, colicky babies. Especially with her mother plopped down next to her, surreptitiously tearing out recipes from the clinic's copy of *Woman's Day* magazine. In fact, that last appointment was four years ago. That kind of time spent mouldering in a loud and overheated waiting room could be used to catch up on her reading. She longs for the days when she would brew herself a monster-sized cup of black tea loaded up with milk and sugar, and spend hours reading a proper book. The pages sliding the story into her hands, the characters more known to her than people in her real life. Time. She will own time.

She heaves herself up from her desk, her knees popping. She should go to her Ballet for Beginners class. She paid for it. She thinks about her sweatpants in the chest of drawers, her runners tossed into the dusty back of her closet with her once-used yoga mat, a badminton racket she thwacked around exactly twice. Just toss the runners on and run to ballet class. Just do it, Edith. Do it. The class only four blocks away. The clock on the computer tells her it's 6:25 p.m. Class starts at 7 p.m. But she needs a good night's sleep. She should have taken her swimsuit to work; she could have splashed a few laps. But she has no time for swimming now that classes have started, the undressing and redressing, the shower, the drying, students seeing her saggy and naked in the change room. It's all too much. She will feel better if she grades some essays. She will *make time* for essays. A glass of wine and twenty-seven one-page essays graded. Or at least four. She eases back down into her seat. Shuts her computer. Draws the teetering bundle of 110 essays to her belly and pulls the cap off her red pen. She also needs to finish Helen Bedford's chapter. She cracks her knuckles. Gulps from her wineglass.

The red pen scribbles and circles across pages until 1:30 a.m., red blobs bleeding into her cuticles, staining the palms of her hands. The heat vent clicks on and off, the soft whirr of the building's heating system warming her up. The occasional, distant ding of the elevator door at the far end of the hallway. The walls ash-grey, silver-grey, cockatoo-grey. The grey walls look like sleep. She rifles one last time through Helen Bedford's chapter. Double-checks the spelling in her own comments. Tries to dab away a speck of wine on page three. She obscures the speck with a red ink scribble, as though the scribble was a comment she had second thoughts about. She lines up the essays in a bundle, taps the four sides of the bundle so the pile is an even, clean hay bale on her desk.

That night a nightmare bangs her eyes open. The same night of studying the cork bits bobbing in her drink like tiny buoys, the night of watching her former mentor, the multiple award-winning, FORT grant–winning Lesley Hughes toasted with huzzahs and ballyhoos from a cheering crowd as she pranced into her role as the new Endowed Chair. The earths lashing out and swallowing the little moons. This night ending in an email from Coral dragged into the trash. Coral is contaminated. But Coral is the only person Edith could ever talk to about tonight, the tentacles and moons, about how disoriented she got in her own office building back in August, how rattled and hopeless she feels, even with her magic shoes and an empty office wastebasket (she emptied it herself), this night ending in drinking two and a half bottles of wine – it only felt like one generous glass, really – and grading. This night of evil stacks of sloppily graded essays still lumping the surface of her desk even though she scraped through at least ten of them just before bed. And none over a page long. The essays like Sisyphus's boulder but with paper cuts. She graded at least ten. Maybe eight and a half, but she can't tell because she kept flipping back and forth between papers she'd already marked, worried her grades are too high and the students and the dean and associate dean will think she's a soft touch. And some of the papers she worries she graded too low and the students will come to her office and squeal with their tight, cross mouths about how they've never received grades this low *ever*.

That night Edith dreams of hares. Hares hanging by their necks, throttled by catgut in a thicket of trees. Someone has executed them, hares the size of small birds, their soft, drooping bodies. All dead. Their long ears dangling, the half-closed yellow eyes. Hares hanging like grisly earrings from the branches. Edith wakes abruptly in her brand-new condominium building of shiny chrome and concrete, the walls painted with interior design catalogue shades of grey she picked herself, the grey of time dripping away as grey water.

She pushes back the covers and swings both feet out of bed. She pulls on her jeans and slides her wallet and her phone into her pockets. Forgets to lock the door behind her.

In the elevator, she leans back against one of the mirrors and regards her reflection, multiplied by infinity in the mirror opposite. A baggy-eyed, expressionless stranger. The face so bland it verges on hostile.

Bev isn't working in the Kaffee Klatsch tonight, and when Edith slides into her favourite booth, the coffee tastes somehow not as succulent.

Edith opens her phone, opens her emails. Coral hasn't written back yet. Edith could send an addendum to her last email and write more of her actual feelings. Like that when Coral was gone she missed running into her the most when they collected mail from the wall of metal department mailboxes in the photocopy room on the fourth floor. On Mondays, for example, Coral would fling flyers and used envelopes into the recycling bin underneath the boxes and ask Edith about Edith's weekend. Coral would have to reach up high on her tiptoes to twist her key in the hole of her box because her mailbox door was so high and she was so petite, while Edith would have to curl down low like a spider playing dead to reach her box because she is tall and her box is at the bottom. They first spoke when Coral told Edith that she'd come across Edith's article in *Canadian Quarterly* and was *dazzled*. Edith blushed so hard she almost swooned and could no longer look into Coral's eyes so light brown they were almost yellow. She smelled Coral's mothball-perfume smell.

She missed Coral's ease. How at meetings Coral never chose the same seat in room D562 every time the way some professors would. Coral sometimes sat up high in the fourth row beside members of the faculty junta like Marian Carson in her authentic tortoiseshell glasses, sometimes off to the side in the second row next to contract lecturers like poor Otis, old-school eccentrics like the often tipsy Angus Fella; she sat next to graduate student reps in the bottom-tier seats, she sat next to Edith. Coral could run with the hares and hunt with the hounds because, unlike Edith, she had gone to the correct university as a graduate student, Carberry University in Ontario, from whence the dean and so many members of the junta graduated. Although Coral was a specialist in an iffy, more contemporary topic having to do with feminism and philosophy.

– Keep calm and write on, Edith, Coral used to say.

Coral was always too near the precipice.

Edith presses Delete Draft. She slurps her disappointing, valerian-infused coffee and texts Bev.

Bev snores. Loudly, lustily. Her arms thrown up around her head. Her nipples buttoned from the chill in the room. Bev snores the way she makes her lattes, heaping with luxurious foam, embellished with artful leaves, flowers, once a panda bear's face. The sheets twine around her opulent flesh like an Italian sculpture. She does not believe in bras but sticks little adhesive rubber caps to her nipples instead. She knows where to buy weed. She has five children. She left her husband eight months ago. Her phone dings with rainfall, sparkles, chimes, chirps, and beeps, because her children and grandchildren are always texting her. So refreshingly non-academic.

When Edith texted to ask if she could come over because she couldn't sleep, Bev wrote back, *Booty Call!*

Edith rolls over onto her back, fighting not to fall asleep. She must get out of this bed. A long cobweb trails from the wire pendant lamp shaped like a dandelion clock suspended from the middle of the ceiling. Bev pinched the lamp in the divorce. They lie on a mattress on a red Persian rug, its edges curling with green and gold tassels. Bev had to buy a new mattress because the husband fought her for the mattress and the bed frame, carved from a single cedar tree trunk.

– It was fucking glorious, said Bev. – God, I miss my bed. But that's the only thing.

But the Persian rug she got in the divorce. – Well, I stole it, said Bev. – Because I bought it. With his money. But really my money. The money I should have been paid to bear and care for his children. Worked like a truck-stop waitress for decades.

Edith pulls the blanket up to her chin. Smells her fingers, redolent with coffee-bean aroma and sticky from baroque, flamboyant sex with Bev, mother of five, new adventurer of life, Kaffee Klatsch barista, and condo neighbour one floor down.

– You're my new adventure! shouted Bev, and she smashed her lips onto Edith's.

Edith has been here tonight for seventy-nine minutes. Now she *must* get up and exit this condo. She scissors her legs under the sheets. Dozes. She has an eight-thirty meeting tomorrow with her graduate student. Her big lecture class is at noon, and there's a workload agenda meeting at four. She hasn't finished grading the one-page essays. Bev offered to help Edith grade essays. Edith declined.

Edith slips out of bed, pokes and peers around for her sweater, her jeans, in the half-dark. She tiptoes barefoot into the hall, slips on her flip-flops.

Two nights ago, the night they slept together for the very first time, before Bev asked her if she wanted to come upstairs to her condo, Edith thought Bev might be a new friend to replace the friendship hole in her life, with her artisanal latte skills and her charming gap teeth. Or like a friendly local bartender, polishing glasses and mugs while Edith monologued her heart out at her favourite table in the coffee shop. The easy way Bev talked about kids, coffee beans, politics, Heinz condiments, and different brands of soy milk. The way she moved so comfortably in her round, Venus of Willendorf body. Edith originally thought Bev was just inviting her over for coffee, that's all Edith thought Bev the Barista wanted. She thought that being invited for coffee to Bev's condo would be maybe half an hour of idle chatting with a neighbour and a cup of coffee made from exotic, gourmet coffee beans, freshly ground, served in some exotic way, like with ice cream or lemon rind or twenty-four-karat gold leaf flakes. Perhaps an elaborate silver coffee pot and purple velvet drapes. Conversation about grandchildren, divorce lawyers, perhaps some listening to music and discussion about percussive syncopation. Edith envisioned a new friend. Edith would occasionally borrow a couple of eggs from her, maybe use her washing machine. But instead the invitation was for sex. And it had been so many years since her ex, Beryl, and the microsecond of Coral-rebound, that Edith couldn't reasonably say no. Bev can't stand coffee because she works with it every day, so Bev didn't even offer coffee.

– I've got tap water? Bev had said, pointing toward the sink. – I didn't know you'd be thirsty.

Bev wrapped herself around Edith the moment Edith stepped in the front door.

Edith has no *time* for sex. But she will *make* time.

– I want your D-cup tits in my face, said Bev, her face close to Edith's, her hands squeezing Edith's waist. – I've never felt another woman's breasts before. Can I? Does it bother you that you're my experiment? There, I said it.

– I don't ... , said Edith, squirming, her back suddenly very straight. – I have work to do, Beverly. This is literally my coffee break.

– Me too, said Bev, whipping off her long apron, then hurrying back to kiss Edith, her hands cupping Edith's face, Bev exclaiming that Edith's cheeks are so soft! Bev exclaimed about every inch of Edith, the softness, the roundness, the smoothness, the bigness of the breasts. – I'm converted, exclaimed Bev. – I officially love women's breasts!

Bev stuck her face between Edith's breasts, and kissed her cleavage and nipples with extravagant smacks. Edith has to admit that being Bev's experiment is very pleasing.

Bev smelled pleasantly of coffee, milk, and lotion made of Bali sea foam.

And now every time Edith exits her building to go somewhere on foot, she by necessity walks by the glass floor-to-ceiling walls of the Kaffee Klatsch. Where Bev will see her entering and exiting the building.

Bev can also get marijuana from her kids. For Edith's father's arthritis. Edith found this out when Bev asked her if she wanted to eat a hash brownie or smoke a joint after their first round of sex.

Edith runs from Bev's condo, down the hall, and punches the elevator button. She's forgotten her underpants. She coughs, her throat sandpaper-harsh. She should have been grading papers if she couldn't sleep, not inviting Bev the Barista to continue experimenting on her. Bev so loud, so non-academic. Not a single book in her entire condo, which disturbs Edith. Not even a magazine beside the toilet. A home without books is like a refrigerator filled only with plastic fruit and a ham shank carved from tofu. Edith's ideal partner should be an academic. Like Lesley's husband, Dino at Carberry University. Definitely Edith's ideal shouldn't have five children. An ex-husband. Work in a *coffee shop*. But Edith can already feel herself dropping into love. She will give this new year a second chance. The reception was just a minor blip. Her new book and her new sweetheart will make this the most stunning year ever, even if it means being sleep-deprived, even if it means having this terrible dean as her boss, and her turncoat old supervisor Lesley as her colleague. She would love to telephone Vivianne about Bev. Crow to Vivianne about her life improvements, how she is architecting her life. But that would eat up an entire free session for no good reason.

As soon as Edith pulls her own blanket up over her chest in her own bed, she tumbles backward into sleep.

Edith scheduled her meeting with Helen Bedford for eight-thirty this morning. She can barely slide out of bed, her head concrete-heavy in her hands. She accidentally blobs mint toothpaste on her hair pick, picks it into her hair.

She will wear the black-and-white version of the shirt today. She will tie on the new scarf.

When she stumbles into Crawley Hall, Edith boards elevator #1 on the basement level, a paper-bagged scone from the cafeteria in her hand. The doors close, and she pushes button #4.

On the main floor the door opens to Lesley, framed by the doorway, her dozing piranha mouth all teeth and dimples as she laughs widely at something the dean's said. The dean hustles into the elevator, brushing Edith with an elbow. Lesley's eyes flick to Edith for a fraction of a fraction of a second, then flick back as the dean punches #5.

Edith smiles in a vague, watery way at them both. She unbuttons, then rebuttons, the top button of her coat. She fingertips the end of her brand-new scarf, the gauzy, Harlequin-diamond fabric.

– You know what, Phil, Lesley says to the dean, – I'll take the next elevator. I just need to freshen up for a second, I was up until late last night preparing for this graduate student talk this morning and I feel like a madwoman in an attic, so why don't you go ahead and I'll meet you up there?

The dean salutes her, mock-clicking his heels together. – Of course, Lesley! Don't take too much time. Your audience awaits with bated breath!

Lesley can't even stand to ride the elevator with her anymore! Lesley thinks she's a monster!

But no. Vivianne told Edith to practise her self-talk. What is your self-talk, Edith?

I am the architect of my life. I build its foundation and select the locks for the attic.

Edith peers at the dean, at Lesley, from the dirty windows of her life.

The dean leans toward Lesley, says – I'll be in Madrid in February. I won't be here that month, come to think of it. But thank you for the invitation, earlier.

– Oh, the CREP conference? I'm being given the CREP award. I'll be there too.

– Ah, well. We'll be doing a cava tasting on day three.

– No one in Spain drinks cava anymore, Phil, says Lesley. – I'll be moving on to France right afterwards to deliver a keynote.

Lesley and the dean natter on. *They are weak*, thinks Edith, sniffing her fingers for vestiges of Bev's musk under her fingernails. *I am strong. My foundation is reinforced concrete. My sub-basement is stockpiled with grenades and hair-trigger booby traps*. The dean wears a tie that looks like stained glass.

It's 8:37 a.m., and Edith is seven minutes late for her meeting with Helen Bedford because of traffic skidding over icy, sleety streets, and Lesley and the dean one-upping each other is making her even later, his hand with its unnaturally hairy thumb resting on the rubber edge of the open elevator door, preventing the elevator from hauling Edith to her floor. The fingernail on his thumb is blue and peeling. Time is an illusion, but it is also gelatin. The elevator door beeps in protest, as though in pain. The grit under Edith's feet powders its way up to the inside of her mouth. The scarf winds around her neck as the dean grins and chatters with Lesley on the other side of the elevator doorway. He faces straight ahead, his marionette-lined mouth smiling in a way that has nothing to do with happiness. Dropping her scone, Edith puts her hand to her throat, the scarf screwing tighter, her fingers clawing, trying to unknot. Neither of them notices her mouth making O's like a koi in a pond, her scone rolling its floury way out of its brown paper bag into the middle of the elevator floor. The elevator door beeps its distress again.

The elevator door slides shut, the dean settles back against the wall, his rooster feathers settling. The scarf collapses in her fingers, just a floppy fabric scrap she's yanked away and balled up in her hands. Her stomach grumbles as she surveys her dirty scone.

She's not unlocking her office door until 8:39, huffing from labouring through the corridors. One hallway blocked with a Construction Zone sign and a warped plywood wall; in the alternate hallway the ceiling tiles have been ripped away the whole length, the silver ducts and metal pipes twisting above her in the dark, and her scarf crushed in her hand. Helen Bedford hulks by the dark blue office door with a mountainous backpack hoisted on her back, a gigantic cardboard coffee cup in her hand, her mouth flat as a slug's.

Edith fumbles at the knob. Drops her keys to the floor with a jangle. Then her scarf tumbles down. She reaches for the keys, the scarf. Her satchel swings forward and thumps her in the temple. She fights the door open, the key sticky in the lock.

She refuses to let Helen intimidate her.

Helen has wide-open eyes, unnaturally wide, the whites of her eyes egg-fresh and luminescent and clear, and not unbearable to look at. Edith tosses her coat onto the coat stand, propels the scarf into the garbage, pulls out a package of curled papers. Edith's desk is lightly powdered with construction dust, and the metal cover from her heating vent is missing. For some inexplicable reason, a grain of rice sits on her desk. Maybe a workman eating his lunch? A remnant from the Cup-a-Soup lunch from last week? But she cannot think about that as she swipes all the debris aside with her sleeve because she has had Helen Bedford's thesis chapter for almost seven weeks and the chapter is only fourteen pages long. Unforgivable! Edith spent the last week chewing through the chapter, a study of sugar in Canadian fiction. Helen is interested in sugar in literature because of her juvenile diabetes. – Research Me-Search! Edith called out gaily when she first heard about Helen's topic.

Helen sits in the grubby chair with the flattened cushion. Grubby and flattened from years of students' and professors' bums. Edith tried to get a better chair from the faculty lounge and its collection of unused chairs, but the office administrator, Alice Z., caught Edith pushing the chair along the hallway in transit between the lounge and her office and chided Edith – Edith needed to fill out the appropriate form, and the new chair should be in her office in six to eight months. Thirteen months ago.

Edith also sits in a tired, squished chair. She talks about Helen's chapter three, that it is shaping up well, but that Helen needs to better prepare for the line of inquiry she's proposed in chapters one and two, and this chapter doesn't seem to be taking into account Lucy Maud Montgomery's numerous inclusions of cake in her *Anne of Green Gables* novels as instances of sugar or the most recent theoretical sources commenting on baked goods as semantic objects in literature. As Edith thumbs through pages eleven and twelve filled with her tiny red-penned comments, Helen Bedford inhales loudly and her cheeks fill up like a puffer fish. Edith realizes that Helen is bored – that momentary, obvious imitation of a puffer fish telegraphing everything Edith needs to know.

Edith desperately wishes she could call Vivianne.

Edith is not sure what to make of her imaginary house's foundation. It feels untrustworthy, leaky.

She inhales, exhales. This is her year. This will be her year. She is a published author. She has a new, proper girlfriend for the first time in nine years. She straightens her shoulders. Crosses her feet at the ankles. Uncrosses them. Crosses them again.

The black hole of the heat vent suddenly belches burning air, moist and smelly. Like boiling eggs. Edith pauses a moment, plucks at her collar to let out some of her own heat.

– Let's continue, shall we? Edith says.

She paws through her notes, trying to sum up two, three pages at a time, and when she reaches the end she looks up at the clock and sees that she's been spouting for almost twenty-seven minutes. She asks Helen if Helen might have any questions.

Helen arranges her hands in her lap. Edith notices for the first time that Helen never took off her backpack, that Helen's hair sweeps strangely thinner along the hairline. Edith has always admired Helen's low and vigorous widow's peak.

– Yes, I do, says Helen. – I'm switching to a different supervisor. Dr. Hughes has agreed to supervise my thesis.

Edith's back suddenly arches from a palpable smack of disappointment, sadness, panic. She flips erratically through the papers, her notes glowing and crawling along the margins, the three-page typed response she wrote resting on top of the stack.

Lesley's tentacled chemise.

Edith should have paid attention to the tentacles and not the Earths. She should have read that creepy, shifting hallway as the evil omen it was. Her scarf. This place is turning against her. The building and the people in it. She's not crazy.

I own you, said Lesley, only seven years ago. The *Titanic*.

– All – All right, says Edith, her throat full of dust. The air from the heating vent blows harder, the boiling-egg smell becoming a hot sewer smell. She pats her nose when really she wants to clutch it, stuff it to stop the horrible compost stench suddenly rising in the room. She wonders how her losing Helen will affect the dean's targeted refreshment strategy. Helen leaving gives her no supervisions at all. She'll have to put *zero* under the MA and PhD Supervision box on her AAO form. She has not a single student to guide. Helen was her very first long-standing recruit to the academy. Edith has already bought Helen a *Congratulations on Your Graduation* card and a forty-dollar pen embossed with a University of Inivea crest in preparation for her and Helen's great day.

The toilet across the hall flushes. The vent blows a frizzing wisp of Edith's hair into her eye. Edith clutches Helen's chapter to her chest.

– But why, Helen Bedford? Edith asks finally. – Why?

– Dr. Hughes said she could fund me. She said she could help me get the FORT assistantship because she's on the long list for a FORT grant.

But I own you.

Helen puffs up her own cheeks, exhales abruptly. – I'm going to be late for my shift, says Helen. – I have to go. Can I have that?

She reaches her hand out for the chapter.

– What do you do? asks Edith, her fingers clutching and crinkling Helen's chapter even more. – Where are you working your shift?

– I do psychic readings, says Helen.

Edith worked so hard on this chapter; she could have graded so many more essays if she hadn't been reading and worrying over this chapter. She could have spent more time with Bev. She didn't even prepare sufficiently for this afternoon's lecture because she laboured so hard to finish reading on time.

A gust of wind blows past the window. The window pane vibrates in its frame, as though the building is exhaling its exasperation with her too. Everyone against her, even Crawley Hall.

Tacked to her bulletin board is a list of all the faculty members' names, and recorded by each of the names is a list of the students being supervised by each faculty member. Alice Q. updates the list each year. Beside Marian Carson's name, six students' names. Eugene Thiessen has five: all scrawny, big-eyed women magnetically attracted to his pottering daddyishness. Even the perennially sick Leroy Hoffman has three. He even video-conferenced in for the candidacy exam for one student from his hospital bed where he was being treated for septicemia. Coral once had nine. And beside Edith's name: *Helen Bedford*. Which Edith will have to strike out. Which the dean will see. Leonardo has two names, and he started only a year ago. Edith will be forced to teach the giant classes that no one wants, that's the punishment. The kind of class that texts and plays video games right in front of her, students who sleep with their heads on their desks. A class with so much grading, there's no time to pee or breathe, forget about writing her second book. She won't be able to make one pan of matrimonial squares with a class like that. And she'll never get to give Helen Bedford that pen.

Helen Bedford, please don't leave me.

Rumpled Baby shouts his kookaburra laugh in the hallway. The toilet across the hall flushes.

– What did I do wrong? asks Edith. – Let me know and I can fix it.

– I need those papers, says Helen, the whites of her eyes glowing. – Dr. Vane, I can take that.

– Helen, says Edith, – your nose is bleeding.

– Shit, says Helen, touching her index finger to her nose. – That's disgusting.

Blood curls around Helen's knuckle.

– Let me get you a Kleenex!

Edith scuffles through her purse for a package of tissue. – Pinch the bridge of your nose and lean your head forward! No, wait, lean your head back! Here! Here!

She shoves a crumpled tissue at Helen. Helen coughs. Blood coats her tongue, daubs her teeth.

A loud bang on the window behind Edith slams her from behind. Helen's egg-white eyes flare.

Hands to her throat, Edith spins to the window.

The perfect residual outline of a bird in flight on the other side of the window, and a smear of feathers, a speck of blood, smushed into the glass.

She turns back around. The tired, squishy chair empty. The chapter gone too. Only a splash of blood on the tabletop.

The scarf has evaporated from the garbage can, probably stuffed somewhere in Helen's backpack.

She dashes back to the window to see if she can tell where the bird might have fallen. The heating vent blows its noxious air so hard the papers pinned to her bulletin board flap. She jams on her coat inside out. Slams the door shut behind her, harder, louder than she intended. The slam ricocheting down the hallway. Helen's blood drops peppering a trail on the hallway floor. Edith's heart breaking.

Coral stands, mannequin straight, at the bank of elevators. The fine, straight ginger hair pouring down past those narrow shoulders can only be Coral's. Edith lurches to a stop, as though an invisible person has pushed a hand up against her sternum. Coral's wearing a wheat-coloured trench coat. Cinched tight at the waist. No pattern.

Edith hovers. Should she call out? Backtrack and plunge herself down the stairwell instead? Tap that bony shoulder? Edith's not ready yet for a full encounter. She remembers the email she sent last night. Why did she have to *send* it?

For Edith has had the revelation that she does not want Coral back, no, she does not. Coral is a psychic hangnail.

But the *bird*. Probably concussed and twitching in agony in the bushes below Edith's window. She could gather it up in the skirt of her coat. Call wildlife officers. Feed it from a tiny bottle and send it flying away, back into the grassy foothills where it belongs.

Elevator door #1 slides open, and Coral steps in. Edith jumps forward, flapping her paddle-sized hands, crying gaily, – Coral! The prodigal daughter has returned!

Coral spins around. Her familiar thin face flushes with irritation, with misdirected blood, eyeliner around her eyes thick and furiously black against her skin, her eyes two holes in her face.

– I freak you out and your therapist says you should approach me with caution? asks Coral, her face so much thinner than when she left, her cheeks painfully sharp. An insectival thinness. The eyes disproportionately large.

Edith's breath stops. If she breathes she will burst into tears and she cannot let the tears gush here. She turns her face to the floor of this enemy space, the dusty corners of the elevator floor, a hair elastic knotted with threads of hair, a torn scrap of grey paper.

– I shouldn't have sent you that email! says Edith, – I was really tired ... I ... Coral! I wanted to live the truth. In vino veritas.

– Jesus. Not again. You don't need to drink two entire bottles *every time*, Edith.

– It was just a couple of glasses.

– Don't you think it's a problem that when you drink you decide *that's* the time for truth? What if you email the dean or the president in your next moment of truth? You'll be screwed, Edith. Seriously.

The elevator machinery lurches behind the doors, and they sweep open to Lesley Hughes and her post-doctoral student, Melnyk, carrying two satchels, two coats. He stands, impassive as a Buckingham Palace guard. Lesley's eyes flick to Edith, but strictly out of reflex, the way one's eyes would flick to a ragged bit of curtain blowing from a sudden gust of breeze. Although it never breezes up here – the windows are unopenable in this squat fortress of knowledge. Lesley ignoring her feels like a pair of scissors hacking away at a pumpkin.

Lesley and Coral regard each other.

– How do you do? says Coral, extending her hand out to Lesley.

– Hello, says Lesley, her smile clicking open like an umbrella. She takes Coral's hand, shines her sun on Coral. The lovely stranger Lesley. – You look familiar.

The elevator doors clunk closed after Lesley and Melnyk squeeze in.

– You're Lesley Hughes. I'm Coral Fletcher. We met once at the POSTE conference in Venice, but I'm sure you don't remember me. I did my PhD with Ted Hudgens at Carberry. I've read your monograph on bullying in the campus novel. It was absolutely fascinating. I've been a fan of your work for years.

Lesley puffs up; Edith can feel her puffing up, the officially recognized cock among the hens. Lesley grasps Coral's hand with both her hands now. They huddle together, Lesley's back to Edith.

The fragile, shiny skull under the coiffed, bright hair. Both women wear Hangaku shoes, the hourglass heels new and unscratched. Lesley's shoes distinguished by a lion's head pressed into the leather at the top of the heel.

– Of course I remember you, Coral, says Lesley. – You were there when that waiter ripped off his pants at the conference banquet. I was at a conference with Ted in Basel last week, as a matter of fact. Is this elevator going down? I could have sworn we pressed the Up button and we were moving up. Melnyk, you pressed the wrong button.

– The pantsless waiter in Venice! says Coral. She clutches her chest in a giggle.

– The Venetian waiter with the flexing buns of steel!

– I was supposed to be in Basel, but I couldn't make it. I was so looking forward to your plenary!

– Well, I'll be doing another one in Vienna in three weeks.

– Vienna! At the QTFR conference? You're one of the keynote speakers? I'll make sure I'm there! How wonderful!

– Yes, I'm looking forward to it ...

The elevator keens to a stop. The doors open slowly and stick partway. Edith and Coral squeeze out between the doors.

– You have a meeting upstairs, Lesley? asks Coral through the gap between the doors.

– An AEX meeting. On the fifth floor with the dean, says Lesley. – I'm late, but I must retrieve my mail. Melnyk, go grab my mail and meet me on the fifth floor. Take the stairs.

And he thrusts open the doors sideways, one elbow on each door as he balances two satchels and two coats, and glides past Edith and Coral.

– You and I, Coral, says Lesley, fiddling with her huge pearls, – we should go for lunch.

– I would love that, says Coral. – I'll tell Ted I saw you.

The doors clunk closed, Lesley's perfume a remnant fog that clings to them.

– Hmmm, says Coral. – I'll *bet* she's a keynote at that QTFR conference in Vienna.

– Which one's the QTFR? asks Edith.

– Oh Edith, says Coral. – You need to stop being so guileless.

– *Please* let me buy you a coffee. Or a poutine. To make it up to you, I didn't mean it, I was sincerely exhausted, I'd only had a drink or two.

– Another one of your truths, Edith Vane.

Coral begins stubbing her toe against the peeling rubber baseboard. – *Everyone's* invited as a keynote speaker at the QTFR conference, Edith. That's how we're all getting money to go. Hughes is advertising herself as the only one.

Coral hugs herself as though she's cold. Her profile sharp. Coral's hands more bony, more veiny, than Edith remembers.

– Did you know, Edith, she says, – that this building we work in is five floors of basement plus a basement. She turns to Edith, her high voice turning waspy. – Do you know what this style of architecture is called? Brutalist architecture. How apt is that, Edith?

She coughs, then yanks out a tissue from inside her cardigan sleeve.

– I looked it up. It's the same style they use for jails and insane asylums, Coral says. She coughs again, into the tissue. – Look, she says, holding out her phlegm to Edith. – Does that look like a normal colour? I've only been back here for a few weeks and already it's affecting my breathing.

– I don't see anything, says Edith, trying to avoid the tissue, looking at the floor, the wall, Coral's pointy nails.

– Of course you do, says Coral, shoving her tissue and its shining phlegm toward Edith's face. – *Look!* All you have to do is look. God, Edith. It's so obvious what's going on here.

Edith wants to leap at Coral and say it too: *The building's possessed.*

– The building's making me sick again, says Coral.

– Oh, you're right, says Edith, pretending to squint. – I see a definite, unnatural tinge.

Coral crumples up the tissue.

– I'm sorry, Coral.

Coral wipes her nose with the tissue. Stuffs it back up her sleeve. – Friday we can go for coffee, she says. – But if you send me any more drunk, truthy emails between now and then, forget it.

Edith propels herself out of the building's front doors. The hard bang on the window. The bird. She scurries to the bushes under her office window, hoping. Nothing but bushes shedding their leaves, discarded cardboard cups, tattered plastic bags. Twigs and branches scratch her hands as she parts the bushes, a plastic bag clinging to her shoe as she tries to kick it aside. She leans back, looking for her window, counting windows up and then sideways until she spots it. She turns a complete circle: grey concrete wall and skeletal shrubs, a metal side door, scraggly pine trees, the view of the parking lot where she parks her car, the brown grass island with its single pine tree in the middle of the traffic circle, a sidewalk marked by pylons where a crack has been sprayed with pink paint, a concrete garbage can with a dented metal hood, glass doors, grey concrete wall. She turns another circle. Right between the concrete wall and the metal side door, a little grey bird lies sprawled on its back, wings outspread.

She's too late.

The earth gives a small heave, and she stumbles. She needs to eat something because she could have sworn the earth just rumbled. Poor little bird. She bends down. The beak's shiny hardness. The tiny curled claws.

A hare lopes away from under a nearby bush. She should really bring carrots the next time she comes to work. Do a little good for the wildlife around here. Atone for the bird's death.

Wind gusts through branches of the tree and near-naked bushes, sighs weirdly as it blows past the doorway behind her.

– Gonna bury it? asks a voice. Dr. Angus Fella. His ragged boots right next to her hands, propped in the dirt.

– No, says Edith, sitting back on her haunches. She no longer cares about dirt on her knees, her hands. She rubs her hands together.

– I could help you dig a hole, he says. – Got a shovel in my office for emergencies. But my back's fucked. You'd have to do all the digging.

– I'd like to, says Edith, standing up. – But there's no time.

– Oh well, says Angus.

– Well then, says Edith.

– Bird couldn't have been that bright, he says. – Trying to get into a building like this. Aren't animals supposed to have some kind of instinct about bad places?

Nutty old white man.

Several days later she has to drive around and around campus to find a parking spot because a Campus Security officer in front of neon yellow plastic barricades waves her away from the entrance of her regular parking lot. She's forced to circle into the Novacrest Library parking lot. She sighs as she eases into a spot between the HUGHES silver Mercedes and a black pickup truck. She wrenches out from the front passenger seat footwell a plastic bag of unnaturally identical GMO carrots and a chopped-up head of iceberg lettuce, upends the bag in the scrubby, frosted grass next to the grille of her steaming car. She juggles her bag, her travel mug of coffee, and a Tupperware container of matrimonial squares. She baked them last night because today she hands back the one-page essays and her students will loathe her. Which happens in every course she teaches; the truce breaks down as soon as they learn she's their teacher and not their nerdy buddy, as soon as she discovers they're only using her to get their Law or Computer Science degrees and not because she's successfully seduced them into drowning with her in the glorious whirlpool of literature. Hopefully the matrimonial squares will sugar away some of the loathing.

She trips and slips across the pockmarked lot, past windshields and bumpers feathered with frost, past the concrete hulk of the Novacrest Library. She crams her nose into her collar, her fingers cracking with cold as she grasps the Tupperware and the mug, her briefcase thumping her buttocks with every step.

There's something very wrong with Crawley Hall.

A crater blossomed in the night right beside the building. Which is what prevented her from parking in her regular space. Part of the parking lot, the traffic circle, the walkway in front of the door on this backside of the building, have collapsed into a giant hole. Part of the concrete foundation of Crawley Hall exposed. Its root. She flushes with embarrassment; seeing the raw foundation feels like accidentally seeing an ancient uncle's naked buttocks.

The brown grass island in the traffic circle collapsed in the night into a cavity the size of two bungalows, and now blue mesh fencing rings the hole with large CAUTION signs wired to the fence, and official-looking women and men in helmets and bright safety vests swarm around the hole, chattering at each other, chattering at the hole, chattering into mobile phones and pointing at things.

She pauses at the edges of the fence. Like the Friendly Giant punched a hole in the ground. For now she's forced to go through Crawley Hall's main front door where she might run into Lesley or the dean. Or Coral. She wishes she had an invisibility shield she could switch on. She pulls a book from her briefcase, props it on her plastic container of matrimonial squares, and pretends to read it, flipping through the pages with one hand as she walks to the front door, her travel mug dangling from her thumb as her briefcase thumps her bum all the way to the elevator. Past the edges of her book's pages, Olivia Tootoo's black-and-white wing-tip Hangakus heel-toe past, Leonardo Baudone's leather Converse runners squeak their rubber soles after her. She closes her book because neither the dean's polished black Rumpelstiltskin shoes nor Lesley's lion-headed Hangakus strut around. Edith nods at Olivia, at Leonardo. They wait for an elevator.

– Did you see the sinkhole? Leonardo asks Olivia.

– No, what sinkhole?

– The one at the back of Crawley Hall. Nearly complete deglutition of the entire parking lot.

– That's insane.

The elevator doors wheeze open. They all step inside. The doors wheeze shut.

– Olivia, says Leonardo. – Please go for dinner with me. I'm going to ask you every day until you say yes.

Edith pushes herself back into the faux-wood wall. She should have taken the stairs.

Olivia pushes her glasses farther up on her nose.

The elevator opens one floor early, and Edith slides out as quickly as she can. Romance is so confusing. She wonders if she should text Bev.

Edith tromps up the ugly stairwell. Her knees clicking unhealthily, the walls coated with strange grit. Her lungs burn.

In her office, she continues panting from her climb up the single flight of stairs as she snaps open her email and wipes the grit off her fingers with a tissue.

She clicks open her email. An email from the dean's assistant pops into her box: William's Engineering reps have been in various faculty offices in order to survey the sinkhole from up high. *In doing so, window coverings or objects on the ledges may have been shifted*, reads the email.

A rep was clearly in her office. A stack of books has shifted from the left side of the windowsill to the right. The bloody shadow of the dead bird lingers on the glass.

She shoves the books back to the left side where they belong, disturbed that a stranger was in her office and fooled with her things. The wall behind her bulletin board abruptly bangs, the bulletin board shivering. Asbestos abatement or renovation, she guesses. Renovation in the building never stops.

She had another nightmare last night. But a predictable one this time. She has had them periodically since the first day she started this job seven years ago.

That she stands in front of a chalkboard in a lecture hall packed with students, wearing nothing but a towel and curlers in her hair; she is teaching on a stage, but the towel only reaches the tops of her thighs and she wears no underwear so the students can see flashes of her pubic hair under the towel. And the curlers keep unrolling and bouncing to the floor, so she has to keep bending over to chase her curlers while keeping the towel down, her breasts from popping out, and her genitals out of sight.

That her students are so fed up with her they start to walk out.

Except that today this nightmare isn't happening in her sleep, today the nightmare is real, even though she's wearing clothes and she's distributing matrimonial squares first thing to cushion the blow of their essay grades because students are always disappointed with their grades. Icing sugar powders between her thumb and index fingers as she offers the squares to each student.

– No nuts except oatmeal, she says. – These squares are also gluten- and dairy-free.

Then she distributes their graded essays, and they flip through the pages of their essays while she starts talking about the first slide she's put up. They sit in horrible silence, absorbing their grades. The students' eyes drilling into their grades, then drilling into her. On this essay she kept the average at a C+, the way she was warned to at the end of last year by the dean because he said her grades were too high. Their faces curdle into hatred and contempt, even as they bite into her squares. A man in a yellow construction hat strides by outside the classroom window, his hands on his hips, along the sinkhole's edge.

She flips to another slide: lines of poetry, with heavy marks above each syllable. The light from the projector turning the students' faces blue. One of her favourite poems glows on the screen. She smiles and spreads her hands wide as she gestures to the screen.

– So as I mentioned last class, in the poem's third stanza ... , she begins, in the semi-dark next to the projection screen.

– Professor, can I talk to you after class about my paper? demands Caprice. Caprice's voice clipped and trembly.

As she explained to Edith on the first day, Caprice intends to go into medicine, and she only needs this course to help her get into medicine.

– Um, Edith says, – yes, but my office hours are only on Tuesdays and Thursdays and today is a Monday...

– This is really important, says Caprice. – I've never received a grade lower than an A in my life.

– Well, even monkeys fall out of trees, Edith says.

A thing one of her favourite Shakespeare professors once said.

– So now I'm a monkey? asks Caprice.

Edith continues on with the stanza, pointing out the way the scansion matches the content. – So here, she says, pointing at the lit screen, her head starting to thrum, her ears getting that special, thrilling poetry tingle, – the accent of the syllable falls right on the word *whoosh*, and then we swoosh on to the next line in the stanza ...

– I don't see it, says Caprice, her arms crossed. – It falls on *pear*, not *whoosh*. Caprice then asks her where is the proof the poem's stanza ends on the next page and not at the bottom of the page. There is no proof! And what does it mean that there can be multiple interpretations of a poem, and there's no single right answer? What is a poem anyway? Dr. Vane still hasn't clearly defined what a poem even is.

– I'm not feeling very centred, says Caprice, slapping closed her laptop. – I'll go wait by your office right now, if you don't mind.

Caprice slings her bag up from the back of her chair. She stalks out of the room, the door booming shut behind her.

Edith continues pointing stupidly at the screen. She doesn't know whether to run after Caprice or move to the poem's next stanza, the best stanza of all because of the exquisite example of chiastic structure in the final line. She can't afford another student complaint to the dean, she just can't.

A boy to the right licks date paste from his fingers.

– Are we allowed to go? asks a girl next to him, her fingers curled around her essay, rolled tight like a baton. – Is that why she left? Because we can go? Or is this poem on the screen going to be on the final exam?

– The class only started five minutes ago, says a woman on the left-hand side of the class who's still wearing her coat. Edith wants to hug her in her zipped-up parka.

– So the *whoosh* propels the line forward ... , she falters, – into this wonderful example of a chiasmus. Does everyone remember what a chiasmus is?

She blinks at the students, at the clock ticking at the back of the room that says the class still has sixty-four minutes to go. If the clock is telling her the truth. The hour and minute hands flip her the bird.

She lunges out the door to hunt down Caprice. The classroom across from hers brims with students enraptured with their instructor, Leonardo Baudone. Coral teaches in the classroom next to his, also packed, students holding up their hands, eager to answer a question as Coral paces in the front of the room. But even as Edith totters through the hallways, clunks up the concrete stairs because the elevator would no doubt be its normal glacial self, her knees streaking with pain, her lungs searing, she cannot find Caprice. Her office door unmolested. Edith clumps back down the stairs in the ugly half-lit stairwell, clumps down the hallway to her classroom. Only a quarter of the students have stayed, texting, fiddling on their laptops, scattered around the room. Little Simon is one of them. His braces gleam as his mouth breaks into a smile, as though he is relieved at her return. She scrunches her hands into fists, raises herself to her full, Associate Professor, *Philosophiae Doctor* height.

– This poem is most definitely on the final exam! she shrieks.

The students bend their heads down to their desks and begin to type and scribble in their notes.

Yes, she is the worst teacher ever.

She steps over the threshold of the elevator, waits for the grate of the elevator machinery lifting off before she presses the button for the fourth floor. The metal doors of the elevator close, and greasy handprints cloud the dull silver sheen. In the midst of them, some bored student has pressed their greasy face against the doors, the smudge of chin, cheeks, forehead, tip of nose, lips. Lips smushed against the door. The elevator's machinery finally starts to churn.

That face's residue leering at her.

The elevator stops on the second floor. A cleaner trundles a trolley heaped with garbage bags into the elevator. Stands silently beside Edith. Facing the filthy elevator doors.

– These doors need some cleaning, remarks Edith.

The digital display above the door counts the next floor up.

– These doors are filthy, said Edith.

– Hmm? says the cleaner. She's wearing earbuds.

– You need to clean these doors. And my office wastebasket hasn't been emptied since March. Is that because of the budget cuts?

The cleaner smiles tentatively at Edith and shrugs her shoulders.

The digital display silently tings the fourth floor. Pauses. The doors not opening.

– Why aren't you doing your job? bursts Edith to the cleaner in her blue smock. – The semester's barely begun. These doors are always dirty, filthy with fingerprints.

Edith waves at the greasy smears, the handprints, the leering face.

The cleaner faces the door.

Edith notices a small pile of dirt in the back corner of the elevator. Not dirt. Little balls. Little brown and black balls. Rabbit turds.

The cleaner bundles the turds in a cloth and stuffs it into one of the plastic garbage bags on her trolley. The garbage bag rustles as the cleaner fusses with it.

The elevator door pulls open onto the fourth floor. The cleaner pushes the trolley out the door, and Edith could swear the bag is still rustling, as though something inside it is settling, moving.

Probably just garbage sliding around. Clearly the building has a rabbit infestation. Edith should alert one of the Alices.

Her next class is her graduate class. She has a half-hour break between classes today, not enough time to do anything except pee and panic that she's not prepared enough for the next class, or give in and sip room-temperature leftover coffee from her travel mug while gawking out the window at the enormous hole by the building where she used to park her car. After twenty-two minutes of watching brown dirt, parked white trucks, and skeletal autumn trees, she gathers up her papers, her briefcase, her Tupperware just in case she needs a snack during the bio-break, and locks her office door behind her.

By 2:25, one of the more senior PhD students has already pissed on a junior PhD student. In graduate classes, the PhDs always interrupt and snarl at the MAs, and the MAs yowl to her in her office after class. Today, both PhDs and MAs snarl at *her*, they yip, they spray her with their frustration and competition, try to jostle her out of the top spot. They all hate her because they smell her panic, how she's bumble-faking key theoretical concepts that aren't in her area: she always mixes up the words *tautology* and *ontology*, and she has to look up what *aleatory* means every single goddamn time. She cringes as they ooze contempt, refusing to take notes, as if everything she says is meaningless. She flips through more pages, starts picking at a thread on the book's spine as she namedrops theorists just to get the students to think she's smart and deserves to be at the front of the classroom, and mistakenly mentions Derrida and *Specters of Marx*. The most innocent-looking of them all, Karis, lingers in the room after the others have left and peers at Edith from under her bangs, her perpetually squinty eyes pencil-eraser blue. Karis asks a question about Derrida. – Did he believe in the supernatural? asks Karis. – Does he mean that the supernatural actually exists?

How the hell should *I* know? Edith wants to say. Who cares? she wants to ask, and she doesn't care what the answer is. All she cares about is Beulah Crump-Withers, but no one ever wants to talk about Beulah Crump-Withers.

Then Karis says she didn't know Derrida believed in the supernatural, and Edith's tongue prickles for the new bottle of wine she bought yesterday, a Cabernet Merlot blend. So red, so luscious. A quick tumble with her new girlfriend and future wife, Bev. A reassuring riffle through the raw manuscript version of her book at home. Yes, that's what she needs.

– It's all just metaphor, Karis, Edith says, not looking Karis in the eyes. – Of course the supernatural doesn't *exist*. There's been no peer-reviewed book or article showing that the supernatural is real.

– Oh, says Karis, her mouth drooping, as though she's been told Santa Claus is only a seasonal contract worker with a polyester beard. – That's disappointing.

Edith wonders if Bev should move into her condo or if she should move into Bev's condo when they finally take the leap. Bev's dandelion clock lamp will have to go. At least Edith won't have to make room on her bookshelves.

Coral always understood how hard teaching is for Edith. Edith could phone Coral, and on cue, Coral would rant in her screechy voice on the other end of the phone about the encroaching post-secondary neglect of women, and that Edith's articles and her book on Beulah Crump-Withers were terribly important, that recovering women's history, making women's work relevant in all its forms was essential to the struggle in this insidiously patriarchal, neo-liberal, dribbling-cock-venerating machine of a post-secondary institution.

Edith slumps against the elevator wall, her throat dry, her arms sagging as they prop up her books, papers, and briefcase. The elevator stops, the door yawns open, and she plods down the colourless hallways to her office, straight, then right past the mailroom, then right again, then left, then another left. She forgot about the second left. The hallways seem to stretch longer and longer, now that she is more tired, she supposes, now that the days are shorter. A trick of the changing sunlight. Her watch says 4:40 p.m. She remembers she said goodbye to Karis and flicked off the classroom fluorescents at 4:26 p.m. It took fourteen minutes to get from the third floor to her fourth-floor office? The fatigue clearly feasts on her.

But as she tries to round the second left, she nearly trips. Books litter part of the hallway, a pile collected against the wall opposite an open office door. A plant flies out of the door, spatters dirt against the wall, peppering the books.

– Fuuuuuuuck, she hears.

Then, – Fuckety fuck McFuckintosh O'Fuckinstein vanFuck-lington!

The office belongs to Jack Froese. One of the creative writers.

A porcelain mug skids across the floor, its handle popping off in a spray of dirt and flutter of pages.

Creative writers are always so flaky and easily offended. Especially the poets.

Dr. Froese's head with its white springy nostril hairs pops out of his doorway.

– Ellen ... Elise ... whatever your name is, he says, raising his finger as though he is about to assault her with a sound poem, – tell Phil Fuckface Ver Mucusdick that may the only pear he ever eat again be a *Pear of Anguish*!

Froese is being refreshed before her very eyes! Her pupils dilate.

She shields her head with her Tupperware container and ducks in the other direction. She can't reach her office except through Froese's hallway unless she wants to retreat the way she came, navigate the hallway the floor below, and climb the back stairs.

Instead she folds herself into a bathroom cubicle, settling herself on the edge of the toilet seat. She picks at the three matrimonial squares. She scrapes a hunk of date paste off a crust. Licks her fingers. The texture gluey. The toilet in the adjoining cubicle flushes, water rushing violently; a mound of toilet paper unspools to the floor. If she stays in her cubicle long enough, maybe the students waiting at her office to complain about their assignments will collapse from boredom and slink on home.

Only five students lined up to complain, which seems like a record. The matrimonial squares worked! After, the sun bloated and sinking, she stumbles around the mesh-fenced sinkhole, her fingers puckering in the nighttime breeze. Where the hell is her car? Then she remembers she parked by the library this morning. She stumps around the mesh fence.

Jackrabbits graze around the edges of the fence, chewing at the brown grass. Their pelts have already started to clot with winter white fur. They lazily hop away whenever she nears them.

The dead bird still lies on its back behind the bush where it landed after crashing into her office window, the eyes collapsed, the body dehydrating. But a hare nuzzles it, nibbling a toe on one of the frozen feet. The foot missing completely from the other leg. Edith clamps her hand to her mouth.

– Ewwwww, she whispers.

She clunks a path in her tired Hangaku feet to the parking lot by the library. She unlocks her door with her fob, and the sound startles a hare out from under her car. It dashes in a frenzied circle between her and the car before bounding away.

The iceberg lettuce she left this morning as an offering for the hares flaps, untouched, in the wind. The carrots still dumped in a heap.

The palm tree beside Coral stretches out its spiky fingers. Coral sips from a cardboard coffee cup. For the first time in their history of drinking coffee in the Jungle, Coral doesn't complain that the coffee tastes like rabbit turd. Unnatural warmth prickles across Edith's skin. From the heat of her own coffee, from the Jungle's muggy air, from the sadness of Coral drinking instant coffee out of a disposable cup instead of her ceramic *Male Tears* mug without complaint. Like a normal person. A person without passion.

When Edith asks Coral if she has any gossip, which is how they always used to start their Jungle conversations, like if Coral knows anything about what's going on with Olivia Tootoo and Leonardo Baudone, Coral answers that she's in a new meditation group, and as part of the meditative practice they refrain from gossip.

A rainbow film coats the surface of Edith's coffee. She gently bites the edge of her cup. She secretly loves the old-fashioned cardboard cups that plop out of the Jungle's coffee machine.

– Umm. The weather this winter's not going to be great for the hares, according to the Farmer's Almanac, says Edith. – Some of the jackrabbits are already turning white but the ground's going to stay brown. They say this winter there's hardly going to be any snow, so I wonder if they'll ever have enough snow for camouflage. Fish in a barrel for coyotes.

– Why would coyotes fish? Your metaphor depletes me, says Coral. – I'm feeling so much more grounded now that I'm in my group.

– Oh, says Edith. – When did you start going?

– When I was refreshed. I've recast being refreshed as a great gift. A time for me to recast, re-evaluate, and reorient. And believe it or not, they're part of the U of I BalanceWell employee health program. I found out about them *after* I stopped being an employee. They offered me a free year-long membership as part of the post-employee outboarding program. Why not.

She purses her freckled lips and sips her coffee. – You should join.

– I'm really worried about my AAO, says Edith. – Phil's read me the riot act.

– Oh, Edith, says Coral, licking her lips as she swirls her coffee around the bottom of her cup, – you just can't sweat the small stuff. Concentrate on the bigger fish. Or coyotes. Whatever. You know what I mean.

She gulps her coffee. – It's not like we're the Fukushima Fifty. This job's not that hard. Just manage your time. Stop dwelling so much on the negative. When we give to this job, we receive so, so much.

Coral brushes something invisible off the tweed grey of her pants.

– Anyway, she says, – I should go to my office and polish off the article I'm writing. I've been working on it for almost three weeks. I don't like taking longer than two weeks to write an article.

Heat crawls up Edith's scalp, envelops her extremities.

– Hot flash, she gasps, pulling open her collar, fanning herself with her hand.

Sweat pools around her ankles, streaks down her arms. Three weeks to write an article? Even those self-righteous, goody-goody how-to books say an article that takes twelve weeks is fast. And during the first weeks of a brand-new semester?

Edith salvages a scrap page of student newspaper from under Coral's seat. She fans herself, aiming inside her shirt's neck hole.

– I control my hot flashes through meditation now, says Coral. – I haven't had one for at least seven months. It's all about self-control. Self-regulation and ownership. I am the architect of my life; I build its foundation and select its furniture.

– Say that again? asks Edith. A rotten banana smell ripples out with the cool air of the newspaper. – What did you just say?

– My BalanceWell therapist told me that I am the architect of my life. I find this useful as an epigram for pretty much everything.

Edith fans more slowly now, then quickens.

– Who's your BalanceWell therapist? she asks.

– A wonderful woman named Vivica. I'm so happy about BalanceWell. What a gift. Isn't it a gift? And you can phone anytime, day or night.

Edith untucks her blouse, poofing out the hem, parachuting the fabric.

Through a dribble of sweat she sees Coral pour the last of her coffee into her mouth, upending her cardboard cup. Handwriting scrawls across the bottom.

Coral stands up to go. Straightening her pants, hoisting up her bag to her shoulder.

– Bye, Edith, she says. – Be well. Be productive.

She crumples the cup. She drops the cup on the floor by Edith's feet. Litterbug!

Coral swings out the glass door, her fine hair flicking.

Edith hoists up her own bag, her own cup, the page of student newspaper. She retrieves Coral's discarded cup.

I'm here is scribbled in ballpoint pen on the bottom of the cup.

Edith hooks together a longer and longer paperclip chain while she talks to Vivianne, the cord leading from her earbuds to the phone gnarled and twisted. The paperclips sparkle in the desk lamplight. She tucks her left foot under her thigh, sways in her chair.

She tries to picture Vivianne in her office talking to Edith, surrounded by plants and sipping herbal tea from an artisan-made ceramic mug while she writes notes in a black, hardcover notebook. But this image collapses into Edith's favourite scene instead: Beulah in her hat, sitting at her kitchen table and peeling potatoes, talking to Edith on the phone. Edith has on her dresser in her bedroom a framed reproduction of the only known image of Beulah: a mugshot of a nineteen-year-old woman in a high-collared blouse and hat with a fabric furl on the brim. One photo shot from the side, its twin shot from the front. A wisp of a smile because her poet's soul could not be crushed. Arrested for vagrancy at the Utopia club in Vancouver in 1917. Profession: *Sporting Girl*. From before her first marriage to that farmer. That set of photos a priceless jewel Edith stumbled upon in the Vancouver city archives.

On the other end of the phone, Vivianne/Beulah sighs.

– You can't help it, Edith, Vivianne/Beulah says, – if your graduate student Helen Bedford chose another supervisor, although I agree it's not a ... welcome ... development. When Helen told you she was going to leave, did you try to talk her out of it?

– I asked her why.

– Next time ... I don't advocate this for everyone, but next time you might try crying, Edith. Show some emotion.

– Cry in front of a student?

– Sometimes it can work quite well to get others to do things for you that they might not otherwise do. It can work quite well for showing individuals in your life how important an issue is.

– Erm, okay, says Edith, upending another box of paperclips. – By the way, I met with Coral.

– Yes?

– It's like she's been neutered. Or spayed. Neutered. She's joined a completely depressing meditation group. And she has a BalanceWell therapist too. Named Vivica.

– BalanceWell has proven itself a very successful program.

– Vivica told Coral that she was the architect of her life, too. Do you all have the same script?

– BalanceWell is a very successful program, Edith.

– I was just making a joke. I really do appreciate you helping me. Coral wrote *I'm here* on the bottom of her cup. Though how she wrote that on the underside of a full cup of coffee, I can't fathom. Weird, huh? Of course she's here. What's her point? Maybe her cup was second-hand. Yuck! She never drinks out of cardboard cups. I guess she's figured out the planet's screwed, so why not one more paper cup?

The phone hums as Vivianne flips pages, clicks and unclicks her pen.

– Hello? asks Edith.

– You're welcome, Edith. We're at the end of our time now. Goodbye.

Edith taps out an email to Coral: *Of course you're here, silly.* Clicks Send.

Edith unhooks the paperclips, dropping each one into a glass jar. She slips into bed, one foot cold, the other numb. Her eyelid tics. She curls herself around Bev's warm, round limbs.

– Did Vivianne say anything useful? asks Bev.

– She's an excellent therapist.

– Hmm, says Bev, her hands climbing down Edith.

– Bev?

– Yes?

– Will you marry me?

– Sure, says Bev. – Now get on your back.

Edith flops onto her back, pulls a pillow over her face, and tries not to scream with joy.

October

October 12. The occasional hare has transformed into a full-fledged ghost, completely white except for the ear tips, the dark contour around the eyes. Others more speckled and freckled.

Friday at 4 p.m., handprints and footprints coat the shiny elevator doors, as though a number of barefooted people ran on all fours up the wall, and the ceiling also covered in greasy handprints and footprints.

Edith slaps her hand against the door. Leaves her own handprint for company.

She checks her mailbox, mostly overdue essays, while Angus Fella photocopies his bank records behind her because he's in the process of remortgaging his house. Coral collects her mail, smiling briefly at Edith while chatting with Iris Bell about bodies without organs. Coral's twig legs poke out from under her skirt. Coral's body is shrinking. Edith wants to force her to eat an extralarge poutine with extra gravy, extra cheese curds, and extra French fries. An entire suckling pig. Their friendship is gently renewing: they haven't had coffee again together, but Coral once high-fived Edith when Edith duct-taped back in place a peeling wall panel by the fourth-floor bathroom door. Another petition's appeared in the mailroom, but this time about the conflict of interest in the dean's hiring of ParTray Catering Co. for sixteen faculty functions even though the dean's wife *coincidentally* works as a food stylist for ParTray Catering Co. Either Daphne Vermeulen should resign from ParTray or Phillip Vermeulen should resign as dean. Once again the petition is signed only by Coral and Angus. Melnyk waits in line with a book in his hand, likely something he has to copy for Lesley. Edith nods hello on her way out, but he barely blinks. At least he makes eye contact.

Jack Froese's rage still bothers Edith. How efficiently the dean erased him, unlike how he tried to erase Coral. Froese didn't even have a retirement reception. His office nameplate has vapourized, his face and faculty profile have been stripped from the department website. Even though he'd been working at the university for forty-two years. His office door stripped of the fading writers' festival posters and flyers advertising student writing contests. Three sessional instructors, plus Melnyk the postdoctoral fellow and Coral, cram into Froese's office now, three women and a man and Coral, who is only *hotelling* in the office as her *touchdown space* while Alice Q. tries to find her permanent office space. Coral's former office is swathed in tarp and is an Authorized Personnel Only designated zone.

All their office hours are taped haphazardly on the door on different-sized sheets of paper, along with conference ads and photocopied cartoons about grammar and climate change. Students' sullen forms line up at the door, they camp out on the floor with smartphones and calculators and iPads.

Bev said she was only kidding when she agreed to marry Edith. Their first fight. Their first luscious bout of make-up sex two days later. In just under three weeks they'll have their two-month anniversary. Edith will maybe propose again.

In her own office, Edith shuffles, stacks, restacks the three neat heaps of brand-new essays from three different classes on her office desk. She snaps an elastic band around each bundle, then angles them all into her P. T. Madden shopping bag. She slings on her coat. She will try to catch up and grade at least twenty mid-term exams a day this Thanksgiving long weekend. She's filled out the Knowledge Mobilization section of her AAO – yay! – and she has printed out the top of a POL grant application relating Beulah Crump-Withers the Amber Valley, Alberta, farm wife–diarist to health, even though there is absolutely no connection between Canadian prairie landscape metaphors and health, but the dean's office manager, Lisa Ives, sent a blanket email about a POL grant opportunity having to do with Health in the Workplace. Edith could argue that Beulah's kitchen was her workplace, the memoir a journalling of her twelve children's and her two husbands' various bouts with influenza, tuberculosis, toe fungus, and bedbugs?

In the elevator, Olivia Tootoo tells Leonardo Baudone that she heard Froese tried to hypnotize his students. Leonardo harrumphs that he drank Bellinis with the dean last week and blathers on that Froese was a dinosaur who reviewed books on the radio, hadn't published a single poem or poetry book in decades, and pooh-poohed academic grants like the FORT or POL as part of the capitalist machine.

– It's a different time now, said Leonardo. – Tenure's not going to help you keep your job if you're not on board with the EnhanceUs plan, putting out a book every year or two, bringing in a FORT or some other grant. Did I tell you Staines-upon-Thames Press has accepted my next monograph for publication? I'm not happy because Staines didn't do a good job with the images in the last book Phillip co-authored, but you know. Staines is one of the foremost academic publishers in the world. If not the foremost. So I guess I'll go with them. Though I hate to compromise.

Then he asks Olivia if she has any plans for dinner tonight because Phil's told him about a vegan, gluten-free tapas and wine bar in Mull Park.

Olivia answers, – The theoretical orientation driving your scholarship repulses me.

Leonardo clasps his hands in prayer, and says, – I don't know what you're talking about but I can change.

Edith raises her lecture notes up close to her nose, pretending really hard to reread the nonsense typed at the top, and Olivia still hasn't answered Leonardo by the time the elevator door opens and Edith squishes herself past them into the lobby. Edith giggles. She's beaten Leonardo in one category: the Love Prize. She giggles again.

Cinnamon perfume crashes into her nose and she sneezes. Edith almost collides into Lesley and Melnyk, Lesley haranguing him because he took her outfit to the wrong dry cleaner. – They are going to *ruin* the buttons on that dress, she puffs.

Melnyk stands, stoic as an Edwardian butler.

Edith composes a mental list: the stacks of essays, the AAO's final section, the FORT grant application, the POL grant application, that too-long conference paper with so many off-topic tangents and dead ends it's a textual Winchester House, the minutes from a CCA meeting she needs to type up and upload to the committee Dropbox by the next meeting. The building electronic wall of untended emails from university administration and committees, and no new book in the works. Not a page, not a paragraph, not a single letter of the alphabet. Every time she types, the letters arrange themselves into a letter to the dean: *Dear Phillip, Please Don't Refresh Me*. Maybe she should follow Vivianne's advice with the dean and cry in front of him. The long Thanksgiving weekend starts tomorrow, and tomorrow morning she has to drive two and three-quarter hours to Red Deer, where her parents live. She hasn't even packed underwear yet. She is so behind, her eyelid threatens to flip inside out.

She wants to phone Vivianne again. But that would be four times in three weeks, and that would put her two sessions beyond her quota. What would Vivianne say?

What do you need to do to make yourself feel better? Vivianne might say.

Rearrange your metaphorical furniture, Vivianne would say.

At her condo, Edith hooks two paperclips together, three. She sips her wine. She could drop by Bev's apartment and water Bev's plants. Pretend to not hunt for Bev's diary so she can read it and find out how much Bev *really* loves Edith. Bev's spending Thanksgiving in Victoria with two of her children and a new grandbaby, but she didn't tell Edith she was going until the very last minute and then didn't invite Edith to come too. Edith feels uncertain about Bev's emotional investment in her. Bev told Edith the last time they slept together that Edith is *a lot of fun*. Edith hates the frivolous sound of *fun*. Edith hooks up three more paperclips. She clicks on a jewellery website, glumly surveys engagement rings, unsure which one Bev might like but certain that if she wants to catch Bev for real, a marriage proposal is the way to do it. Women love that stuff.

What does she need to do to make herself feel better?

She needs to grade papers. She needs to read graduate student applications and try to nab a graduate student to supervise. She needs to write a birthday card for her mother because the weekend is for Thanksgiving but also for her mother's birthday. She needs to exercise. Edith will walk the long way around Crawley Hall, snap on her flippers and go paddle in the university's Olympic-sized pool. She will swim!

No. The ballet class she signed up and paid for. She pulls her sweatpants out from under a mound of dusty shoes.

She attempts pliés and jetés, pirouettes, and tries to reach her toes above the level of her waist, she tries not to judge her gangly, angular flamingo self in the long mirror reflected in the high sparkling windows. Her quads and buttocks ache, her neck sweats, she sweats into the tangling, frizzling roots of her hair, while her ballet teacher counts out loud, tells them, – Move with propulsive strength and purpose! Don't flop around like dolls!

Edith chugs her breaths like a train, the inside of the windows veiled in the students' condensed sweat and breath, her joints straining until they tear and pop. *Exercise is my furniture*, she chants to herself as she sweats and pains. *Exercise is my furniture.*

The teacher plays the first strains of 'Dance of the Little Swans.' She and the other women in the class link hands in two human woman chains, the teacher presses Play on the CD player, and they hop and clump sporadically in and out of sync while the teacher shouts directions, trying to keep in time to the stabbing notes of the flutes. Edith towers over all the women, her hands and the two hands she desperately holds on to slippery and hot.

The lack of coordination, the sweat trickling around her ears, the puffy fingers of the other women clutching her own, the clumping of their feet on the shiny wooden floor. The ceilings in this room stretch very high, and she wonders what part of the train station she is now galumphing around in. The old waiting room? A storage room? She can hear the whistle of the train as it crashes toward her while she hoofs from side to side, pretending to be a little swan, the train's scream splitting her open.

The teacher crashes the CD player off and emotes at them, – I want to see the electricity crackling out of your fingertips!

Edith sags.

She stops in a 7-Eleven on the way home to buy aspirin, when she sees Angus Fella using tongs to pick up a wiener from the rolling rows of greasy, withered hot dogs in the corner of the store.

She has never seen him off-campus. She is like one of those children who believe their teachers live at school, are shocked that teachers do things like shop for packets of French onion soup mix or aluminum foil.

– Angus! she calls.

He fumbles his hot dog, startled. It squelches to the floor and rolls, picking up layers of dust and dirt.

– You'll have to pay for that, sir, declares the pimply clerk.

– No, interrupts Edith – I'll get it!

But even as she says it, she remembers she only has small change in her sweatpants pocket; her wallet and credit card are back home in her hallway closet.

– That would be super, says Angus.

She jingles her hand in her pocket, anyway, fruitlessly. – I can't get it, she says, – I don't have enough money on me.

– Well, that's just *great*! says Angus, he claps together his thick, wrinkled hands.

– I'll buy you a hot dog another time. Tomorrow. Will you be at school tomorrow?

– Someone's going to have to pay for that food, pipes the clerk.

– I'll *pay for it*, you ninny, says Angus. – A hot dog isn't even real food. Really, you should be paying *me* to eat it.

– It's not company practice to pay customers to buy food, sir, says the clerk, barricaded behind the counter. – That'll be $3.99.

– I haven't had a chance to put it in a *bun*, says Angus. – I haven't put any *ketchup* on it yet.

He scoops up the wiener from the floor with his fingers, jams it into a bun. Holds the ketchup container upside down over the dusty hot dog and squeezes. A glob of ketchup blats out of the container. He takes a giant bite.

– Dr. Fella! squeals Edith. She gags.

– That'll be $3.99, sir! yelps the clerk.

– Here, says Edith to the clerk, digging her new bottle of aspirin out of her pocket. – I'd like to return my aspirin and get my money back and pay for a new hot dog. Angus, please put that hot dog down, I'm buying you a new hot dog.

Angus, still chewing after the first bite, takes another extravagant bite, pink hot dog particles, the tinfoil edge of a gum wrapper, and wet bits of white bun spilling from his mouth.

– Has the aspirin bottle been opened? asks the clerk. – I can't accept a return if the bottle has been opened. I will also need the receipt as proof of purchase.

– I haven't opened the bottle!

– I'm afraid I have to disagree, says the clerk. – The safety seal on top of this bottle has been broken.

– But someone else must have done that. I didn't even ... You've seen me standing ...

– Have you ever considered a job in government? Angus asks the clerk.

– I am completing my degree in business administration, as a matter of fact, says the clerk.

– Even better, says Angus. – Even better, a fine, law-abiding young man like yourself.

– My hot dog tastes great, by the way, he says, chewing with his mouth open, his lips glossy and a dust bunny hanging from the corner of his mouth, waving the hot dog in Edith's direction.

She draws herself up to her full height, taller than the clerk, taller by far than Angus Fella, and in her best angry Associate Professor, *Philosophiae Doctor*'s voice she instructs the clerk to exchange the hot dog for the aspirin. His face blinks red from blushing and his pimply whiteheads pop out.

– Only this time, he mumbles. – Whatever.

She hands the new hot dog, warm, withered, and greasy, to Angus, who splats ketchup and mustard all over it.

– Thank you, Evelyn, says Angus.

He chomps into the hot dog, squirting mustard onto his moustache.

– Name's Edith. My pleasure, Angus, says Edith.

She holds the door open for him as he passes into the night.

– Killed any more birds? he asks.

– No.

– The job killed *you* yet? asks Angus, chewing his brand-new hot dog. – Or made you crazy? Or both?

– It's a long weekend coming up.

– You're the one who wears those strange flowery blouses.

– Um. Sorry?

– I can't abide patterns. Just another way for it to make you doubt your worth. Make you think you're seeing things all twisty.

– *What?*

She hates to think she knows what he's talking about because if she knows what he's talking about then she is the same as him. *She is not the same as Angus Fella.*

– Oh, forget it, he says. – We're all mad here, Evelyn, he says, shoving his Cheshire Cat watch into her nose. – Heh heh heh.

His lips shine with grease, a speck of hot dog lodged in his scraggly beard.

– Yes, says Edith firmly, – but there's free psychological help via telephone, twenty-four hours a day, and subsidized exercise classes.

She draws back her shoulders and takes in a confident breath. – Plus, my psychologist is amazing.

– One of the head shrinkers hired by the university, am I right? Saying all the perfect, inspirational things? They tell you what administration *wants* them to tell you.

– That sounds like a conspiracy theory, she says.

She titters, shakes her pocket full of change. Presses a finger between her eyes to try to push away the ache. She wants her bed. She wants her bedmate.

– No, says Angus. – It's not a conspiracy theory. Spittle flies from his mouth as he enunciates the *p*.

– Oh, Angus.

Such a white man.

– I'm not joking, says Angus.

She keeps walking, swinging her arms, electricity shooting from her fingertips and toes, her limbs loose and swanlike. Still proud she told that pimply little business major what for.

Angus blathers on, – The University of Inivea is just a machine that eats people. The shrink and the pool are bait. They want you to give until they've sucked you into a husk. They want you to splatter your brains like that bird on your window.

Edith shakes her head. – Heh heh heh, she says, pretending to laugh at his joke.

– Oh, come *on*! he says, – haven't you noticed how sick all our colleagues are? The medical leaves? Froese's nervous breakdown? The general nuttiness about semicolons and rampant incompetence? You think that's all a coincidence? Don't *you* feel like what we're trying to accomplish is becoming more and more impossible?

– I'm just happy to have a job.

He grumbles.

– What am I trying to accomplish? she asks.

Angus stumbles as he steps down off the lip of the sidewalk. He mumbles as he plods away from her, the second half-eaten hot dog in its paper clutched too hard in his hand.

– If it's so bad, then why haven't *you* quit? she shouts, her words climbing into cold mist. – It's not like we're the Fukushima Fifty!

– It's too *late* for me, he shouts. – *Obviously!*

He shouts some more words sounding like *kangaroos* and *paddock* and waddles across the street in a fury, white scraps of hair fluttering out from under his hat. He marches past a clump of pine trees. A hare hunched among the tree trunks lifts its ears, tilts its head toward Angus as he plods by.

At home, she pulls off her sweaty clothes and stuffs them into her broken washing machine while she phones her mother.

– What would you like to eat for your birthday Thanksgiving, Mother? she asks. – I can bring down anything you like that you can't buy in Red Deer.

– All I want is my beloved family around me, says her mother. – Nothing else. Oh. Your father would like to speak to you too.

Sounds of rustles and fumbles. Her father clearing his throat.

– Does Chicken on the Way deep-fry turkeys? he asks. – Your mother's craving Chicken on the Way.

– I think Chicken on the Way only does chicken, says Edith. – Seriously? That's what she wants for her birthday Thanksgiving dinner?

– It's the best in the province, he says. – That would be some birthday Thanksgiving Day, now wouldn't it, Sondra? Edith hears her father say. – Edith! Your mother says that's a smashing idea. Let's shake it up! Also, bring me a bottle of Armagnac. That would be nice too. Not the cheap one like last time. Your old father doesn't have many years left and he needs to enjoy them. Also spring rolls. Your mother loves spring rolls.

– Okay, says Edith.

– Get a cake too, he whispers. – And candles, because I can't find the candles. And a birthday card. Make sure it's signed for both you *and* me. Corn fritters would go well with the chicken. I'll pay you back. And don't forget flowers. From both you *and* me. And more weed. My arthritis has been really bad lately.

That night, dreams of dead things speckle her sleep, of her hands stretched out to catch a falling crow, clutched around the throat of a kicking, struggling rabbit. She wakes up in the night to pee, and when she reaches out to wash her hands at the sink, cannot comprehend the long scratches up and down her forearms. She will wear long sleeves at the birthday Thanksgiving dinner so she doesn't have to explain herself to her parents.

Saturday. Her mother's birthday. And official/unofficial family Thanksgiving Day.

For her mother's birthday gifts, Edith dashes to the mall first thing and buys a bucket of caramel corn, the superexpensive Victorian hand lotion, a new bathrobe with matching slippers, and a box of chocolate truffles from the Hudson's Bay. Just like she does every year. Only this year the bathrobe is silk, the terry-cloth slippers embroidered with a gold crest. She starts crying as she picks out delicate, hand-made wrapping paper and a card embedded with flower seeds in the stationery shop.

She also buys a box of deep-fried chicken and corn fritters from Chicken on the Way, spring rolls from Golden Happiness restaurant, and from Sandersams she buys a pre-tossed salad in a double-sealed plastic container, a pre-packaged birthday cake, and a paper cone of bedraggled chrysanthemums because they're the only kind of flower left. From Sandersams liquor store, a bottle of Armagnac, the cheapest one at only $75.63 with tax – $75.63! She packs it all in her P. T. Madden and Hangaku bags and stows them in the trunk of her car. Her essays in a third bag. She slams the trunk closed. Manoeuvres her Taurus onto the Queen Elizabeth highway and aims her nose for Red Deer.

Edith would like to have her mother to herself. She would like to take her mother out for a nice birthday dinner in a bistro with cloth napkins and servers in uniforms, silver buckets to hold the ice for white and sparkling wine, amuse-bouches and palate cleansers between the courses, a long list of chocolatey, creamy desserts they could share. The chance to impress her mother with her fancy salary, her taste in foodie food, but she knows her mother would insist her father come along, and she knows her father would order the most expensive wine and the most expensive food on the menu because that's what he used to do before he lost his job, that's what he did *for* his job, and her mother would look at Edith as though she'd been stabbed in the spleen when Edith tells her father he can damn well pay for himself if he's going to insist on ordering a $300 bottle of wine.

Once her parents answer their front door, she can tell that the reason her mother is probably craving fried chicken and spring rolls is because both she and her father are stoned on marijuana tea. At 3:07 in the afternoon. The marijuana Edith has started buying from Bev who gets it from her drug-dealer son. Edith puts her job at risk for this marijuana; she sleeps with a woman who fraternizes with drug dealers to relieve her father from his arthritis.

– Medical marijuana is so weak, her father insists. – It's as if they think only five-year-olds will use it.

As soon as Edith enters the house, her father presents the chrysanthemums to their mother with a flourish and a wet kiss on the lips. – For my best friend and lover, my crocus in the snow, he says.

– Happy birthday, Mother, says Edith, kissing her mother on the cheek.

Her mother hugs and hugs Edith tightly. Edith savours her mother's warm squishiness.

– Where's the wine? asks her father, rummaging through the bags.

– Thank you, Edith Lynn, says her mum, pulling away. – Any wine? No wine! When's your book party? Date picked yet?

– My daughter the author, says her father. – I've always had a book inside me. Just haven't had the time to write it. Maybe you could drive up next weekend and I could dictate while you type it out?

Edith darts into the kitchen. She extracts forks and knives, clinks out plates from the cupboards and drawers.

Her father has already torn open the bags in the dining room. He rips open the top box, packed with deep-fried corn fritters and an overflowing container of gravy, cranks open the box and fritters, and begins biting into corn fritters at an Olympic rate.

– Father, don't you need a plate? Don't you want to heat the food up first?

He chomps, his cheeks and fingers greasy, bits of fritter catching on his chin. Her mother uses a fork to nab a spring roll from the greasy Golden Happiness paper bag, and devours half the roll in one crunch. Her father grabs a drumstick like he is Henry VIII and begins gnawing. Her mother pecks out a chicken wing from the greasy, chicken-fragrant cardboard box in front of Edith, and nibbles at the skin. She tosses away the wing bones and tears her teeth into a chicken breast.

The tattered bouquet of chrysanthemums salutes them in the middle of the table among the detritus of oily Golden Happiness paper bags and cardboard Chicken on the Way boxes.

– There's also a salad, says Edith. – I don't want you two dying early on me.

– We're fit as fiddles, Edie, says her father.

She slides the vase of flowers to the side, plops down the plastic container in the middle of the table.

Her father pauses in his mastication. – That is so environmentally unfriendly, he says. – I can hear the last of the polar bears screaming in agony as I look at that thing.

Edith peels the lid off the container. Lettuce, mandarin orange slices, sliced blanched almonds.

– That thing is so solidly plastic, it could be a kiddie pool in the summer, says her father. – Hey, Mother? A kiddie pool.

Her mother laughs, her mouth spilling plum sauce, her fingers cramming a fritter into the gravy container.

Edith spoons salad onto her father's plate and hands him a fork. She pats him on the head.

He obediently stabs into the greens and fishes them up to his mouth.

– Yeah, says Edith, – because the former oil business exec suddenly cares about plastic pollution. Why don't you go hug a tree.

– Namaste, my daughter, says her father.

– Namaste, my father, she says.

Her parents' half-drunk cups of marijuana tea cool and congeal on the sideboard, a layer of oil skimming the top.

– I've fallen in love, says Edith.

– I don't know why you couldn't hold on to Beryl, says her father. – It's not the getting the girl, it's the keeping the girl. Beryl, she was a catch. Made over a quarter of a million dollars a year.

– A catch! says her mother, raising a chicken breast.

– What does your new objet d'amour do? asks her father.

– She's a coffee barista.

– So she's young, says her father. – Good for the cardiovascular.

– No, she's older than me. She has five children in their thirties. She left her husband six months ago.

Her parents chew, their clicking jaws, the dissolving, disintegrating meat in their mouths the only sounds in the room.

– She's the one I bought the last two batches of marijuana from, says Edith.

– From what I am deducing, this is the last wing, her father says, waving the chicken limb. – Anyone want this wing? No?

He plunges his teeth through meat, gnaws on bone.

– That was simply delicious, says her mother. – Too bad you forgot the wine.

– How's your arthritis, Father?

– My what? Here's what it is, says her father. – I drank some tea, I watched an episode of *Cosmos* with Neil deGrasse Tyson, who I must say is becoming the spitting image of me the older he gets, and an hour later I had a crashing moment of clarity about the universe. Nothing matters. We're all just microscopic blips with no effect whatsoever. This is what you need to do, Edith. You need to give up control and follow the currents of the universe. That way, maybe the world will stop shitting on you so much. Or when it inevitably does, you won't mind so much. Or get so excited by ... mediocrity.

– Daddy!

– All you need is a cup of the home brew. Here, he says. – You can have the rest of mine.

Edith's eyes prickle with tears as she accepts the cup.

She takes a sip. Bitter. Greasy.

– Now maybe you'll stop being so hypersensitive, he says. – You're a lovely girl when you're calmer.

– Excuse me? she says.

– All I said was that maybe you don't need to take everything so *seriously*. Manage your time better and have more *fun*.

– My job is very demanding, she says.

– But are you having fun?

– Of course I am.

She thinks of Beulah Crump-Withers and blushes with pleasure.

She takes another sip. She settles back into her chair. Cat hairs stick to her lips, poke up her nose. She sneezes. Her parents' cat, Aldous, steps onto her lap and starts to knead, his feet occasionally poking her belly like he is conducting an external exam of her ovaries. She hates cats for their presumptuousness, their furry slitheriness. She sneezes again.

– The cat gets it, says her father. – See, even the cat gets it.

– The tea's not doing anything, Edith says. – It's not working. Pointless.

– Stop talking and listen to the universe! says her father, gathering Aldous up into his arms.

Her mother in the meantime has slid away from the table and is so engrossed in repotting a plant she doesn't even notice they've brought out the cake.

– No candles? mutters her father. – This flightiness does not come from *my* side of the family.

– Mine either! retorts her mother, her hands deep into a bag of dirt.

Moving the plant back and forth between the old pot and the new pot they bought at the mall today, changing her mind each time about whether the plant looks better in the new pot or the old pot, the new pot or the old pot, the new pot or the old pot.

Edith surveys her parents, her father with his ear cupped to the cat's belly, her mother gardening in October. She loves them, but she is a woman in her forties with deadlines.

– I have to go, says Edith.

She grabs up her bag, her coat, her car keys, her empty cloth bags.

Her father smiling at his cat as it sucks at the tassels on a fraying pillow. – You're leaving already? I thought you were staying overnight.

– I've got too much work to do, says Edith.

– Time management! shouts her father as Edith bangs out the front door.

Edith drives, in the growing darkness, for two and three-quarter hours, furious at all the time she wasted, belching gravy. The streets of Inivea dim and empty when she finally pulls into the city. At the Novacrest tower downtown she turns right, in the direction of home.

Tuesday morning, the red, blue, and white lights of an ambulance, a parked fire truck, a police car, revolve close to Crawley Hall. She parks her car in the Leung Hall parking lot. She trudges through the quad, past rusting iron garden sculptures, the dirt heaps and looming concrete skeleton of the future Sandersams Supermarkets School of Business. The closer she gets to Crawley Hall, the more obvious it is that the entire backside of the building has been blocked by temporary fencing. She'll have to enter through the main door again.

She peeks at the action, the police officers in their hulking uniforms, the ambulance.

She sidles closer to the building, to a side door, far from where she needs to be but also far from her colleagues' regular entryway. She will take the stairs again today.

She has to drag her briefcase through three different hallways to get to the proper stairwell, but she is still early for her meeting with Simon from her Canadian Literature Before 1950 class. But the hallways smell worse than usual. Like boiled eggs. Not just boiled eggs, but eggs boiled in manure soup. She wonders if someone had a particularly potent diarrhea in the washroom across the hall. But this smell has a dull, bitter quality, not like diarrhea or the regular boiled-eggs smell, but like an exploded garbage bag cooking in the sun.

She taps opens her email while she waits for Simon. A note from the dean's assistant to the entire faculty and staff: *It is with much regret that I must inform you that Coral Fletcher was involved in a vehicular accident when her car drove into the sinkhole behind Crawley Hall. Coral has suffered minor injuries but has not yet been released from hospital. The as of yet unidentified male passenger died at the scene. I will inform you of the details when I receive more information. Flowers and a card have been sent on behalf of the faculty to Coral in the hospital.*

Edith leaps to the window, yanks up the crooked blind.

In the hole, the butt end of Coral's white car points up at her. The roof and doors ripped off and the edges jagged. The hole and its edges swarming with more humans, fences, yellow police tape.

Edith presses her forehead to the glass. Coral. Edith's eyelids flutter, tears coiling, congealing. *I'm here.* Was this Coral asking for help? Why was Edith so stupid? Why didn't she *see*? She needs to find out what hospital Coral's in. Right now.

A tap at her office door. Simon.

Edith digs through Simon's essay, babbling about thesis statements and topic sentences so that she doesn't have to imagine hearing the noise of the car in the hole, its choking exhaust, the faltering engine sputtering. She circles moments of illogical reasoning, *thesis* spelled as *theses*, *ficus* spelled as *feces*, shows him misplaced commas and a faulty parallelism.

She ticks off his name on the class roster: Simon (Emma) Leavitt.

A toilet across the hall flushes three times in a row.

Simon pulls the neck of his T-shirt up over his nose. She suspects he probably thinks she's farted when it's just the regular smell. She can think of no way to broach the topic. She resists turning to the window, resists sharing her panic with this student.

A grain of rice drops onto Simon's essay. He pulls the T-shirt away from his face.

– That's a maggot, announces Simon, pointing.

– It's a what? she says.

– Yup, says Simon.

His lips curl. The braces on his teeth sparkle. Simon pulls the T-shirt back over his nose.

They both turn their faces up to the ceiling. Between the edges of the adjoining panels, another rice grain drops out and plops on the desk. She pokes the rice grain with her red pen. She squints, draws her head back so the focus is better. Simon is correct. One rice grain has segments. The rudimentary beginnings of eyes, jaws. The grain abruptly flexes.

She flicks the one maggot off the paper into the garbage. The other she slides off into the garbage with the blade of her hand. No way is she moving offices again. No way. She will kick and scream and cling like ivy to stay the architect of her own life.

– Let's move to this side of the office, she says, and drags her chair to the bookcase next to the door. She brushes the top of her hair with her hand. To make sure nothing's dropped on her head.

Simon slide-thumps his chair across from hers. She props his essay on her ancient edition of *The Riverside Shakespeare* and keeps talking. Once Simon's left she'll plug up that hole with her handy roll of duct tape.

But that afternoon she's dumping the books she has into her P. T. Madden bag and sliding her boxes, still packed, into the hallway. Her floor's C wing is being temporarily decanted and jammed into her floor's D wing. *Faculty members will have to double up in their offices*, writes Alice Z. *Try to be a rainbow in someone's cloud (Maya Angelou)*, reads Alice Z.'s signature.

Edith's office ceiling wasn't the only one dropping maggots. Other people in offices on her floor were just more sensitive about it. *Please bear with us as we undergo this transition phase.*

She now shares an office with Leonardo.

Thank you so much for your patience during this transition phase.

She lines up with other displaced, maggoty professors and contract instructors at the main office. Alice Z. is even more clippy and sneery than usual as she hands out new office keys, her desk littered with a pyramid of empty Pepsi cans and photos of her Russian blue cats.

– Do you know which hospital Coral's being treated at? Edith asks Alice Z. as she takes her new key.

– Like I know. The university hospital?

– Didn't the faculty send her flowers?

– You'll have to ask Lisa upstairs.

– Do you know how Coral's doing?

– Think she broke her arm or her leg or her collarbone something. No idea. Next in line please.

Leonardo's office smells like armpits and musty bike clothes because he cycles to work every day and drapes his sweaty cycling clothes around the office to dry. His *second-best bike*, his words, sits in the corner by one of the filing cabinets. He recently stuck a line of silver fish stickers leading from his office door down the hallway, all the way to Olivia Tootoo's door, in an attempt to persuade her to love him.

Edith unpacks her stapler and box of Kleenex and lines them up with the edge of the new old desk. *I am the architect of my life; I build its foundation and select the furnishings*, she scribbles on a Post-It and tucks it inside the top drawer.

Edith is on the same side of the building as her last office, but she has a radically different view of the sinkhole, closer, more north. She is kitty-corner to the south-side fourth-floor washroom instead of across from it, which she guesses is an improvement. She notes the rough kidney shape of the sinkhole. She wonders how Coral is, where she is. Another, smaller pit deeper inside the sinkhole, as though another sinkhole occurred inside the sinkhole. A shattered fragment of Coral's rear bumper shining up out of the hole in spite of the dust and death.

She tries not to listen to Leonardo's phone conversations, usually about going for martinis with someone, anyone, at the newest, most chic downtown restaurant. She tries not to dislodge or bump the many award trophies and excellence plaques and mounted magazine articles with photos of Leonardo on the walls and bookshelves. He's arranged his bookshelves with the spines facing inward so the covers won't fade.

– How do you know which book is which? she asks. She slides two out of a shelf. – They're not even alphabetical.

– I have a system, he says, taking the books from her hand and sliding them back in. – And a photographic memory.

His bookshelves are arranged in a multi-layered maze. Her boxed materials are in storage in Crawley Hall's basement. Every day she will meet his bicycles and sweaty clothes, a garbage can overflowing with Kleenex from she-doesn't-want-to-know-what. His glittery fish stickers and unrequited love for Olivia Tootoo. The constipating, robotically neat handwriting on his file labels.

The heating system whooshes in Leonardo's office even worse than in her old one. Rhythmic. Rasping. Sighing like a pensioner. Fever-hot when it's on and sinew-freeze-drying cold when it's not.

She misses the sounds of the faculty lounge microwave beeping out canned soup. She recalls the smell of canned spaghetti or recycled restaurant biryani as far more appealing than the smell of sweaty, unreciprocated, overpaid nerd love.

She calls the university hospital, but no Coral Fletcher has been admitted to any unit there. She calls the Inivea General. No C. Fletcher admitted there either.

A week passes.

Edith stumbles into the mailroom, the fragrance of Lesley's spicy perfume so formidable her eyes water.

Lesley wrenches her key in her mailbox keyhole, stonily ignores Edith. Edith thinks furiously about furnishments, such as the bookcases, rolltop desk, kitchen table, armoire, and L-shaped chesterfield that populate the architecture of her mind. She remains the architect of her life. She sets her table with human-sized bouquets of flowers so she cannot remember the pain of having her dissertation called the *Titanic*. Lesley wears a knee-length coat, an elaborate petally ruffle around the neck making her head look like a grumpy stamen. Lesley tugs the key, whispering *shit shit shit*. Edith's mailbox swings open without even a squeak. She could recoil to her office, or she could pretend to be absorbed by her flyers while Lesley wrestles with her mailbox. Edith shuffles junky envelopes and postcards from scholastic publishers, newsletters from the LEPE and POL associations, three books she ordered online, the confidential Mandate Visioning document and ballot from the dean's office. Maybe Lesley will speak. Will ask Edith for help with her jammed mailbox, then they will burst out with a shared tee-hee in their shared frustration. Throw their arms around each other. Invite each other to the student bar for rum and Cokes.

– Take a Polaroid picture, *Edith*, says Lesley, her teeth gritted, her fingers gripping the jammed key. – It lasts longer.

Lesley snarls at the mailbox, strikes the wall of mailboxes with her palm, dives in again at the little metal door. Edith moonwalks backwards, folds herself out the doorway.

– Melnyk, Lesley calls. – Melnyk, I need you!

Edith nearly crashes her face into the door jamb when Melnyk pushes past her into the mailroom.

– Coming, Lesley! he sings. He pulls at the key. – I think you've bent it.

– Don't be ridiculous, huffs Lesley. – Obviously *you* bent it.

Edith slinks away. She should have heralded the warning smell of Lesley even before she entered the mailroom. She sniffs her wrists. She believes she smells the vanilla-pudding eau de cologne she spritzed on this morning. Worries that the sweaty bicycle pong of Leonardo's office has rotted out her sense of smell.

Toward the end of her degree, when things started to crumble, Lesley called her *hare-brained*. Over the years since then, Edith has done a little research into the hares that nibble among the buildings throughout the campus grounds, these members of the genus *Lepus*, the family *Leporidae*, the mammalian order *Lagomorpha*. She wants to tell Lesley that hares are not actually dumb at all, they are precocial, the *leverets* born with their eyes open and their legs ready to run. From predators, thank you for the nice compliment, Lesley.

She rushes to the elevator, mail and books in her hands. The button already lit up.

The door opens to the dean fiddling with his tie. She hugs her papery bundle. She steps backward, then, embarrassed, forward into the elevator. The doors jerk closed. She tries not to peer at the dadlike bald spot on the back of his head.

– I heard on the radio there's a cold front coming in tonight, she says.

– God! Let's hope not! exclaims the dean, stroking his crisp yellow tie, probably expensive, over his belly. Hugo Hilfiger? Tommy Lauren? Anderson & Shepville? Did those stores even make ties? She can never keep the brands straight. Her father used to flap around with silk ties and platinum tie pins before he was fired for mismanaging funds. The dean presses the elevator button twice.

Her laugh idiotically high. Her father told her that people in superior positions like their jokes laughed at. Which is why he doesn't understand why Edith and her mother never laugh at his jokes.

– Did I say something funny? the dean asks.

Her laugh stutters to a stop. She made a mistake, she laughed when he didn't even tell a joke. She can never get it right.

The silver elevator doors reflect nothing. Edith suppresses a cough. The elevator redolent with older-man aftershave. The dean clasps his hands behind his back.

The elevator dings.

– Good night, she says.

He doesn't answer. He must not have heard her. The dean's hard-soled shoes tick-tock off the elevator, a toy cuckoo-clock man clicking away. The ceiling above him ripped open, and sinuous silver pipes and other shiny guts leer out from the darkness overhead.

She presses the > < button to close the doors. Frantic footsteps gallop toward the door. She scrambles at the < > button, and the doors freeze, then wheeze open. She waits. Pokes her head out the door. No one. Even the dean's echoing footsteps have dwindled away. Nothing but an orange pylon next to a hole in the wall and the view of a cabinet stuffed with taxidermied birds and prairie rodents. Vermin.

She taps the button to the main floor and the doors grind shut. The elevator wheezes, then launches downward. Its gears start to whine, like an old-fashioned fan belt, then shriek. The elevator abruptly lurches, then stops.

She punches the #3 button again.

Sweat trickles down the back of her ear.

She presses the Emergency button. The wall emits a telephone ring tone.

A radioed voice answers the invisible phone: – Maintenance.

– My name is Dr. Edith Vane. I'm trapped in the Crawley Hall elevator, she says. – This elevator isn't moving.

– Do you know about which floor your elevator has stopped? crackles the voice.

– Between third and second. Or fourth and third. Just below the floor with the taxidermied owl and blue heron.

– We'll be there right away, says the voice.

Is the floor undulating? The impossible waves are only in her head; she is probably only going to faint and the floor isn't really moving at all.

She has a night class in thirty-five minutes and she hasn't finished writing her lecture notes, she has a CWA meeting tomorrow at 9 a.m., an IT connect session right after because her electronic interface with her students hasn't been working, she has marking to do, and she hasn't read the books she's teaching in her two other classes this week. She tucks her mail and her books under one arm, and pulls her thumbs. First her left, then her right. Her left, then her right. She once saw a group of students emerge from stuck elevator #2, their hair plastered to their heads from sweat. Condensation from their breaths and heat dribbling down the walls.

Clangs echo in the elevator shaft above.

– I'm Dr. Edith Vane, she shouts.

The clanging stops.

– We're going to get you out very shortly! shouts a voice above. – Are you all right? Can you cope with being in a confined space?

– Yes! she shouts.

The clanging resumes, then stops. Clang clang clang, then nothing. Silence settles, an overstuffed down blanket, in the elevator. She leans against the wall. She flips through her books, one called *Foundations of Business Analysis* to help her with her second book, one on dense theory she desperately wants to care about, the other a book she heard Leonardo nattering about that she assumes is important. She notices that his name appears at the end of the long string of authors. Of course. She wishes she'd been trapped with a decent book. A book of poems. She never gets to read poetry anymore. Or her laptop. At least then she could have gotten some work done. She needs to fill out the External Service box in her

AAO! So many things she could be doing now, in this time. Time dropping away. Her scalp starts to tingle. She can't tell if she's getting hot because of the air in the elevator or because her hormones are about to mutiny.

She lays the side of her head against the wall. Rolls her forehead against the coolness to tamp down the approaching menopausal bonfire.

She digs in her pocket for a piece of gum or a Kaffee Klatsch breath mint. Nothing but old Kleenex. Lint. She dumps her books on the floor. Bev! She could phone-sex Bev! She dials the number but only reaches Bev's mother-of-five, harried-sounding voice-mail message.

She leans her head against the wall again. She unbuttons the top three buttons of her blouse. Pinches the neck of her blouse and flaps it in and out. She turns her other ear to the wall.

A building erected in the 1950s. Air pockets in the walls, heating ducts. Sounds like humming wires, like wind. Pushing one way then the other.

– Soon? she shouts at the ceiling.

Distant banging. Muffled shouts.

A wail.

A sudden chill zigzags up her spine. She can't be hearing that right.

She tries the silvered elevator doors, wiggles her fingers into the crack between them, crams both sets of fingers into the crack, trying to tug the doors apart, the flabby muscles in her arms straining, the joints popping as she tries to pry apart the doors with her bare hands.

The tips of her fingers ache – weak, useless fingers only good at typing and shuffling paper, not even tough enough for paper cuts.

That wail sounded human, sounded awful. A trick of the air moving through the heating vents.

The crack between the doors opens partially onto a concrete wall. She will not panic. The oil from her sweaty hands and fingers smeared translucent along the doors' edges, among the regular fingerprints and smudges the cleaners refuse to wipe off.

She lays her cheek against the wall in the large crack. She closes her eyes. Cold, sweet rock. The flames lick her shoulders. Her forehead, her armpits crackle with sweat.

Remote clanging from above.

She tugs off her cardigan, ties it around her waist. Rams up her sleeves. Wipes away sweat trickling by her ear.

A tap. On the ceiling. A workman must have dropped a screw down the elevator shaft.

The stony cool fades as the wall absorbs the heat from her face. The hard concrete tepid, then warm, almost fleshy. She fans her blouse, presses her other cheek against a lower section of wall, flinches. The wall exudes unexpected heat. She places her palm against the wall on her right: also uncomfortably warm. All the walls too warm, as warm as she is. The walls moist, condensation beading. Sweat drips into her eye.

Her watch face gawps at her. She has sat suspended in Crawley Hall's spinal cord for eighty-eight minutes. Her class is now almost half-over. She wonders how long the students will wait for her.

The overhead light buzzes.

The ceiling taps. Not at all like an errant screw dropped from a height. More like a set of ten fingernails descending all at once on a tabletop.

– *Oh fuck off*, she whispers.

The fingernails tap again.

Above the watch, the flowers on her sleeve begin to pinwheel.

At first as though nudged by a breeze, lazy flowery circles. But then a wind picks up. They begin to spin.

She tears off the blouse, a button popping off and clicking into a corner. She kicks the blouse away. But now all she's wearing is a bra. Not even a good bra. A grey, peeling, old bra. A new bra her perverted washing machine chewed.

She flips the shirt inside out, the lurid black flowers inside, the milky interior outside. The shirt ruined.

The elevator suddenly jumps.

She unties her cardigan, shoves her arms into the sleeves, pulls the front panels closed, buttons it willy-nilly.

The concrete wall files past, and a floor with pairs of workboots slides toward her at head level, then chest level.

Another grinding halt.

– You okay? asks a set of feet.

– I'm Dr. Edith Vane, she says. – Dr. Edith Vane!

The doors crank open further. She tries to pull herself up the wall, the wall suddenly chilly concrete again. A giant workman hooks her by the elbows, another hoists her armpits. One grabs a big handful of her bum, and she bumps her chin on the floor. She writhes on her chest across the floor, away, away.

She clutches at the edges of the cabinet of dead animals. In the cabinet, among the taxidermied owls, mallard ducks, and the blue heron, a stuffed jackrabbit she never noticed before, posed, ears erect.

She will never ride in an elevator again. Ever. Little pods of evil.

She splashes cold water on her face in the washroom, her hair broken out of its bun, halo-ing her face in the mirror. She hooks her coat over her arm, the handle of her briefcase hooked around her elbow, her books clamped against her chest. Deliberately clomps down the staircase to the main floor and to her car. Along the way she passes her classroom just to check if any students waited for her. The lights on, the chairs crooked at their long tables, but otherwise empty.

She hauls herself up five floors in her shiny Plumtree Condominium Towers staircase, but when her lungs start to sizzle, her knees click, and her quadriceps throb so hard they feel like they're oozing blood, thirty-one more flights of stairs, yuck, and the elevators in her condo have never gotten stuck or out of order as long as she's ever lived here. She chokes the neck of her bag as she steps into the sleek little box of an elevator, lights up the number 36 under her finger. She holds her breath. The doors slide closed, the elevator shoots up into the building. She hovers in the middle of the machine, not touching the walls, the mirrored walls reflecting her reflection of a reflection: a tired and saggy-faced, fortyish brown woman, flashing crooked cleavage in a stinky sweaty cardigan. Nothing but gears and a one-way whoosh of the box up the shaft.

The elevator door opens fluidly, professionally. She digs for her keys in her purse as she steps on the mossy hallway broadloom.

Her apartment door stands ajar.

She forgot to lock the door, some burglar's jimmied the lock, she's been robbed!

She crashes into her condo, her cellphone in her hand, 911 already dialled, all she needs is to press the green button, the condo door wide open behind her so she can scream for help.

The TV bright and noisy, the kitchen island spilling Styrofoam food containers, a pizza box with the lid sprawled open, the pizza littered with red- and green-pepper chunks.

Is she being robbed by a cooking show? She's allergic to peppers; they make her gassy! A man reclines on her chaise longue, facing away from her, toward her blaring television.

Edith screams.

– Edie! says Bev, hustling out of the bathroom, her hair tied back in a red babushka. She holds out her pink, kewpie-doll arms to Edith.

– Bevvy! she cries, and squishes Bev tightly.

The man planted at her coffee table watching television, his feet up on a stack of essays, one of Edith's red pens tucked behind his ear.

The curve of that ear. The spiky greying hair on the young face. She knows him. How does she know him?

– Bev! says Edith.

– Edie, I thought we could do dinner tonight now that I'm back.

– Okay? says Edith.

– This is my son, Arthur.

The man unfolds his long, thin legs from the chaise longue.

Melnyk. Lesley's post-doctoral student. Her protégé. Her lover? It sure seems that way, Melnyk following Lesley around like a pot-bellied pig at every event, in her office constantly, nagging the admin assistants on her behalf for space heaters, air conditioners, a mini bar fridge.

– Melnyk?

– Dr. Vane!

– Melnyk's his middle name, says Bev, bustling about with paper napkins and dirty plates. – I thought Arthur could keep me company. Edith, I've come out to Arthur, he's the first of my children I've told. Arthur, this is my partner, Edith. Edith, this is Arthur.

– Okay, Mom.

– Edith is an author! She has a book coming out very, very shortly. Its release date's been delayed for some reason, some mix-up about getting the rights for the art on the cover or something, but it's coming.

Edith stops putting away her coat and shoes, and instead presses a long kiss onto Bev's mouth for being so wonderful.

– Why are my essays piled in front of the TV? asks Edith.

– Look! says Bev. – Artie and I marked all your essays. I knew you would say you were too busy. Are you happy with me?

– Bev!

Edith scrabbles through the papers with their paperclipped corners, their lumpy, barbed-wire stapling.

– But you have no experience, Bevvy.

– Yes we do, says Melnyk. – I should go now, Mom.

– Arthur, please stay. This is important to me.

Edith has walked into a daydream masquerading as a nightmare. She dumps her briefcase, her coat, her purse on the floor. Dumps herself on the sofa. Pulls the essays toward her.

– Would you like a slice of pizza, Edie? asks Bev. – I wasn't sure what you liked on your pizza. I've also brought up your laundry from my washing machine and put it in your dryer. Should be dry in about five minutes?

Edith scans front pages, back pages of the essays, the comments brief but precise, the grades matching the students she can remember on the few papers she leafs though. She is on the verge of sobbing from being trapped in the elevator; she is also so happy she could cry. The sobbing howls wrench from her mouth as she succumbs to waves and waves of hopelessness, confusion, gratitude, nervousness.

Arthur asks if he can smoke in her condo, and because she is so embarrassed by her violent crying fit, so afraid of what Arthur might report back to Lesley, Edith slides open the balcony door. She worries about how much or what Lesley's told Melnyk about her, and what a failure, a *hare brain* she is. The glittering window lights sharpen in the forest of buildings fencing in her condominium tower.

Melnyk taps open a slim cigarette case. Extracts a hand-rolled cigarette, a yellow plastic lighter.

The sweet, cabbage, skunky smell of the marijuana twists through her living room. Her clothes, her furniture will stink of pot. She narrows her eyes at the first sinewy line of smoke. Does he smoke weed at Lesley's? Does she smoke it with him and then they make stoned, May-December love?

He inhales; the joint's tip brightens.

He passes the cigarette to his mother. Bev pinches it between her lips, pulls in a breath, holds the joint in the V of her fingers. Bev leans over to kiss Edith, tries to blow the smoke into Edith's mouth. Edith can't help opening her mouth, kissing her back, inhaling.

Who is this man, sitting on her carpet so casually in his pointy hipster shoes and spiky hair? This is Bev's son, Lesley's current protégé. Melnyk is what Edith was. Melnyk will report to Lesley every detail about Edith, her condo, her manner. The same way Edith once dutifully reported to Lesley.

She wonders if he's slept with Lesley. If he likes having sex with a woman at least thirty years older than him. Maybe it's his thing. Maybe it's a fetish. Is she being ageist? Maybe the sex is just that good. Maybe if they all smoke long enough, she will work up the courage to ask him if he's Lesley's boy toy, and he will be high enough to tell her the truth. He hovers the joint under his nose, deliberately sucking the smoke into his nostrils.

Such an angular young man, such smoothness, such leanness. She can see why Lesley would want him as her servant.

The television hums and snaps.

– My head is killing me, she says, slumping her face into her hands.

– What happened to your shirt, says Bev.

– I Botox my forehead to stop the migraines, Arthur says.

– Do that trick with your forehead, says Bev. – Edith, look at Artie try to raise his eyebrows. It's so funny.

His eyebrows sit. Bev yelps a laugh. He hovers the joint next to his nose.

– Yeah, Alice Z. told me it worked for her so I tried it, he says. – Worked after only one session.

– Alice Z. in the main office?

– Yes. You know she breeds Russian blue cats? She won the lottery when she was eighteen but then spent it all by the time she was twenty-three. All she had left from all that money was three purebred Russian blues.

Edith will ask him. She is going to ask him. She can pretend she's stoned. He owes her after sucking all the oxygen out of the room and making her high. Spying on her.

– Have you and Lesley ever slept together?

Melnyk studies his yellow lighter. Flicks on the flame, flicks it off. – Well, he says.

– Have you, sweetie? asks Bev, her head in Edith's lap, her eyes glassy. Turning her face to Melnyk, – Yes?

– Not that it's anyone's business, he pauses. – But yes. And no.

Bev pops up, her babushka askew. – I have to go to work. I have a shift in ten minutes.

She folds a slice of pizza in half and shoves it into her mouth.

– I thought you were going to give me a ride, says Melnyk.

– I can drive you, Edith blurts. – I would love to drive you.

– So nice! mumbles Bev through her half-chewed pizza. – But aren't you too busy?

Edith slows her car to a stop in front of a four-storey, lipstick-red, 1912 gutted and renovated chimera of a house, a picture window stretching up two floors. A faux-sandstone finish and faux-antique lamps. A giant abstract painting spanning both floors.

– Thanks, he says. – I'll get you the weed by Monday. I'll ask Alice Q. to put it in your mailbox.

He leaps out of the car, his courier bag slung over one shoulder. His tall, lean form loping toward the house, pausing, then loping back. He opens the car door, sticks his head into the car, his cheeks rosy, his breath smoky.

– We can't ever be friends, he says.

His head disappears and he gallops for the front door.

He hasn't hurt her feelings. She knows he has only furnished her with stony fact.

The door opens to warm incandescent bulb light, walls painted mauve, and rows of bookshelves. An artsy chandelier composed of broken bottles arranged in a bouquet. Suspended from the ceiling in the front hall.

Edith knows that chandelier. Its owner bragged that she bought it in a glass studio in Venice, and that she slept with the artist, Lorenzo, who made it.

She pulls away from Lesley's house, her eyes on the asphalt road, nothing but the asphalt.

As part of her new routine, she leaves the house thirteen minutes earlier than she used to and winds her car through the narrow corkscrew roads of the campus, hunting for a parking space because her parking lot is still a collapsed hole. She trudges on lumpy, frozen grass to get to her side door of Crawley Hall. She shifts her books to her other hand.

– Edith! cries a voice.

Crawley Hall has sprouted a gargoyle in the night. She clings to the top ledge. The gargoyle is the shape of a woman in black.

A black blot against the brown concrete planes of the building. The geometrically precise rows of tiny slits for windows. Edith cannot believe what she is seeing; the more she sees, the less solid the ground becomes. Her throat closes and she cannot shout the word *no*. She hesitates beside the mesh fence circling the sinkhole. Then she strides toward the building, trips, kicks off her shoes, then dashes around the large fenced-in-area of the sinkhole. A grazing hare on the grass startles and bounds away; Edith trips and tumbles over the concrete edge of a scrubby grassed meridian strip, on ice, bits of snow, feet in ripped stockings, her head dangerously light as she runs, for what she has no idea, to catch the woman, she supposes. She is the only witness to this woman so high up, clutching the side of the building. Edith reaches toward her, tumble-runs to the bottom of the building, grips her hands together in prayer, her eyes cemented to the horrible bird perched on the uppermost windowsill.

– That's not allowed! shouts Edith.

The woman in her long black gown, clinging to the side of the building. She lifts her hands away from the building, fits them together like a swimmer on a diving board, and dives toward the concrete sidewalk.

But no. This is impossible. Because the windows on the building were never designed to open. The woman in her black gown is not a tragic gargoyle poised on a window ledge, not a woman in rippling clothes smashing her hardened fontanelle into the rippling sidewalk below.

A spread of bones and cloth abruptly pile at the edge of the sinkhole. Edith stops, tries to hold herself upright by digging her fingers into the mesh of the blue metal fence, then leans over to gag into a shrub at the edge of the pit. She falls onto her hands and knees, dirty snow, twigs, and little rocks digging into her palms, her jaws cranked open, waiting for something, anything to expel.

She wonders if she can cancel her classes. She has to prep the students for their mid-term exams and she needs to interpret chapter nine with them or they'll be floundering.

She fumbles her phone out of her bag and edges herself around the fence so she can see the face, the body so awful it glows behind the blue mesh.

– Campus Security? answers the voice.

– There's been a terrible accident!

The heap of dress, the face twisted away from her. The woman isn't wearing a black dress, she's bundled in graduation regalia: a tasselled cap, a pleated black gown and blazing red hood. Edith edges over, stoops, and peers through the mesh at the woman's face.

The face is Edith's face. She jumped off the building.

She clutches her head, presses it with both hands, *hard*, the way she tries to press away headaches. She squeezes her head between her hands, willing it to burst like a melon.

She turns back to the body behind the mesh fence. She doesn't want to see the face again.

But there is no body, there is no woman in black, there was no jump.

Just caved-in sidewalk at the edge of the stupid, stupid hole.

– Ma'am? asks the phone. She hangs up.

Opposite her, inside the fence, on the other side of the sinkhole, a jackrabbit stands perched on its hind legs, ice-still, studying her with one yellow-irised eyeball.

– You, she says.

You know, she wants to say.

She looks up. Crawley Hall's top floor is as empty and plain as usual. Except for a new concrete bulge in the corner that looks like an outsized, mottled carbuncle, probably from some kind of long-term water damage. She is not crazy or on a lingering high.

The rabbit drops to its forelegs, continues to survey her.

Crawley Hall's doing this. Crawley Hall threw Edith off the ledge, threw Coral down the sinkhole, makes patterns crawl. Why does it want Edith? Because it can tell she is one of the weakest, the slowest, the softest. *Hare-brained*. She is easy prey. Sicko. *Sicko*.

Edith retrieves her shoes from where she threw them and edges toward the door. Pauses. She doesn't want to touch the handle and catch the sickness. But probably it's too late. And Crawley Hall knows she has work to do.

She shivers as she waits for the elevator. All she wants is to make herself a cup of tea with the kettle in the lounge, sit on her side of Leonardo's sweaty office, reread her lecture notes, google plot summaries on Wikipedia. Forget what was obviously a waking dream because she didn't sleep enough last night and smoked too much bad weed. She will phone Vivianne today. Yes. Admit she's on the verge of a substance-abuse problem because she is unable to turn down cannabis whenever anyone offers it to her.

The door slides open. She enters. The door slides closed. A greasy handprint on the buffed silver inner door. A leftover from her horrible night. She leaps for the < > button.

She trudges up the stairs, heaving herself up past Angus Fella as he bumps, slow motion, down the staircase, wheezing and pausing for breath every second step. The air in the staircase is damp, chilly. She pulls her coat collar up around her neck. Her breath rises in white vapour. Another hallucination. She will never smoke weed again. Never.

In her office, she clicks open her email. As she reads the first one, Edith has to lower her head between her knees in case she faints in her seat. She tries not to hyperventilate, her hands clutching her chest.

– What are you doing? asks Leonardo. – Please don't throw up in here.

An email from the dean's assistant, Lisa Ives, requesting a meeting between her and Dean Vermuelen. Tuesday at 7 to 7:10 a.m. or Thursday at 4:20 to 4:30 p.m.

She picks her way down the staircase to the Jungle for a coffee, wishing she could collide into Coral and launch the H-bomb of anxiety crowding her throat, hoping at the very least that in spite of Coral's absence, the green and the chemicals secreted by the phony rainforest will reorient her.

She pauses in the stairwell, her phone pasted to her ear. – Vivianne. Please, she whispers, – I need to book an appointment.

I have to meet with the dean and I'm on the verge of a panic attack. Vivianne.

Vivianne's voice mail tittering on about how Vivianne can't come to the phone.

The air in the Jungle is juicy and rehydrates her lungs almost immediately. The coffee cup plonks down from the machine, coffee whizzing into the cup. Angus Fella reads a book in the corner by the palm tree, a coffee cup balanced on his knee between his flaky, wrinkled fingers.

She presses the cup's edge against her lips. Slinks out, pretending she hasn't seen him. She has nothing to say.

Thursday, 8 a.m. Lecture Theatre room D562. As usual, her Canadian Literature Before 1950 class is as exciting as a buckwheat pancake, no matter how hard she tries to pick out funny images, chortling to herself, or asks directed questions. When she asks the students questions about *Sunshine Sketches of a Little Town*, they fiddle on their laptops, observe her like she is a strange sea creature. They nod in their baseball caps and yoga pants, their parkas sliding to the floor. *Sunshine Sketches of a Little Town* is not her favourite book, but it's a Canadian classic by the father of Canadian letters, it says so right on the book, and when she thinks of its role in Canadian literary history she feels a small bubble of pride. One of the students, Joffrey, responds irritably that the book is far too long considering the frivolousness of the content. She tries not to be afraid of Joffrey, but cannot help it, cannot stay immune to his rising voice, his heavy beard that makes him look thirty-five even though he's only eighteen, the strange way he only ever wears T-shirts even when it's sub-zero temperatures outside. Joffrey's told her he's going into law. She has not yet given him a grade below a B, strictly out of fear. She tries to draw him into chapter eight, the characters of Zena Pepperleigh and Peter Pupkin.

– Aren't those terrific, meaty names, Joffrey? she asks.

– Okay? says Joffrey back, and she can't tell if he's asked an actual question.

Only Simon's finished the book, bless his heart, his hand popping up so many times she's tempted to ask him to just settle himself at the front of the classroom and teach while she leaves for a coffee and a frustrated weep. She stands, lumpy and undercooked, on her side of the classroom. She wants to be a better teacher. She has the passion. But all the students except Simon sit, bored and silent to the point of catatonia, on their side of the classroom. She arranges them into groups and asks them to go through the first chapter together and come up with three humour clusters to talk about. Anything. Please. She putters around on the computer in the podium, checking her email.

Four p.m. Room D562 again. Professors and instructors dribble into D562 for the monthly AJX faculty meeting the dean likes to hold fortnightly for some reason. This time Edith sits on the other side of the lecture theatre, the student side. She opens her laptop and drapes her cardigan on the back of her chair in the top tier of the giant horseshoe of seats, a seat away from Ian Bell red-penning a stack of student essays, and Iris Bell pounding the keyboard of her open laptop. Leonardo's curly head leans in to Olivia, and Olivia gestures to Leroy Hoffman, who wears a clavicle brace. He broke his shoulder when he slipped in a puddle of water in the men's washroom. Angus Fella has planted himself opposite her in the horseshoe, his fingers curled together into a single, outsized fist.

The dean calls the meeting to order, his hairy fingers tucked in the waist of his pants. The room drudges through the minutes from the last meeting. Edith rereads her AAO, which is due next month, and which she's completed except for proofreading. Leroy Hoffman comments in his puddingy monotone about the TUP plans, and notes the colon used instead of a semicolon in section 5.4 about the Hawaiian-themed December holiday reception.

Ian Bell skips his pen through his student essays, curling the pages back as he scribbles, sometimes flipping back and forth. Iris Bell taps her keyboard, raising her hand during votes for and against changes to the minutes. Marian Carson has stationed herself in the row below Angus. Edith tries not to stare at Marian's breasts, the nipples poking through the beige jersey fabric. Edith once saw Marian in her office reading Deleuze and Guattari and smiling. Edith briefly imagines Marian and her, side by side under a rumpled pile of blankets in a bed, reading Deleuze and Guattari together, chatting, naked, in a bedroom spilling with books. Academic, romantic Elysium. Marian has an outrageously shapely bosom when she wears jersey fabric.

Edith scrubs her pen in an inky circle. Lesley clunks open the room door, followed by Melnyk of course, carrying her briefcase and a Holt Renfrew shopping bag. Edith ducks her face behind her laptop and almost smashes her nose against the Knowledge Mobilization section of her AAO. Lesley manoeuvres herself past colleagues, empty swivelling chairs, to the centre of the front row. Melnyk slides in beside Lesley.

Edith colours in the circle so violently she punctures the paper and inks the desktop. She flaps her hand at Melnyk in a subtle wave hello – she will probably be his stepmother one day whether they are friends or not – but he is too busy arranging Lesley's coat into comfortable folds behind her back.

Edith rereads the most important line of her entire AAO:

Vane, Edith. *Taber Corn Follies: The Memoirs of Beulah Crump-Withers.* University of Okotoks Press. 343 pages.

Dean Vermeulen begins an anecdote about the time he was at an intimate dinner with the Baron and Baroness of Renfrew as a way of segueing into the budget update.

Edith presses Save, then Submit AAO.

Submit AAO? asks the program.

Yes, she presses.

AAO Submitted, the program responds.

She wants to shriek her lungs raw, she wants to kick up a flamenco, she wants to drink mojitos until she turns peppermint-green. She doodles a happy face with her blue pen.

Olivia drones about the study coming out of the University of Inivea School of Sociology about the statistic regarding the increasing rates of suicide and depression among professors. Dean Vermeulen reminds them of the U of I BalanceWell faculty and staff Care and Well-Being support program.

– And of course my office door is always open if you have any issues you would like to discuss with me. I'm not just your dean, he says, spreading his arms out wide, his pocket watch chain glinting at his breast pocket. – I am also your first stop for institutional *support*.

Sharon Silver the Food Anthropologist begins to sniffle when the dean reminds them about the approaching deadline for the AAO and the progress on the EnhanceUs Refreshment Strategy. Edith overheard Olivia telling Leonardo that Sharon's being indirectly pressured by Sandersams Supermarkets to retract damning articles she wrote about how modern North American grocery stores isolate community members from each other, unlike the food markets of ancient civilizations.

Edith wants to cackle, for she is free of her AAO, at least for another two years. And this time her VI score will be astronomical.

Angus raises his hand and asks, his words tight, – Is anything going to be done about the sinkhole? It's been stewing there for weeks. Crawley Hall will slide into it any day. One of our own's still in the hospital from falling into it!

Angus rabbits on about how he's seen a crack in the basement that travels along an entire wall, and a urinal detached itself from the wall while he was pissing into it and nearly crushed his foot.

Marian Carson shakes her head. Most of the faculty smile and shake their heads. Leonardo clucks a laugh. The Bells chuckle, lean against each other that way long-married people do. *Poor dotty old Angus.*

Dean Vermeulen abruptly stops his pacing.

– Angus, he says. – As I've informed you on numerous occasions, I'm not going to address an issue like building management and other non-curriculum issues at an AJX faculty meeting.

Angus slams down his stack of papers, and pushes himself to standing.

– While *you're* planning yet another fully catered, host-bar reception, he bellows, – as professors we're being forced to subsidize photocopying and pencils and p-p-paperclips! We're two and four to an office while the C wing vomits vermin. That goddamn elevator #1 is getting more erratic and was stuck between the basement and main floor for three hours last Wednesday, probably because the building is literally falling over, and my eight-months-pregnant teaching assistant nearly gave birth in it! Why don't you meeting that, ol' Phil.

He shoves himself past the other people sitting in his row, bonking Leonardo's head and ruffling his cherub curls. Angus shoves out the door, a sheet of paper fluttering behind him.

– Well, I guess that's that, says Phil.

The room chuckles. Chairs squeak as faculty members shift in their seats. The dean chuckles, coughs. Pulls his handkerchief from his suit jacket pocket and dabs his mouth.

At the end of the meeting, Edith slings her bag over her shoulder and skips down the steps out the door, her burden lighter because she has submitted her AAO. She'll pour herself a double rum and Coke when she gets home. Maybe she'll go exercise like a normal person! She will *not* smoke a joint with Bev. She hovers behind the pack of her colleagues, keeping Lesley's golden bob in her sight. The professors and sessional instructors cluster in front of the elevators. Edith skulks past them to the staircase door, and flits down the dark stairs. Goosebumps leap out all over her chilled arms, and she remembers her cardigan. Which she left in D562.

She climbs back up the flight of stairs. Even more lights in the stairwell have fizzled out, creating a definite *murk*. In D562, the Bells are still flumped in their seats behind his stack of essays, her open laptop.

– Meeting's over, Edith calls out, as brightly as she can.

Of course they ignore her.

She sweeps up the cardigan from the back of the seat, bundles it under her arm. A patter. Like dropping grains of rice. Edith pivots back to the Bells.

The Bells haven't moved. They aren't moving at *all*.

– Iris and Ian? she asks.

Iris is slumped in her seat. Ian sagged into Iris's shoulder. Not Iris. Not Ian. Their mouths slack, Iris's eyelids drooped and still. Ian Bell, who is closest to her, is *heaped*, as if his bones are an afterthought. He sags, like a drunk in a still-life. Edith has seen dead bodies before, but they were in caskets, neatly arranged, posed, coloured in.

Above them, the ceiling gapes, the tiles blistered and ragged. Rice grains dropping, spitting from the ceiling.

Edith stumbles down the five tiers so quickly she catches her foot on a patch of duct tape holding down a carpet seam. She bashes her shin on a chair, the pain slashing to the tips of her toes, her brain popping from the pain.

She scrambles for the Campus Security phone at the front of the room, her hands, her teeth chattering so hard she can barely form the words, – I ... what ... I ... , she burbles into the receiver.

– Campus Security? answers the receiver.

The Bells' faces, hands, their faces ... the Bells are dolls now. Horrible, grey, meaty dolls. Their exposed selves are unthinkable, but their clothes writhe with life. Edith cowers, the phone crushed to her cheek. The green checks of Ian's shirt crawling and undulating, the paisley of Iris's blouse bumping, twisting, and sighing. Their clothing alive, and now Edith is officially losing her mind. Like doppelgänger Edith's leap from the fifth-floor window, the ivy on Coral's dress, the flowers on Edith's P. T. Madden blouses, but this hallucination lingers too long, this hallucination clings and clings.

Crawley Hall has possessed them.

Edith's cardigan crushes and wrinkles in her hands. A warm, dusty draft ebbs from the hole, ruffles her hair. She throws her cardigan over her head to block the awful breath exhaling from the ceiling. Shoves the heel of her shoe into her mouth to block her teeth chattering. Tastes grit and salt.

Iris Bell's chest heaves as she gasps in a breath.

Edith sprawls up the steps toward her.

Edith sprouted itchy patches on the backs of her hands in the night. She thrashed her legs between her sheets, sucked on the corner of her pillow, trying to block the sight of the inanimate biological package that used to be Ian Bell, and Iris's doll-like, prostrate form as the paramedics swarmed her back to life. The maw in the ceiling that seemed to have sucked them up then spat them back out. She was only sitting two seats away from them during the meeting. Did they collapse during the meeting? When? How could she have not noticed them dead and almost-dead? Why didn't anyone else notice? She'd assumed they were napping or thinking hard with their eyes closed. Was it a coincidence they were sitting under a vast and ragged hole in the ceiling? Was the ceiling ripped open before the meeting or did the ceiling rip open after the meeting? So many ceilings in the building were exposed, nothing but pipes and ducts and wires, she can't remember. Did someone poison them? Did carbon monoxide ooze out of the hole and envelope them? Then why wasn't anyone else in the room killed? She didn't notice larvae dripping from the ceiling during the meeting.

She gulps once from her kale smoothie, gags it into the kitchen sink, then shoves the smoothie into the fridge. Kale and chia seeds pooling on the stainless steel.

As she navigates traffic on the way to school, she picks and picks at a flaky spot on the back of her scalp, her fingernails chipping through the skin. Her fingers twist and pinpoint a pimple, which she picks. Blood under her fingernail. A habit she had as a child that has now returned. Surveying sections of her hairline, portions of her face in the rear-view mirror, she stuffs her hair into a ponytail with the elastic she'd snapped around a pack of student essays so she won't be tempted to pick at her scalp while she's teaching a class. The way she wore her hair when she was a teenager, a big poof at the back of her head.

Edith crashes into Leroy Hoffman in the photocopy room.

– Whoa-ho! said Leroy Hoffman. – You almost dislodged my clavicle brace!

– You okay? she asks.

– I've been better, he sighs, scratches at a spot under his brace, – I've been better... You found the Bells.

– Yes.

– That's tough, he says. – Poor Iris and Ian. What a way to go. They say she's stabilized now, but still not able to eat on her own.

Suddenly colleagues like Leroy and Alice Q. and Olivia are initiating conversations with her and giving her eye contact, not excusing themselves immediately when she starts talking. Marian Carson and Leonardo, she enthralls them. Leonardo wheels his bike alongside her in the hallway to their office, his tires unfurling muddy tracks, his bike pedal biting her calf, her ankle. They want to know details, to know if she has any theories. They want to know why she couldn't save them.

– What exactly did you see, demands Marian.

Edith can't help glancing at Marian's chest. Marian's wearing a jersey again.

– I'm late for a meeting with the dean, she tells Marian. – I really must go and prepare.

In the office, Leonardo drapes his damp bicycle shorts over her coat hooked on the coat tree, then wheels his chair in front of his computer. He starts battering his keyboard so hard it clatters against the desk's hard surface. He abruptly stops typing, then asks her, – Did you give them mouth-to-mouth resuscitation? Did you check for heartbeats?

They work on their opposite sides of the office so she has to turn to talk to him. She tries to speak. Tears blur her eyes. She swivels back to her computer.

– I would have done mouth-to-mouth, says Leonardo. – Or CPR.

– They looked like old meat, she says, her lips dragging around the words. – Ian was *decaying*.

– That's impossible, says Leonardo. – It's biologically impossible for decay to set in that quickly.

He clatters his keyboard some more.

– Was it carbon monoxide poisoning? he asks rhetorically. – Coincidental and simultaneous heart failure? Poison? Did you notice them ingesting anything at the meeting? Did you try to talk to them? Call their names? Wouldn't there have been death rattles? You say their skin looked grey. Do you mean their skin was red? Or are you sure they weren't actually tinted blue? I am sure they must have been blue, given the circumstances you've described. Yes, they were blue, which suggests asphyxiation of some kind.

Edith's lips crush, her mouth filling with mucus and tears.

– I have to go now, she says, and she slams the office door behind her as best she can. Cinnamon chemicals envelope her, trumpeting Lesley's imminent arrival and just one more nauseating addition to this day. Edith's not sure which way to turn down the hallway. She dives left.

Lesley sails toward her, lips a violent red slash, Helen Bedford and her gigantic backpack cantering alongside her, humping Lesley's flowery coat and briefcase. Edith flattens against the wall as they hurtle by.

She is 3.5 minutes late for her meeting with the dean.

– I'm sorry you witnessed the Bell tragedy, says Dean Vermeulen. – But it's good you were there for Iris.

– Thanks, says Edith.

– But notwithstanding all that, frankly, says the dean, his chair swivelling back from the window to face her, – it's been a full two years since you received tenure, and I'm seeing zero percent improvement in your teaching evaluations, and here we are again, with seven undergraduate and graduate students as separate, organized groups using up my valuable time to complain about your classes.

She shakes her head. The view from the window shows the bleak stretch of thrusting concrete buildings, wide swaths of dead grass, churned dirt on the construction site, the steel lace of still and silent construction cranes. The punching bag glowers in the corner of his office, a witness to her humiliation. Why is it so hot in here? Like an oven set to Self-Clean. He has no books in his dark wooden shelves. No papers, no files. His desk as clean and wide as a prairie plain. How could a university dean not have a single book in his office?

– And your negligible involvement in higher-level committee work, your lack of success with a FORT or POL grant or any other kind of funding, I wonder if it wasn't a mistake to hire you in the first place. I'm not sure how you were awarded tenure – only one book to press in seven years? I was brought in to clean house, says Phil, wiping the air, pretending to scrub a wall, she guessed. – I'm cleaning house. The dropout rates in your classes are extraordinary. Ninety students dropped down to thirty in your Introduction to Literature course. That's more than 50 percent. Complaints from graduate students. One more semester of this and you'll be due for a third official warning, book or no book. AAO or no AAO.

– Third?

Edith dabs her forehead with her sleeve. She would like to rip every stitch of clothing off and streak into the snow, Phil's severed windpipe dripping in her hands.

– This is your second, says Phil. – One more warning and I will be forced to engage the EnhanceUs Refreshment apparatus.

He grunts and slaps closed her file.

Edith twists her hands compulsively in her lap. Her hands are a thrashing baby rabbit, its throat slashed by a bored cat. So hopeless, everything puddling into hopelessness. Her study on Beulah Crump-Withers is being relegated to the irrelevance pile even before it's had a chance to break open a single bud.

– Lesley once mentored you as your supervisor. She says you've never been exactly prolific, and that this book is exceptional only because she believed you had no chance of ever finishing it, he says.

– But it's still a book. And it was due out this month, she squeaks. – It's been delayed because of some printing issues, but it *will* come out.

– Ah, but that was your dissertation. That is how you first got the position, that is how you sidled in to being awarded tenure with the last dean, whose standards were evidently at a basement level. Because you had a book coming out. Lesley tells me she essentially co-wrote that book. Now you need another book, he says, spreading his hairy fingers out across the desk surface. – A proper book. Or at least four publications per year in top-tier journals. A FORT grant for at least $75,000. An award of some kind. Supervision of a graduate student who actually completes the degree with you. Surely you can manage *one* of these things. That's what you're paid for. If you don't make things happen, then things will happen to you. You'll scrape by this AAO cycle because of your book, but next time I'm not so sure.

She can imagine her father's excruciating sympathy, possibly his secret delight, if she lost this job and had to go work in a coffee shop like Bev. Him fired, then Edith fired. Comrades in failure. Her mother would remain the only one who managed to not get fired before retirement. Although her mother did have to give that free $800 hair weave after she burned off the client's hair with straightener because she was too busy gossiping with her sister on the phone. Or maybe her father would be glad because he could blame it on the economy rather than his dodgy expense claims and fraternizing with a competing company for payoffs. Her mother's disappointment, the ulcers Edith would develop trying to pay down her student loan, her credit card bill, her gigantic mortgage, by working in a coffee shop. She isn't even qualified to work in a coffee shop. Probably Bev will dump her too.

– Leonardo Baudone only has one book, she mumbles, – and it was his dissertation.

– I refuse that kind of response. I refuse to make comparisons. But I will note that Baudone's book came out with an international press. It was mentioned in the *New Yorker*. His book has high Impact Factor. And he's had a second book already accepted: two books in three years!

She dabs her temples with a square of Kleenex. Her cuffs soaked with sweat. She should leave before she starts crying. No. She will take Vivianne's advice and cry openly, in front of the dean. She squeezes her eyelids shut. Tears spurt from her hot face. Beryl once told her she was an ugly crier. If she were a beautiful crier, would it make a difference? What does a beautiful crier even look like? A bubble of snot heaves in and out of her nose. All she wants is to do right by Beulah.

– Oh, come now, says the dean, tapping the desktop impatiently. – Is that necessary?

But with his South African accent, so it sounds like *Eess thet nessissree?* Which only urges her to cry harder.

I am the archaeologist of my life; I build its fountains and dig the nuclear bomb shelter.

– Phillip? she asks, remembering advice her father once gave her. She wipes her nose on the back of her hand.

– Yes?

He picks up his phone and pushes a button.

– What kind of soup did you eat with the Prince of Cornwall again?

– Prince of *Wales*, *Duke* of Cornwall, he sniffs. – Duke of Rothesay, Earl of Chester, Baron of Renfrew, Earl of Carrick, Lord of the Isles, Prince and Great Steward of Scotland. Organic watercress soup, of course.

He stands up from his gleaming desk, straightens his shirt cuffs, and whisks out the door. He does not return, but instead his administrative assistant, Lisa, poses in the doorway, her long hair curling around her shoulders and chest in a lanky, Catherine Middleton fashion, and guides her into the reception area.

– The bathroom's over here, says Lisa. – You'll probably want to freshen up.

Lisa steps back from Edith, as though Edith might vomit on her.

– You found the Bells? says Lisa.

– Yes.

– Such nice people. Poor Iris.

She frowns, a Kate Middleton dimple sweetening her right cheek.

Edith unbuttons her blouse and fans at the heat frantically. Drops her head into the washroom sink and bawls, miserable wails that twist up from her innards. She has failed Beulah. *I am so so sorry,*

Beulah. She smears snot all over her hands and wipes her hands up into her hair, then frees her hair from the stupid elastic band, her hair a comforting black, hot mass cushioning her cheek, her neck, her jaws. She's dribbled water from the sink down the front of her shirt, her mouth agape, she doesn't care. She surfaces from the sink, faces the mirror. Her eyes are the size of grapefruit seeds. Ugly crier. She looks like she belongs on the cover of *Creepshow*. That's another thing she remembers Beryl once told her. Oh god, she misses Beryl. Beryl collected old comics. Maybe she should call Bev. But Bev might tell Melnyk, who would tell Lesley that she's a loser.

A woman in a stall behind her sighs.

Edith sniffs. She should probably pee. She rebuttons her blouse. Perhaps the woman will come out and ask Edith what's wrong. Perhaps the woman will say something hopeful or magical and Edith will feel better instead of such a dreadful failure. Both the stall doors are closed. She waits, rinsing her hands again in the sink, blowing her nose. It's been a minute, maybe more. She blows her nose again.

She peeps under the doors to see the feet of the women in the stalls. To see if one of the stalls is actually free.

Leather lion heads mounted like figureheads on Hangaku heels: Lesley's shoes. Edith didn't smell Lesley because her nose was so plugged up with tears and snot.

The pattern in Edith's sweaty olive-green blouse froths. There's so much wrong with this place, this building that asphyxiates people, spits maggots, makes her blouses weird. Her mother was right: patterns *do* look terrible on her bosom! She can't pull off the professor masquerade and she never will – the clothes, the confidence, the publish-or-perish pukiness. She isn't like these people, Crawley Hall knows she isn't like these people, and it's chewing her up and planning to pick the remaining shreds of her out of its teeth. But she won't let it win. *Beulah* wouldn't let it win.

The bathroom door clunks behind Edith on its broken hinges as she bolts.

She swings down the staircase banisters like a rabid gorilla, two steps at a time, the banisters icy, slippery. *Lesley says she co-wrote Edith's book?* Is that what Lesley is telling everyone now? And why is Lesley on the fifth floor? Is she meeting with the dean to talk about Edith? Conspiring to get Edith *refreshed*?

Edith pulls on the door handle to the fourth floor, but the door sticks and she nearly yanks her right humerus out of its shoulder socket. The stairwell's trapped her inside its hollow grey horribleness, this echoing concrete bowel of a stairwell. Everyone in this building hates her; this building hates her too, and it has been telling her it hates her for months.

– *Let me out!* she shrieks, and the door flies open.

She screws her key into her mailbox, her hands shaking, her nose running. Perhaps a reassuring promotional postcard from her publisher. A free book she might bury her nose in.

Nothing. Just the metal slope of an empty mailbox. That's incorrect. A letter from Parking Services. Its stiffness suggests it's her new, overdue parking pass. For a parking lot that's a people-eating, car-eating hole at the foot of a building that's methodically destroying them all.

She bangs the mailbox shut, pinching her index finger, the pain lightning up her hand. Yanks out the key. A crooked key juts out from Lesley's box.

She rubs her face in her cardigan sleeve, trying to unravel the horrible ball of hairy crud the dean has lobbed at her.

Her mailbox door pops open.

She shoves the key into the door, turns it, and slams her door closed. Hard.

The whole wall of mailboxes, including Lesley's mailbox, snap open. Envelopes, papers, packages slither out. Lesley's spicy smell slithers out.

Edith bends down to gather up the papers, manila envelopes, the parcels. A thunk on her crown. A shower of thunks.

Papers, envelopes, catalogues, flyers cascade onto and around her. The mailboxes yawn open, mail spewing and fluttering.

She tries to gather up the mail, but cannot keep up with the envelopes, boxes, fliers slipping, whiffling out.

This isn't her job, cleaning up after dysfunctional mailboxes. Or is it? She can't imagine Alice Z. on her hands and knees, chasing envelopes under the photocopier.

She chases an envelope under the photocopier.

Dr. Lesley Hughes, Leung Endowed Chair, CONFIDENTIAL. She holds the envelope between her fingers. She wants to drop it and pretend she never touched it. Or put it in her pocket and keep it with her forever. She gathers more of Lesley's mail under the photocopier along with gobs of dust, paperclips, pencil nubs. Desiccated rabbit turds.

She stuffs Lesley's mail into her bag. Scoops up two more pieces of mail, a large manila envelope, a postcard, next to the mailroom filing cabinet. Flees. The mailbox doors continue spewing and vomiting.

She ducks into a utility closet: plastic pipes, a dry mop bucket, jars of bleach, and stacks of folded garbage bags. She huddles with her phone. Vivianne's line keeps ringing, a repeating burr that bores into Edith's eardrum. She needs Vivianne to tell her what to do. Cure her. Explain to Edith why she stole Lesley's mail and how to give it back without anyone finding out.

She skitters to her office. Grasps the doorknob but cannot understand why her hand slides off.

She doesn't understand the mottling on her office doorknob, the lumpishness. Her key parked in the middle of it.

It must be a prank, peanut butter? Dirt?

But the smell.

The doorknob smeared with dog feces. A terrible, spirit-crushing prank. Aimed at her, she knows it.

She sits in her car now, her hands still trembly and smelling. She got some on her hands when she first pushed in the office door key, she can't wash the smell off; even after blasting hot water on them in the women's washroom, even after soaking them in dish soap in the faculty lunchroom, her fingers still smell of shit. She suspects one of the students from Canadian Literature Before 1950, Joffrey, or the white boy with the half-shaved head, or maybe the marsh-mallow-faced kid with the goatee in her night class. Or Karis the graduate student who only got an A– on her presentation. Or Lesley. Or the dean. It could be one of them. Or all of them.

All she has ever wanted to do is read books. Write books. Talk about, sleep with, breathe, shit, and eat books. Maybe find true love with someone like her who understands the crucial, necessary, life-giving essence of books. That's why she thought she'd chosen the right job, because understanding books is what professors do. She inhales an uneven breath. She digs her nails into her steering wheel and squeezes her eyes shut, trying not cry. She still doesn't know where Coral's gone.

Edith careens out of the parking lot in the dark, zips round the curves in the playground zone near the university daycare at sixty kilometres and clips a jackrabbit. The low white flash of hare against the dark of the asphalt surface, a jackrabbit eye glinting red in the light from her headlights just before impact, one of Crawley Hall's spies, she just knows it; the thud of impact, a bump, but when she gapes into the rear-view mirror, just black road tinted red in her rear lights. She jams down the brake. Squints in the rear-view mirror again. There.

She pulls the car off to the side. Opens the car door.

She's crushed its skull. The eyeball that faces up has popped out of the socket, bloody and engorged.

The fluffy white paws. She is a filthy murderer. Her face collapses as the tears spill and then flood from her face; her chest crumples with grief and shock.

Edith wobbily strokes the hare's soft fur, the body still warm, blood and matter splashed from its head all over the road. She touches the throat. She slams on the brakes on her crying. Wimp. Pansy. Beulah would never cry like this over a jackrabbit. Edith loops her fingers around the rib cage, her fingers pressing the warm lines of bones, swings it up, and carries it to the trunk of her car. Drives away. She will bury it properly somewhere.

Bev helps Edith scoop the stiffened, dripping hare out of the trunk with a black garbage bag turned inside out.

– I dunno, says Bev. – The city has a road-kill pickup service. They could have taken care of the body. Now the inside of your trunk's covered in blood and gunk. Eeeyuck!

Edith cannot abide Bev's callousness. Blood sprinkles and drips down Edith's forearms.

– Maybe we should smoke a joint, says Bev.

Instead, Edith drinks two bottles of wine while Bev eats funky brownies made with Melnyk's grade A marijuana. When Edith asks Bev if Bev wants to have sex, Bev says, – No. Wrestling dead, crunched rabbits kind of doesn't do it for me.

Bev licks the last of the brownies off her fingers and stands up because she has to be at her shift in twenty minutes and she still has to iron the apron of her uniform.

– Where should we bury it? asks Edith.

– The sinkhole by your building? says Bev. – At least it'll be close to home. Or the garbage bin?

Like ensuring the proper burial of the hare Edith murdered is some kind of joke.

– At the very least put the body outside now, in the cold, says Bev, – so it won't rot.

Bev hoists up the black garbage bag full of dead hare, slides open the balcony door. She tosses out the garbage bag onto the balcony. Steps back inside and slides the door closed.

– I'm pretty sure my building is possessed, says Edith.

– The condo? asks Bev in alarm. – Did you see a ghost?

– No. The building where I work is alive and has got it in for me.

– As long as it's not the condo. The condo fees are already astronomical. It's been fun, Edie, says Bev. And she pecks Edith on the nose.

Fun. Edith wonders if Bev is getting ready to break up with her.

After Bev leaves, Edith brandishes her letter opener while contemplating Lesley's stack of mail. Two literature journals in transparent plastic envelopes, a newsletter from the university teachers' union. An invitation to a reception at the Inivea Petroleum Club. And five envelopes of varying sizes, thin and fat, provenance ambiguous since several sport names she doesn't recognize or lack names entirely, and one seems to be from Carberry University. *I am the architect of my life; I build its foundation and design the cellar crawl space within which I hide the bodies.*

Her fingers shrink cold as she contemplates opening Lesley's mail. She's positioned the shredder between her feet so she can destroy the evidence immediately.

She slices open the envelopes one by one.

The first envelope holds a letter asking Lesley to renew her subscription to the QTFR association. Edith has never been able to clearly google what the QTFR is – the results are always in German or French, even though Olivia, Coral, and Leonardo namedrop it. So do the Bells. So *did* Ian Bell. She chews her thumb. Edith crumples up the paper in irritation. Palms it smooth again, then feeds it to the shredder.

The second is a notice informing Lesley that she's been banned from Stenson College, California, or even contacting any Stenson College employee without permission.

The third a submission from Helen Bedford. Lesley is old school. Of course she'd make Helen submit a hard copy of her crappy sugar chapter. Edith would print out Helen's emailed chapters. Edith bets Helen's regretting Lesley as her supervisor! The shredder grinds as Edith feeds sheet after sheet into its eager, cavity-laden teeth.

The fourth a CONFIDENTIAL copy of Lesley's budget so far as the Leung Endowed Chair, and how Inderdeep in accounting has found several expenses that cannot be adequately accounted for: flowers delivered to Lesley's home address, a banner produced by a non–University of Inivea–sourced printing company, a three-week car rental in Italy, an $817.44 restaurant bill, two first-class return airplane tickets, one to Rome, the other to Hungary, and an unspecified clothing purchase from Coco & Violet for $3,499. *Please forward detailed explanation for the receipts and credit card statements as soon as possible.*

The fifth envelope, return address Carberry University, decorated with the Carberry chimera crest, holds a handwritten letter and a gold signet ring. Hurried handwriting on Carberry letterhead:

Lesley –

Since you refuse to share your home address with my lawyer, I am sending your father's ring to you care of the U of I address.

– Dino

Dino. Lesley's husband. Edith slides the ring onto every finger on her left hand until she finds one the ring fits. Her thumb.

The last package holds a cloth-bound book: *Geneviève Masson, Poems: Métis Balladeer of the Red River* by Lesley Hughes. Another new book. One of the few Lesley's written not co-authored with Dino.

Dear Dr. Hughes,

Please find enclosed a copy of the book with the erratum included, as we discussed.

Sincerely,

Duncan Wu

Staines-upon-Thames Press

Edith flips through the book. Glued inside the book's front pages, a paper rectangle with a doubled black border:

Erratum – Lesley Hughes gratefully acknowledges Arthur Melnyk Jones, post-doctoral scholar, for his meticulous research assistance and for co-writing the book's introduction, conclusion, and prefatory sections in Geneviève Masson, Poems: Métis Balladeer of the Red River.

Edith holds the Erratum page up to her nose, inhales the glorious glue smell. She brushes the page across her lips. Arthur wrote and edited this book. But Lesley took all the credit. Then Lesley somehow got caught.

Edith lays out her trophies: the book, the three delicious letters, the ring. She should shred the letters. She should pawn the ring or toss it into a gutter grate. But they make her heart explode into petals and pearls.

Her email pings on her phone. An email from lhughes: *edith my office tues meet me at 10 we need to talk hugs lesley*

Edith retches so hard she drools on her carpet. Lesley knows. Lesley *always* knows. How does Lesley always know?

Edith stands in the doorway of her old office, now Lesley's office. Edith frowns.

– Edith, exclaims Lesley. Lesley throws her perfumed arms around Edith.

Edith perches herself across from Lesley on the very edge of the seat of a new leather-upholstered chair. Through the window the view of the crackling mountains, of trees, of blue sky. But Edith is chilled from the breeze of the pendulum blade swinging above her head.

Lesley chatters as if they never stopped being friends, as if she had never soured on Edith, frequently placing her hand on Edith's upper arm, her fingernails so glossy red they look like they might drip, talking about her gardener, her cleaner, the keynote she gave recently in Denmark, the conference she's organizing in Portugal, her new book about Genéviève Masson which will be coming out shortly.

– How's Dino, says Edith, her tongue flat, sticky.

– Oh he's wrapping it up at Carberry, preparing to move here and putter around in the garden and on the golf courses like every other retired man I know. For the first time in our entire marriage we'll be living in the same city!

Lesley laughs, her mouth wide, showing off every single tooth in her head. Perfume billows from the folds of her clothes. She pats her gold victory roll.

– He's talking about taking up scrapbooking, says Lesley. – Insists he'll be a househusband. He needs to find better hobbies.

Edith stews in her chair, lumpen.

– Now, Edith, says Lesley, leaning in toward Edith, settling her elbows on the arm of her chair. She picks at something lodged between her teeth with a pinkie finger. – I know you stole my mail.

– No.

– Edith. Don't be dumb. I saw you digging through all that mail, and what a coincidence, when Alice Z. cleaned up the mess, no mail for me anywhere.

– I don't know what you're talking about.

– You poor, sad thing. Did you find what you were looking for? Pathetic little bug.

– I would *never* do such a thing, insists Edith.

– Oh, Edith. Do I need to tell your story to the dean?

Lesley twists her wedding ring. Pats Edith's knee.

– Edith, I have a proposition for you.

She hands Edith a sheet of paper. Edith nearly chokes.

– I don't understand this email, says Edith, shaking the paper.

– Edith, says Lesley, settling her bottom into her seat and folding her perfumed arms, crossing her perfumed legs. – You and I both know how hard you worked on this book, but also how hard *I* worked on this book. There would be no book if it weren't for me. I introduced you to Beulah Crump-Withers in my graduate class. I led you to the archives. I suggested the methodology. I gave you the structure. I edited the writing, drew out your ideas and, frankly, gave you many of my own. My name as co-author is only fair. After all I've done for you, the tears I shed, the arguments I had with your examining committees to have you pass your candidacy exam, your final PhD defence. I was on the committee that admitted you into the PhD program in the first place. I never told you this, but no one else wanted to admit you into the program. I cried, Edith, I *cried* and I fought because I knew your potential.

Lesley kicks up to standing. Floofs the hair at the back of her golden head with her fingers. Rubs her hands together, flips through papers on her desk, then settles herself on the other side of her desk. Pounding in the ceiling. A muffled shout from someone upstairs.

– I wrote to the University of Okotoks Press, she says. – I know the acquiring editor, Terry, from years ago at Carberry. I forwarded Terry all the emails, drafts I kept because I keep the drafts of all my students' work, and Terry knocked together a new cover that includes my name, and they've put a rush on the printing.

– It already has art on the cover!

– I've never liked William Kurelek. A Group of Seven painting would be more appropriate. Mona Leung owns a Lawren Harris. She's delighted we're using a reproduction of her painting for the book jacket. She's very excited about the book and the attention it will bring to the foundation. And I will take the book with me to the University of Vienna at the end of December. See the publicity Beulah will get?

Edith's eyelid so frenzied it threatens to jump off her face and down Lesley's throat.

A crash on the floor above them reverberates. Construction and asbestos abatement. Or someone's knocked over a bookshelf.

– You *know* the Beulah Crump-Withers book was a collaborative effort, says Lesley. – You're devoted to books, Edith, but devotion only takes a woman so far. *Nuns* are devoted. You've got no heat. You couldn't have finished it without me.

Edith's body reacts without her brain, without consent, with automaton decision and intention. She leaps across the desk, her clawed fingers only centimetres from Lesley. Lesley doesn't move.

A handful of larvae drops between them. A short shower that tip-taps onto the desk surface.

The ceiling tiles bloat, crack.

Edith slings her briefcase over her shoulder and shoves past leather chairs and bookshelves for the door. Both hands tugging the doorknob, she tries to pull open the door, but Lesley crowding behind her makes it impossible. Edith turns, grabs for Lesley's arms, but all she can grasp is quilted fabric and handfuls of hard, biting pearls. She yanks open the door.

Behind her, a creak, then a cavernous thunk as the ceiling collapses. Followed by plonks of plaster. Sprinkles of dust and debris.

An overriding smell of boiling eggs and synthetic cinnamon.

The office a mound of white ceiling tile, cottony insulation, and uncoiled silver ducts and coils. A dusty brown hare scuttles between Edith's legs, a bullet of breeze and muscle, and sails down the corridor.

The only sign of Lesley is the palm of a hand that blinks open in the middle of the pile of debris.

– Lesley! she shouts.

She trips and slips over ducts, stumbles and falls onto crumbling tiles that collapse into dust. Grabs hold of the hand. The hand clutches back.

Edith speed-dials Campus Security.

November

Edith sleepwalks through the first weeks of November. Her forearms so deeply scored from her fighting herself in the night she has to buy gauze to wind around her arms to stop the blood. She shreds the three letters addressed to Lesley. Pointless. The blackmailer blackmailed. Lesley's father's signet ring she drops into an ancient jar of pickled beets at the back of her fridge. A jar of beets she keeps for sentimental reasons because she made the beets following a recipe in Beulah Crump-Withers's journals. Maybe she should give the signet ring to Bev as an engagement ring. Edith still hasn't had time to shop for a proper engagement ring.

Once she even ventures into the University of Inivea pool, hoping freezing-cold water will wake her up again, but Angus Fella with his round fish belly and genitalia-red trunks outlaps her again and again. She floats face down, irritating the other swimmers so much they shout at her and accidentally on purpose bang her with their flippers and flutter boards. Finally the lifeguard descends from her high chair and asks Edith to leave.

Sometimes after teaching her classes she sits at her desk in Leonardo's office and thinks so intensely about the blankness of her life she forgets to go home until deep into the night; roaming Crawley Hall as a nocturnal being almost provides a kind of solace, as though the evil of the building, of the job, approves of her so long as she doesn't try to indulge in a life elsewhere. That bewitching self-righteousness and validation that come with physically being on campus and at her desk nudge her when she stays late, or arrives early in the morning when the moon still hangs in the sky. If she is in the building then she looks like she is working, even if she isn't working at all. She looks busy and devoted to her job if she sits in the office. Busy is good. Wearing clothes without patterns is good. Thinking about her book and about Beulah is bad. She never runs into Lesley or the dean or anyone except old Angus in the stairwells. Sometimes Angus shuffles past her office door in his bedroom slippers.

– I've always worked better here than at home, he says.

She suspects he's sleeping in his office every night. Swimming every morning in the pool for his bathing and morning libations, and eating Egg McMuffin breakfasts in the food court in Leung Hall when it opens at 6 a.m. She notes that he never arrives late for morning meetings.

The silent corridors and rows of locked doors. The deserted nighttime campus almost hums it is so empty, the floors somehow shinier, more hopeful, in the vacant hallways.

One night at 10:59 p.m., Edith wheels Leonardo's second-best bike from the office doorway after she collides into one of the pedals with her shin. She redrapes his crusty, second-best cycling shorts over the handlebars when they accidentally slip to the floor. She settles herself at her desk in Leonardo's office, draws toward her chest the motley, ragged stack of essays she's had for almost four weeks. The essays have almost beaten her because she has been staring at the wall too much. She will not let them.

She peers into her reflection in the window. The view outside calming, luminous in its darkness. The sinkhole deep as outer space. Nothing but occasional street lights stringing along the highway at the edge of campus.

She extracts her red pen from her purse and slowly begins scribbling and ticking her way through the wildly ungrammatical pages, miles of faulty logic, the written-the-midnight-before wool gatherings.

Soon she is a marking powerhouse, she has graded seventeen essays in fifteen minutes, she is a marking automaton. She should grade papers at three in the morning every single day! Her mind vinegar-sharp, a slayer of dangling, squinting, and misplaced modifiers.

Until she hears the dripping. A steady drip of the tap in the bathroom across the corridor. A drip that intensifies, pokes into her concentration, fragments her midnight genius. She pushes the exams away, stands up from her desk, slips her keys into her pocket.

She pushes open the washroom door into moonless black. The sound of water running from a tap. She flicks on the switch. Only one fluorescent light flickers on. The ceiling gutted and cavernous.

Her heart startles, clatters in her chest.

A woman in a yellow dress bends over the sinks. Coral, rinsing her mouth.

Coral's hand stops, mid-rinse, her hand still cupped over her mouth, water drip-dripping, her bloodshot eyes gazing at Edith through the dim reflection in the mirror.

– I'm sorry, Edith half shouts. – I didn't know anyone else was in here. You scared the stuffing out of me. Coral! You're back, she sighs. – You're back from the hospital. I'm so glad to see you.

Edith sighs again, holds out her hand.

Coral's hand stays cupped to her mouth.

– I was so worried about you, Edith says.

Vestiges of water curl down Coral's forearm, drip from her elbow into the sink. Edith drops her hand.

Edith knows it would look stupid to leave the bathroom without using it, so she shuts herself into a cubicle, shoots the bolt of the door, and pulls down her pants. Sits down.

She hears the faucet turn on, then off. Then on again.

She pees, wipes, stands up, and refastens her pants. She swings open the cubicle door.

Coral is still standing there, her back still to Edith. Her hair straight and shiny as a red toy car.

Coral's fingers over her mouth, red.

– I like what you've done with your hair, says Edith. – The colour, I mean. Or maybe it's the light in here. Is it?

Water drips from Coral's hands, rivulets in the sink.

– Have a good night, whispers Edith, and she scuppers out the door without washing her hands, her urine-speckled fingers firmly pushing into the middle of the orange poster that trumpets *Please Wash Your Hands.*

Edith inserts her key into the office lock. Just before she turns, she hears from inside her office a pale intake of breath.

She unlocks the door, swings it open.

Her room spills with paper. Paper and exam booklets tossed around, pages ripped and crumpled. Edges frayed, shredded, almost as though they have been chewed. Leonardo's bicycle mangled and upside down beneath the windowsill.

Blood rushes to her feet, her head suddenly frothy. This is what fainting feels like.

She stumbles back to the washroom. – Coral, she squeaks.

The washroom dark again. She flips on the fluorescents. Only her reflection in the mirrors. A puddle on the floor by the sink.

She bounces side to side down the hall, yanking and twisting doorknobs on offices, boardrooms. Runs to Coral's office and bangs on the door. Locked. Dark. She needs a telephone, an emergency phone.

In the elevator lobby she trips over a mop bucket. The bucket only jolts and splashes, but Edith spills to the wet floor. The night janitor shakes his mop in Edith's face.

– You okay? he asks.

– My office has been vandalized!

He stoops down, scrutinizes Edith's face.

– You high? You're high!

– I'm not!

– You're in the office with the muddy bike tracks all the time.

She learns his name is Wing Lau. After he helps her sit up, they concur about what a slob Leonardo is, then call Campus Security.

Burrowed into her car seat, she dials Vivianne. Vivianne's voice mail oozes her placid voice. She texts the word *URGENT*, pressing so hard her thumbs nearly puncture the glass screen on her phone. She will visit the BalanceWell offices tomorrow first thing because this has gone on long enough. The universe is pulling her apart. Her book, Coral, the paranormal catastrophe in her office, her scratched-up arms, Lesley blackmailing her. Her therapist has obviously quit and *no one told Edith*. She snuffles, then erupts into tears. She drives from the library parking lot to Crawley Hall. Stops her car. The orderly, symmetrical lines of Crawley Hall's empty lit rooms suggest an order, a reasonableness she has not known for months, for years.

She digs through her briefcase for a Kleenex to stop up her runny nose, her tears, when the silhouette of a stick-figure woman stumbles out of the building. The woman steps unsteadily, as though drunk, then splays her limbs wide as she clings to the mesh fencing around the sinkhole with her fingers. She begins to climb, fitting the toes of her shoes into the mesh, her torso, her arms moving like a jerky spider's. She reaches the top of the fence, then rolls herself over the top. Abruptly drops into the pit. It has to be Coral. *We're all mad here.*

She's imagined Coral into the pit. Again.

Edith's right foot punches down onto the accelerator and the wheels spin on the night frost before plunging her out of the parking lot and onto the campus road. Crawley Hall's taken over Coral. Edith's lost Coral.

The next day, Edith climbs the staircase. She fears the washrooms in Crawley Hall, fears the elevators, fears her own office. She cannot help but wait for the plink of maggots in her classrooms when she's teaching, and what about all the jackrabbits? The only place, ironically, that she feels safe is in the stairwells, where the naked concrete and pipes are exposed and vulnerable and true, not costumed with drywall or mouldings or tile and glass.

Paper shields the inside of the window in the BalanceWell office door. She has never approached the physical office before. The doorknob is locked. Edith assumes the staff are attending an important meeting, or a coffee-break birthday party in the lounge, and they don't want to be disturbed. They didn't even leave a sign.

She stands at the door, pressing the edge of her phone against her lips. She checks her voice mail again. No message from Vivianne. Her eyelid tics. She tromps down the stairs all the way to the main floor and out the side door. She hasn't been to Leonardo's office yet. She figure eights in the snow. She figure eights too close to an evergreen, and a jackrabbit dashes away from under the branches.

She stops pacing, squints through the fence mesh around the sinkhole and into the hole's apparently empty depths. Where

Coral spends her time. Time spent. Time lost. Out of time. Oh, Vivianne.

Edith slept hardly at all last night; her arms are so scratched up this morning she could hardly stop up the bleeding.

Dr. Angus Fella ambles slowly around the other side of the stiff metal fence, the broken and slack yellow police tape. In his puffy down winter jacket, the grimy cuffs and collar, the fedora settled firmly on his head. Edith notices that the jackrabbits ignore him; he walks close to them, between them, she even sees him step over one, but they continue nuzzling the stubby grass under the light stretch of snow as though he is invisible or just another hare, this perpetually inebriated, perpetually hatted man, as he perambulates in what she guesses is the direction of the library.

Edith skids and slides over the ice after him.

– Angus! she calls.

He wheels around. Touches the brim of his hat, then wheels back and continues walking.

– I owe you a decent hot dog, she says.

Striding to catch up to him. Her breath thick. She tugs his arm.

– There's something wrong, says Edith. – I understand what you were saying now. About the bird trying to fly in instead of away. The Bells. Ian's death was unnatural. Coral Fletcher's losing her mind too. Crawley Hall is not a good place.

She takes a deep breath.

– I think Crawley Hall's evil, she says. – I think Crawley Hall killed Ian Bell. It's killing Coral. It's making all of us crazy.

– Would you like a glass of rum? asks Angus.

Rum! Does she have time for rum?

– Yes, says Edith evenly, puffing. – Should we head to the bar?

– Bar's the wrong direction.

He turns back to Crawley Hall. She toddles after him like a duckling, a cygnet.

Angus opens the bottom drawer of his filing cabinet and pulls out a bottle of Bundaberg and two cardboard coffee cups. The same cups that plop out of her favourite coffee machine. He pours too much rum into both cups and hands her one, his hand shaking slightly. She accidentally gulps her first sip, nearly chokes.

– Tasty, she says.

– Is it? says Angus absently.

He fingers a mangy stack of battered hardcovers on his desk.

Behind him, on the face of a filing cabinet drawer, a smudged, muddy handprint. Angus pulls open a filing cabinet, offers her a cookie from a peeling blue and red plastic packet.

She crunches on a cookie.

– Neat-tasting cookie, she says, dipping it into her rum.

– It's not a cookie. It's an Anzac biscuit.

Edith crunches. Coconut.

– Do you believe that Crawley Hall is possessed? she asks, spitting out crumbs. – You're here at night. I've seen you. You live here.

He grunts. The office stinks of their rum and biscuit breath. She wishes she could open the door.

– Crawley Hall isn't possessed, says Angus.

– I've seen chairs move by themselves. The patterns on clothing... She looks down into her cup, can feel the blood rush to her face. – You know how the patterns on clothing go all wrong. You know what I'm talking about because you talked about it before.

– Crawley Hall just is who it is.

– *Who* it is?

– What it is. Chairs moving and patterns on clothes are beside the point.

– So then tell me what the point is.

He turns to his filing cabinet. Contemplates the muddy handprint. – I've said too much already. I'm going to get in trouble.

He exhales. Clasps his hands in his lap.

– I want to go home, he says.

Edith swirls the rum in her cup, biscuit crumbs circling the bottom. She dashes the remainder of the rum into her mouth. Stands up. He will only ever talk *around* things, and she will just have to resign herself to the fact that he is only capable of administering drips of truth. She will talk to him as often as she can. She will force him to teach her what he knows.

She also understands now why some people might want just a little drink before work. The rum runs down inside her chest, kindles inside her hands and feet. She will confront the fact of her office and begin the cleanup. She will have to come up with an excuse for Leonardo. Blame it on vandals even though there was no time for vandals, and no noise, and the only reasonable, rational answer is that she tore up Leonardo's rubbery bicycle shorts and mangled his bicycle with her bare hands, threw the papers around herself in a mad, sleep-deprived, 180-second frenzy, and blocked it out. That's all.

She checks her phone for a message from Vivianne. Or Bev.

– Don't you and I have an AJX meeting right now, Angus?

– Do we?

He checks his Cheshire Cat watch. – Och. They laughed at me.

She licks the edge of her sadly empty cup.

He pours more rum into her cardboard cup, into his own.

– This building is a ship, he pronounces, – steeeeeeered by a lunatic, and a wilting economy and collapsed oil prices that are toooossssing us through stormy seeeeeas.

The glow of Angus's desk lamp is reflected in the window, in the encroaching, early night. He turns his face to the window, leans back, his hands cupped in his lap.

– Well, someone, *something*, threw my student exams and papers all around the room and crumpled them up! The office is a mess. Leonardo's bicycle looks like a five-hundred-pound man sat on it.

She bites off the edge of a fingernail, then nibbles the fragments. A shred of nail travels to the roof of her mouth. Angus takes a swig. His cardboard cup crackles.

– I don't know what I'm going to tell my students, she says, clutching her hands around her cup, crumpling it. The fingernail has lodged in a groove in the roof of her mouth, and she is dying to pry it out. – I told one class I'd have their papers back to them on Friday, and the other class expects their quizzes back tomorrow!

– So just tell them your car got broken into, the bag the quizzes were in got stolen, and their next assignment is worth double. Or give them all A's.

– Have you ever done that?

– Of course! The students don't care about the *essays*. They just care about the *grades*. Your problem, Evelyn, he says, – is you care too much about the wrong things.

Edith gulps. Angus's rum has washed away most of the panic. Maybe tomorrow she could phone in a bomb threat and buy some time that way. *Buy time, waste time.* But that would just buy her a single day. She could say a car thief stole the assignments. Yes, she could. Yes, she has no choice.

The click of the doorknob's tongue darting into the strike plate booms intolerably loudly down the corridor. Angus whistles a fragment of a Sousa march inside his office. At the same time, Coral whirls into the hallway, her heels clicking tick-tock, her head lowered as though she is an arrow shooting straight for Edith under the twisting silver ducts in the gutted ceiling. An angry bony silhouette growing more brooding and more alarming with each step. Coral's had a bath. Coral looks almost normal.

As she approaches, the frown hammered on Coral's face takes on sharper and sharper focus, as do the outrageous dark rings Coral has smudged around her eyes; her hair's vibrant colour from last night bled out, her lips pale, chapped. Coral clawing herself out of the pit. Coral sleeps at night in the pit.

– You missed a faculty meeting again, Coral whispers as she whishes by Edith. – Today *you* were on the agenda. Congratulations on your and Lesley's new *book*.

Edith's chest clenches, her mouth opens but utters no sound.

Coral's fingernails are broken and uneven. Dirty, as she tugs her blazer closer around her.

Edith inserts the key in the office lock. The lock so sticky she has to jiggle the key. The door sticks. She has to push it open, push against heaps of paper collected against the inside of the door. Leonardo is already inside, grunting and hoisting books onto his desk.

– Look at this! he says. – I hear you contacted Campus Security. You could have warned me too about the mess I'd have to face.

Snowflakes straggle by outside the window. She checks her phone. Still no Vivianne. No Bev.

She heaves up a stack of tattered paper onto a tangle of exam booklets. Scattered among the chewed-up papers and booklets, drywall dust and little black marbles of rabbit shit. She picks up one of the marbles between index finger and thumb, studies the tiny brown planet, bundled with dehydrated plant fibres. The hares.

Leonardo harrumphs.

– This is completely unacceptable, he says, slotting his books backwards into the shelves.

– I know, she says. – Frat boys are the worst!

– I had no problems before you moved in here, he says. – Now it's vandals, feces on doorknobs, interminable lineups of grumpy students.

She ignores him.

Between the rustles of paper and thunks of books pushed back into shelves, as she tries to distinguish between the chewed and the unchewed, the fluorescent lights secrete their usual low buzz. These papers on this sliding stack, these quizzes on that sliding stack. Leonardo hoists his mangled bicycle above his head and grunts out the door for the day. The rustle and thump of paper, the office floor growing quieter as the staff pack up for the day, as students depart classes and office hours dwindle, the buzz loudening into a rhythmic hum. This first stack dumped into a black garbage bag. That sixth stack on a salvage pile. Her forehead hot. She wipes it with her shirt sleeve. Her reflection in the window sharpens in the afternoon's waning light. Or perhaps the hum of the lights sounds like breathing in and then breathing out. Does she care? She thinks that maybe she just doesn't care. She stands with her hands on her hips. Surveys the mess. The lights breathe in and out in their electric way.

The heel of a shoe sticks out from under a burst box of her books. She hesitates, sussing out the shoe, whether it's still got a foot in it or not. Is there a body under there? She pounces on the shoe. A green suede Hangaku. An older style: she can tell because of the year punched inside it. The suede powdered with drywall. The inside dusted with what look like animal hairs. The shoe far too small for her own foot. Iris Bell's shoe.

December

Even though the book isn't available in bookstores yet, Lesley commands the dean to host a book reception for their book. It's at 4 p.m., immediately following the final AJX meeting for the autumn semester, hijacking the regular end-of-semester, December faculty holiday reception. December 3.

Books will be for sale because Lesley had Terry from Okotoks Press express-ship her three boxes. All faculty and students are invited.

Taber Corn Follies: The Memoirs of Beulah Crump-Withers
By Lesley Hughes and Edith Vane

A heap of books salutes Edith on the table by the doorway, presided over by Helen Bedford, who operates a tin box of cash. Lesley, thirty stitches on her forehead decorously healing, her broken leg tastefully hidden under a long, black velvet skirt, poses for a photo with the book hovering next to her face, her open-mouthed snarl-smile and her pearls gleaming. When the photographer gestures to Edith, Lesley tosses her head back with an exuberant laugh and throws one of her arms around Edith's waist for a photo, holding the book just below and between their faces. The shutter clicks. Lesley hobbles over to the dean and Mona Leung, flourishing a copy of *Taber Corn Follies.*

– Hello, Edith, says Coral.

Coral has folded herself into the windowsill. Thin as a stick man.

Bev heaps her plate with miniature cupcakes loaded on a tray carried by a student server. Bev stopped answering her phone for a while after the dead jackrabbit debacle. But then Edith texted Bev about her book and Bev shot up immediately in the condo elevator to Edith's place, furious on Edith's behalf.

– Boo! Bev had said. – Shame, shame! she'd shouted when she first saw Edith's author's copies on Edith's kitchen counter. Edith grasping the X-Acto knife she used to cut open the package of books, the knife glued to her sweaty palm because she had no idea Lesley would be first author on the book because of alphabetical order. *First* author.

In Lesley's interview with the university's electronic newsletter, *UGotIt*, she talks about the years of research she did on the book. – I knew Beulah Crump-Withers was gold the moment I read the first bit of archive. Just a recipe for good, old-fashioned pickled beets, but in the margins I saw clear evidence of an exceptionally sophisticated brain, someone who was clearly a savante. Her wit, her self-awareness, are breathtaking, even in the margin of a canned beet recipe! Beulah Crump-Withers is a Canadian gem. What a boon for Canadian feminist prairie studies.

– Well, she *is* a good-looking woman, said Bev on her stomach, studying Lesley's photo on the *UGotIt* website, her pink-soled feet waggling in the air off the side of the bed. – Very fine. But why didn't they interview you too?

– Shut up! Why can't you shut up!

Bev bolts Edith's bathroom door.

At the reception, Edith's mother and father line up at the bar, her mother chatting with Alice Z. Her father strutting in the only remaining CEO suit he owns that still fits him. But he's lost weight in the neck, and the neck weight has slid down to his gut so his neck looks like a wet magpie's. The neck hole gaping. The shirt fabric stretches painfully across his stomach, the buttons ready to burst. Edith would like to introduce them to Bev, but Bev disappeared after the first round of mini cupcakes stopped circulating.

Lesley greets Edith's parents like a society hostess in a movie, her arms wide and welcoming. The jolly, jolly laugh she carts out for special occasions crescendoing at something Edith's father says. He adjusts his cufflinks and pops meatballs into his mouth while whispering in Lesley's ear.

A student bartender in a bow tie and black vest doles out glasses of red and yellow wine, pop and bottles of water from white plastic bins full of ice. Her hands whizzing as she scoops ice, pours drinks.

Angus Fella carefully and deliberately asks for a bottle of water. He props himself against the bar, unscrews the bottle, and sips. Then he fades away.

Servers with round trays of canapés – cherry-sized meatballs on toothpicks, satay chicken skewers, spinach phyllo triangles – wander among the academics, students, and staff. Edith doesn't care anymore; she holds a glass of red wine in one hand while she tears with her teeth at a skewer before spitting the meat back out into a napkin, tipping her wine out onto the carpet in the meantime. Her stomach as unsettled and devastated as she is.

She wonders when this ceiling will cave in. She wishes it would cave in right now.

The dean glides about the room with a glass in his hand, moving among the clusters of professors and senior students. He stops at Leonardo and Olivia. Leonardo cups his hand in the small of Olivia's back.

– Funny seeing you two here together, he smirks.

Leonardo erupts in an appreciative laugh.

Edith escapes to the bathroom, locks herself in a cubicle. She sits on the toilet seat, her hands between her knees, rocking at this joke of a book party, this toilet of a day, this toilet of a life.

Whispering in the next cubicle. A giggle. A zipper unzipping.

– I want your double D-cup tits in my face, whispers a woman.

– Stop it, another voice whispers. – You're so funny.

– I've only felt one other woman's breasts before. Can I? Marian? Does it bother you that you're my experiment? There, I said it.

– Oh. My. Jesus. Chrissssst, whispers Marian Carson.

– Mmm hmm, murmurs Bev.

Edith flushes the toilet. Water swirls back into the toilet. She flushes it again. And again and again and again, and watches her pulped heart twist down the hole. She slaps her cubicle door open and yanks open the main door. Don't Forget to Wash Your Hands, proclaims a sign.

Leonardo hands Phillip his wine. An old white man in a black suit strides by. Phillip trails after the man.

– I'd like to say a few words, Phillip says at the front of the room.

He clears his throat.

– I'd like to say a few words about this wondrous occasion, he repeats, opening his arms to the crowd.

He brings a hand to his mouth.

He coughs. He coughs so hard his whole body vibrates. The next cough makes him drop his wineglass, white wine kicks and sputters across the brown broadloom, a cough so hard it blurs into hack, into retch. He draws his hand away from his face, a handful of bloody pudding pooled and spilling from his palm.

The crowd freezes.

Edith always assumed the dean was made of concrete, was hard and cruel concrete, and would last forever like the Roman Colosseum. But now she sees he is nothing but a paper bag of rusty blood. They are all just paper bags of blood. Silly paper beings.

A sparkling headache seizes her. She needs to faint. She cannot faint here, in front of these people who crash as a wave into the dean.

Edith hobbles down the stairs, her hands on her knees, bright sparkling spots in her sightlines. Coffee. Caffeine is good for migraines. And stolen hearts. And stolen books.

She flops against the wall, crawls down the hallways toward the faculty lounge, trips over limp philodendrons, paper recycling bins, confronts a whitewashed plywood wall with an Authorized Personnel Only sign. She has wandered back to her old hallway, where she used to have an office, her crappy little cubbyhole of C454, but at least it was her own crappy little C454 cubbyhole.

She crawls toward Leonardo's office, clutching door frames as she goes; she will lie down on the floor of the office, she will rest. She will curl into fetal position and mourn her precious stolen Beulah. Then she will buy herself a cardboard cup of coffee.

She nears Coral's office, the office Coral shares with four other people.

The door stands slightly ajar. Edith peers into the dark.

She hears the sound of air rushing from a vent. Or a woman's wet exhale.

Edith steers a U-turn, tiptoes quietly and quickly down the hall, her head thumping, stars popping, to the emergency exit, the stairs, and pulls open the heavy metal door.

She presses her spine, the palms of her hands, the pointy back of her skull against the concrete wall, as the door sinks closed behind her. The harsh fluorescent light in the stairwell, the sharp grey edges of the stairs leading up to the next floor. She tries not to peer through the window in the door down the hall, the wire security netting embedded in the glass.

Edith hugs herself with her long arms. It is late, she wants to go home, but there's nothing at home. She wants to stay in the stairwell. The wall cools her head, the stars do not pop so painfully. No one ever bothers her in the stairwell.

Through the netting in the door's window, she sees Melnyk saunter into the elevator lobby, push the button. Edith can smell the hard synthetic fragrance of his cologne. He exhales once and decides to take the stairs. He heads toward her door. She dithers too long, not sure if she should head up the stairs or down or pretend to be entering the lobby. He opens the door. She stands, wobbles there stupidly.

– Dr. Vane.

– Oh. Hello. Melnyk.

She wipes her nose on the back of her hand. An itch. She pinches and unpinches her nostrils.

His mouth crinkles. – Are you all right?

– Just a headache.

– Botox, he says. – I'm telling you it's magic. You're here late.

– Book party upstairs.

– Oh yeah. Lesley's do.

Lesley's do. It's her do too.

He gallops down a flight of stairs, his thighs flexing through his tight jeans. He stops. Calls her from the landing.

– You got enough? You need some more? Your father's arthritis okay?

– He's got enough for about another month.

– I'll get you some more. Next week okay?

He jogs down more steps, his footsteps echoing.

– I thought Lesley didn't like you speaking to me, she shouts down the stairs. Her head throbs with each syllable.

– I have been found surplus to requirements. Yes, let's just say that.

– Oh, says Edith – Of course. Helen.

More echoes of footsteps.

– Bye now, calls Melnyk up the stairwell.

She leans over the stairwell, watching him spiral down and down the well. The main floor door snicks shut behind him. She hovers alone in the grey.

She feeds coins into the coffee machine. Behind her, fountain water trickles, the green rustling in the artificially moist breeze of the Jungle. The door opens. Coral creeps into the room. She reaches the edge of a plant bed, drops on hands and knees, and crawls into the plants, winding her way around trunks of palm trees, banana trees, under and over ferns. Edith rushes to the side of the plant bed. Coral has chosen the furthest, darkest corner. Coral pads in a circle on her hands, her knees, scraping away fallen leaves and twigs, digging with her hands, forming a depression, then curls into the dirt. Her eyes glitter among the fronds.

From: 'Lisa Ives' <lives@uofi.edu.ca>
Subject: Sad News
Date: Monday, December 10, 8:52 am
To: allstaff@postal.uofi.edu.ca

Sent on behalf of Dean Phillip Vermeulen:

Dear Faculty and Staff,

I am very sorry to have to announce that our esteemed fellow faculty member Dr. Angus Fella passed away last night after a sudden illness. I will keep you abreast of the developments regarding a memorial service as they become available. Flowers have been sent to his boarding house.

Lisa Ives
Dean's Office Administrator
lives@uofi.edu.ca

Edith rocks back and forth in her chair, clutching herself, weeping. Then stopping, then weeping and rocking some more. She should have known. She spent weeks oblivious to the danger when she should have known.

Leonardo and Olivia kiss and purr in his swivel chair on the other side of the office, their loud smacking kisses, rustling clothes. Giggling. Giggling!

She is completely alone.

In the stairwell, Melnyk told her as he handed her the oversized plastic bottle marked *Tangy Orange Flavour! Chewable Vitamin C* that Angus was in his office on the weekend and suffered a heart attack, but still managed to dial 911. The paramedics tried to get to him, but elevator #2 was broken, so they took elevator #1, and then elevator #1 stuck on the way up, and by the time they were free, Angus had passed away, wrung dry by cardiac arrest.

– Angus didn't have long anyway, Melnyk said. – What with his testicular cancer.

Of course he had testicular cancer. She should have guessed.

– You okay? asked Melnyk. He tapped Edith's elbow. – It's not like Angus was the healthiest guy. He drank like a pirate. Believed his Australian cookies qualified as a vegetable because they had coconut in them.

Edith unscrewed the vitamin C bottle, sniffed. Tugged out the baggie to check the amount. Unfolded $500 from her wallet and handed it to Melnyk.

Crawley Hall did it. *It* did it. It was Angus's time. He had become surplus to requirements.

She accidentally on purpose throws a pen at Leonardo and Olivia. They continue giggling and whispering. The pen plunks to the floor, bored. Edith paws through her office desk drawers for a tissue because the box on her desk is empty. A fortune-cookie fortune catches under her pinky fingernail. *A thing is not necessarily true because a man dies for it.*

The paper yellowed and smelling of ... clay.

December 11. She huffs up the stairs to the fifth floor. She should be getting in better shape with all the daily stair-walking, but every time she breathes, her lungs fill with murk. The staircase is, frankly, starting to smell like wet dog.

She tiptoes into the hallway on the left, hoping no one in the right hallway leading to the dean's warren of offices will see her; she doesn't want to collide with the dean and the gold-tipped cane he's taken to hobbling around with or waving in faculty members' faces. His weight loss has been astonishing. She wants to break him over her knee. She sneaks past walls taped with flyers, glass cabinets filled with books, hates herself for cringing when she hears his voice soaring from one of the rooms. Passes by the old display case that seems to shift from floor to floor. A case populated by a taxidermied mallard duck and mate, a blue heron, a single loon, a cockeyed gopher, and a jackrabbit, standing on its hind legs in the alert position. The jackrabbit is so alarmingly large the tips of its ears would reach to her waist if she were to set it on the floor beside her. *Fauna of Inivea* announces the blotchy, oxidized plaque at the base. Her face hovers so close to the glass she clouds it with her breath. She abruptly turns away.

The door to the BalanceWell office suite is still locked. But she can see inside. Sweeps of tarp, whitewashed plywood, the floor covered in duct-taped cardboard. A Construction Personnel Only sign under a single light bulb suspended from the ceiling. Ragged rolls of broadloom, plywood flooring.

Only the ghost of the BalanceWell sign normally above the door: dusty outlines of the L and the W.

How could Vivianne do this to her?

To the right of the door, just beyond her line of sight, a hammer rat-a-tat-tats.

Edith bangs the glass with the palm of her hand.

The hammer stops.

– Can I make an appointment with Vivianne? she calls. – She's a psychologist. I don't know her last name. She works here. No one's answering the phones.

She bangs her palm again, the glass hollow-sounding.

The single light bulb blinks off.

Hiding out in a corner of the Jungle, she cries wildly into her cardboard cup of crummy coffee. Fella's gone, now her therapist has absolutely and thoroughly disappeared, Coral's turned into a jackrabbit, her book's been stolen, Ian Bell has been murdered and Iris Bell is on life support, her love life's imploded, she can't go to her regular coffee shop anymore, and Leonardo and Olivia are canoodling all over her office. And no one except Edith notices that there's anything wrong.

And she's officially run out of underwear and clean shirts, especially now that she's sent her three new blouses off to a landfill where they can't ruin her mind anymore. And she can't ask to use Bev's washing machine because. *Because.*

Handwashing clothes in her bathtub reminds her too much of grading essays.

Today she *will* buy a washing machine. She has no time to slog dirty clothes to and from laundromats, and her last water bill crashed through the roof and shot into the stratosphere. She imagines it's because she's been washing her clothes four times each time, just to get the powdered soap out. She'll buy the first washing machine she sees, get in, get out.

She navigates the broken escalator stairs at Bull Head Shopping Centre. The stairs' sharp metal teeth bite into her shin when she misses a step.

Dishwashers, refrigerators, microwaves, stoves, dryers. Washing machines. She wraps her arms around herself as she beholds the vast sea of metal boxes. She was going to buy the first one, but at least two hundred of them stretch out around the giant room. Does she want white or stainless steel? Front or top loader? Energy efficient for more money or energy horrific for less money? What is her price range? She doesn't know, she hasn't looked at her credit card bill or her student loan balance in months.

She doesn't want to talk to a salesman because he'll try to upsell her. Talk her into a new dryer and refrigerator too. Does she need a new refrigerator? Maybe she does.

She'll say no to any salesman who comes near her.

A salesman with *Arnie* stamped on his name tag sidles up to her and asks her if he can help her.

She grits her teeth, ready to say no.

Arnie. Arnold *Nash*?

– Edith, he says, – lovely to see you.

Dr. Arnold Nash specialized in Shakespearean tragedy. He used to eat kippers out of the tin with his fingers at AJX meetings, and he actually sounded reasonable sometimes. He always smiled. When he was angry or someone was being ridiculous he smiled even harder. Then one day he wrote a letter of resignation. Edith thought she would never see him again.

Arnold explains to her the difference between agitators and washing drums, Quiet-by-Design technologies, vibration-reduction technology, AutoBalance suspension systems.

– All I want, Arnold, she says, – is for the patterns to stay put. Not change from florals to giant bacterial entities. I want the inanimate to stay inanimate. Things like that.

He pulls a Kleenex from his shirt pocket and wipes his glasses.

– I would recommend then, he says, – the SenseClean technology on this model.

He leads her to a hulking cube of stainless steel.

They both disregard that he once worked at the university, that she sometimes waited in line behind him as he xeroxed books and forms or in line to ladle pineapple and ginger-ale fruit punch from the bowl at the December winter party; that once upon a time he was referred to as *Dr. Nash* rather than simply *Arnie* as printed on his red plastic name tag. She's never met someone who voluntarily left the profession. She wonders if he is happy, if he misses the money, the social status. She is slightly embarrassed for both of them even though he opens and closes washing machine doors as if it's no big deal, showing her digital displays and the energy efficiency symbol. Her washing machine started washing so hard the bras splintered into wire and polyester wrecks, the arms started tearing off blouses, she wants to tell him. Her colleagues are dying. She is seeing letters of the alphabet in the clothes. Once the powder crusted into an E, nestled in the knee of her flannel pyjamas. Another time a K in the small of her back.

After twenty-five more minutes she settles on the K25-200 front loader by Novacrest.

– Novacrest does washing machines too? she asks.

– Novacrest does everything, says Arnold, handing her the receipt. – Pleasure doing business, he says, pulling his business card out of his breast pocket and handing it to her. – Delivery will be on Saturday between 12 and 4 p.m. Let me know if you need any more household appliances.

She accepts the tiny slip of cardboard. Dr. Arnold Nash. *Arnie.*

– Everything good at the U of I? he asks.

– No, she says, folding the receipt into her purse. – It's a horror show.

– So nothing's changed then, he says.

The last week of December classes.

Her phone tings. A U of I Emergency Bulletin:

Crawley Hall must be evacuated immediately. This is not a drill. Please assemble at Muster Point D.

An alarm honks and echoes through the corridors. A fire has broken out in an electrical room in Crawley Hall – only a small fire, quickly extinguished – but it smokes up the entire building. The scorched plastic smell trickles up through the vents all the way to her fourth floor office where Edith tries to ignore Leonardo and Olivia's bickering over conceptual versus lyric poetry, the smell thick and man-made. Edith and everyone else in the building trickle down the grey stairs, a growing river of people as the alarm honks. Their voices an echoing, bouncing cacophony. Their eyes rolling in exasperation, all of their bodies so soft, suddenly so aimless, so naked in the blaring, possibly incinerating building. They stand huddled in cold clumps just outside Crawley Hall's side doors. Leonardo storms out the doors in his yellow neon cycling jacket and stalks away in the direction of the student pub. Olivia strolls over to the smokers, bums a cigarette, and lights up. The smokers lean against the sinkhole fence, glancing casually at the orange tarp cobwebbed over parts of the sinkhole. Inside a ring of bright orange pylons, Lesley regales graduate students with stories of her time in the Galapagos. Edith huddles next to a concrete planter filled with crusted ice and dirt and studded with cigarette butts. The dean rests feebly on another concrete planter, huddled inside a big black overcoat, his knobbly, hairy knuckles poking out as he clutches his walking stick. He coughs into his hanky. His assistant Lisa gathers up the hanky, hands him a clean one.

After the fire department allows them back into the building, Edith sits in her office and keeps her appointments with her first-year Canadian Literature Before 1950 students in spite of the smell. Holding her nose between appointments. The smell so acrid it should have a colour, it should emit a sound. Because her students have the final exam coming up in a week and a half, and it's important that they know how to properly write an essay when they've completed her class, and now is their very last chance. She refuses to leave until she has met with every single one of them and discussed their progress so far and what they each need to do to prepare to write their best essay on the final exam. Like a good teacher would. This is day four. Only seventeen more students to go.

Edith breathes in the fumes of the burning plastic as she sits in her office with its brutally sealed window, waiting for the students who line up to sit in the squishy-bottomed chair across from her, some of them fidgeting with their binders or laptops. When they sit down across from her, she uses open body language the way she learned in that mandatory teaching workshop years ago so she looks like she cares – eye contact, her body facing fully toward them, arms and legs uncrossed – and hops her fingers across the desk to them sometimes. She tries not to clench her teeth too hard as they list the excuses for why they haven't started studying for the exam yet: because they're working on law school applications, because of wisdom teeth extraction, depression, the flu, sisters' weddings, dead grandparents, grandparents' wedding anniversaries. After the fourteenth student, an older woman with boots that gob dirty slush all over the floor, the melting slush trickling in meandering streams toward the window, Edith feels a little dizzy, the smell a wall of scorched chemicals winding up from the heat vent, like someone is reaching his fingers up her nose and clawing out the inside of her head.

During a little break between student appointments, she writes out *Back in five minutes* carefully with thick black pen then tapes the sign on her door and runs to the bathroom. She pushes open the door and retches, heaves air into the sink, the stench finally unbearable. Saliva dribbles onto the porcelain. She splashes her mouth with lukewarm water. Dabs her eyes. The burning smell lacquered inside her nose. She runs back out the door.

Coral has nested in the coffee room. Edith rinses out her travel mug, crusty on the inside, dusty on the outside.

– Hello, Coral, she says.

Coral ignores Edith, sits fixated on her laptop. Edith dries out her mug with a paper towel. Coral isn't even looking at the screen, just the keyboard. Coral's thinner than ever, her cheekbones, the hollows around her eyes, veering her face toward the extraterrestrial.

Alice Z., Alice Q., and all the other administrative assistants and office managers closed up the front office and went home because of the stink.

Her last student meeting is with Joffrey, who doesn't show up of course. She places an X beside his name on the roster: Joffrey John Bain. She catches up a library book titled *Business Optimization* from her desk and trundles to the photocopy room, marvelling at the empty hallways so early in the afternoon. She empties the output tray on the photocopy machine: someone's printed out Shania Twain concert tickets and forgotten them. She photocopies her book, pages 26–27, pages 28–29, pages 30–31, pages 34–35, the bar of light in the machine sliding left then right, pages 36–37, pages 38–39, pages 40–41, the light a green as bright as an eclipse. The new dusty smell of the paper sheets sliding about in the photocopy machine, pages 42–43, pages 44–45, pages 46–47. There. She's done. She folds the book closed, a job well done. The machine light has left a black bar hovering in front of her eyes wherever she looks; she shouldn't have watched the bar over and over again as it brightly slid back and forth, but she couldn't help it, such hot, embracing light, almost sunshiny. She notices that she's accidentally cut off the left side of the last three pages, and she missed pages 32–33 entirely, distracted by the burning smell, she supposes, her eyes still watering. Tonight she will try to mark at least ten exams over a late dinner she'll buy from the university food court. Maybe on her way home for the night she'll eat an ice cream cone from the 7-Eleven. Or a piece of cake from the Kaffee Klatsch, if Bev has her evening shift. Maybe tonight she'll propose to Bev. Neither of them has texted the other since the day of the ... betrayal. Edith realizes she's pretending she didn't hear what she heard in the washroom that day. She can't imagine Bev asleep while Marian Carson reads Deleuze and Guattari between Bev's sheets, beneath the cobwebby dandelion clock lamp. No. She will not believe it. The conversation she overheard was Crawley Hall trying to make her insane as usual. An evil auditory hallucination. Bev doesn't own a single book. Marian would never go for that.

She photocopies the rogue pages, the light sliding left then right.

The sleeve of her blouse glows in the green light. The tiny stitching on the cuff. A safe, solid blue.

She flips through the papers, those tiny stitches at the edge of some of the papers, once or twice the bottom of the heel of her hand. One where her watch face is showing.

But she isn't wearing a watch.

Her scalp prickles.

She studies the photocopy of her wrist. It's a Cheshire Cat watch on a thick, scaly, man's wrist, the cat's paws at ten and at three. Angus Fella's watch on Angus Fella's wrist at the edge of the photocopy of her pages. Her eyelid spasms.

She flips through more of the sheets, her stitched cuff, her bony wrist bone. Her breath stops. The Cheshire Cat watch again, this time the watch paws wilting, the smile melted into a frown. She jerks the paper away. Dumps all her papers on the floor.

Not until she's turned away from the machine, the warm papers scattered on the floor, does she scream.

A bearded man stands in the doorway.

Her heart stops, strangles as it misses too many beats.

– I'm sorry? says the man.

Not an older, bearded man. Godammit! Only eighteen-year-old annoying Joffrey in a Hello Kitty T-shirt, pimples peppered along his left temple. How long was he watching her photocopy her book? Why doesn't he care that she just screamed? Chivalry is truly dead.

– You missed our final exam meeting earlier, she says.

– Dr. Fletcher left for a bathroom break during our class, and she never came back? he says. – We don't know where she is?

– I saw Dr. Fletcher in the faculty coffee room just minutes ago, she says.

She stomps over her spilled papers, and returns with him to the classroom and the empty front of the room. Calls Security, checks the coffee room with its dead coffee machine and trailing cloth plants. Joffrey follows her, chirping like a baby bird, offering suggestions of where Dr. Fletcher could be. She keeps open body language to his suggestions, to his peeling lips, his constellated pimples, his T-shirt decorated with a bloody cartoon cat. Coral gone missing. She knocks on Coral's office door, striking her knuckles among the curling office-hour notices and comic strips. The glass above the office door shows the light's off, but she knocks on the door anyway. She knocks again, knowing Coral won't answer. She knows exactly where Coral has stowed herself, but she cannot out Coral to strangers.

They march up and down stairs. Joffrey doesn't ask her why they aren't taking the elevator.

She marches down the hallway.

She instructs Joffrey's class to go home. That an office administrator will contact them about a make-up class.

She enters the Jungle.

– Coral? she asks the room, the trickling fountain.

She circles, parting bushes, peering behind trees. She steps into the ferns, rummages through curling leaves for Coral's form. She looked it up: hares sit in shallow depressions called forms.

– Oh hi, Edith, says Coral from her form.

Coral's eyes are puffy, her face streaked with dirt.

– Coral, says Edith, placing a hand on a tree trunk, – your students were wondering where you went during the bathroom break in your class just now. I sent them home.

– This is not a good place, says Coral.

– What do you mean? asks Edith. – Do you mean this building's haunted? I believe you, Coral. But a long time ago you said *I'm here*. Of course you're here.

She wants to hear the truth ring from someone else's mouth. She crouches down.

– They're all lying to us, Coral whispers.

– Who? whispers Edith.

– You know who was in the car with me when I drove into the hole? You know who died?

– Who?

– Our therapist.

– *Our* therapist?

– The programmer for the BalanceWell phone therapy bot program. His name was Jonah. He went to MIT but got kicked out for plagiarism.

– Coral, can I call someone for you? Or do you want to get your coat from your office and we can drive for a visit to the hospital? Just to check you over and make sure you're okay.

– Edith, the dean cut too many things when he was hired. I found out what he cut, and I made it worse. I shouldn't have come back. I should have resisted. This wouldn't have happened if I'd stayed away.

– Oh Coral, no. You haven't done anything. You're my hero.

– Edith, I am the architect of my life. I've finally figured out where I'd like to put my furniture, Edith.

Edith kneels into the dirt. Smooths Coral's hair away from her sad, lovely face.

In the stairwell, Edith dials Vivianne's phone number, for what she knows will be the very last time. Vivianne's voice mail clicks in, Vivianne so self-assured, so *present*. More present than any flesh-and-blood human being Edith has ever known. She hangs up.

She feels a crunch under her heel. She turns up the sole of her shoe. A hare dropping. She continues up the stairs, counting the fourteen steps of each flight before the loop around to the next flight of steps. She looks up from her feet to the top of the stairs on the third-floor landing. She stops. On the top stair, a hare, hunched down, its ears plastered to its back. Her eyelid clicks. The hare's fur is brown, one bulging yellow eye appraising her. The hare's ears slowly lift. Her chest tight, she can't remember how to breathe, her eyelid battering so hard she can barely see. She holds the banister with both hands to keep herself upright, wondering if a hare in its trapped wildness could ever be dangerous to an adult female human. *Rabbit*, she wants to call, *brother rabbit!* Abruptly the hare pops up its hind legs, its white rump a signal, and streaks up the stairs away from her.

But the hare was *brown*. It's the third week of December. All the hares outside, congregating in the sparse patches of snow of the parking lot, on the stretches of dead grass during this abnormally warm winter, the rectangular quads between buildings, are *white*.

From: 'Lisa Ives' <lives@uofi.edu.ca>
Subject: Missing Persons Alert
Date: Thurs., Dec. 14, 12:09 pm
To: allstaff@postal.uofi.edu.ca

Sent on behalf of Dean Phillip Vermeulen:

Dear Faculty and Staff,

I am very sorry to have to announce that English Department faculty member Dr. Coral Fletcher has been classified as a missing person. Any faculty or staff who may have had recent contact with Dr. Fletcher are required to speak immediately with the police about information they might have. Thank you for your co-operation.

Lisa Ives
Dean's Office Administrator
lives@uofi.edu.ca

Saturday.

Edith unrolls her long-neglected yoga mat on Leonardo's office floor and pulls out a blanket, a pillow, a single sheet, from her Hangaku and P. T. Madden bags. She lays out her makeshift bed between the two desks, her head at the window.

She brushes her teeth in the fifth-floor bathroom, fingers her hair up into a bun on top of her head. Back in the office, she changes into her pyjamas and slides under the blanket. Rolls onto her side on the yoga mat, her bones collapsing into assymetrical, uncomfortable triangles on the hard floor. She rolls onto her back, her spine happily cracking and elongating. She's forgotten to turn off the lights. She pushes off the blanket, gets up again. Flicks off the light. Thumps her seat back down onto the mat and lies back, nuzzling the back of her head into her pillow. She marinates in the pong from Leonardo's cycling clothes. Studies the light from the street lights shot across the ceiling. The heating vent intermittently chokes and sputters between its longer, boiled-egg exhales.

She fears and hates Crawley Hall, but has to find Angus and Coral and protect them. And she will give Bev space, and let her get Marian out of her system so Edith and Bev can return to the simple Kaffee Klatsch they once had.

Today, she graded essays and final exams all afternoon in the Jungle, during breaks digging through the Jungle garbage bin for other discarded cups, drinking cup after cardboard cup of coffee, looking for messages scribbled on the bottoms of the cups as they thunked out of the coffee machine, hoping for rustles of Coral in the palms and ferns, hunting for traces of Coral in the dirt, a stray red hair, an earring. Edith wandered the weekend-empty hallways, the stairwells; she shrugged on her coat and paced along the edge of the sinkhole, hunting for handprints, Hangaku heel prints along the edges of the pit in case Coral has decided to take up permanent residence there. She photocopied hundreds of pages, hoping for a glimpse of Angus or his Cheshire Cat. Ashamed that she was so frightened when he might have been trying to tell her something important. Someone, probably Alice Q., cleaned up all the papers she dumped on the photocopy room floor, and now Edith wishes she'd kept those papers. Maybe she would have found some answers. She dug through the cupboards in the coffee room and found an empty package of Anzac biscuits, nothing but crumbs. She licked her index finger and dabbed the crumbs into her mouth, savoured the coconut aftertaste. She's not afraid. She just wants to see her friends again. She won't let this crummy old building win.

Once, she almost collided into Melnyk in the stairwell. His face gaunt, his eyes raw.

She nodded hello and continued prowling, pressing her ear against the walls, dipping her head now and then between the bannister railings to peer down into the stairwell depths. She told him to send her regards to his mother.

Sometimes she caught the ghost of a whiff of Lesley's perfume in the empty, skinned corridors, but Lesley has already flown to Vienna on the first leg of her Beulah Crump-Withers quasi-book tour, so the odours must have only been Lesley's oil traces left behind.

Her eyes blink open to the office door bucking into her feet, morning sun shrieking in the window. Leonardo wheels in his bicycle, gawps at her on the floor tangled in her blankets.

– What the fuck! he says.

She yawns.

– This office smells like a hobo's camped out in it! he says.

Behind him, Olivia sighs.

The best sleep Edith's had in months. And she's even early for work!

Edith can't help notice that she's drinking wine out of a plastic cup at Angus's Celebration of Life reception. At Ian Bell's Celebration of Life, the bartender poured and spritzed drinks into glass wine goblets and tumblers. The dean must have a serious illness if they're drinking from plastic cups again. If anyone deserves glass at his Celebration of Life, Angus does. His sister Barbara flew all the way from Adelaide to be here. The university should let her toast his memory with wine in a *glass*. And Ian Bell got shrimp skewers and salmon pinwheels! Leroy gets canned salsa and nacho chips, and dried-out, skinned carrot and celery sticks. People sip their wine and crunch their sad carrots as they pick over the tables and tables of books transferred from the bookshelves in Angus's office.

Help Yourself, trumpets a sign above the books.

The dean slowly inches his walker to the podium. He stops behind the podium and introduces the eulogists one by one. Edith sobs loudly, dramatically, during the speeches, when Barbara mentions that Angus hated Anzac biscuits until he moved to Canada. Edith's Kleenex dampens all the way through, so soggy after the third speech she has to blow her nose into a handful of napkins. It's both Angus and Coral she's crying for; Angus and Coral knew all along the evil of this place and they were punished. Because they tried to do their real jobs as *teachers* and teach Edith.

Crawley Hall swallowed them up. They taught her enough that Crawley Hall would not destroy *her*.

December 20, Edith dismisses her very last students for the semester. All that's left is grading more final exams and late end-of-term papers. The other professors, the sessional instructors, have camped out at home for the holidays, their offices and the washrooms deserted. Edith drives to the university every day anyway. Word has it the dean has camped out in the hospital until at least January because of a mysterious, debilitating respiratory condition.

This afternoon, Edith drops a pen to the floor in Leonardo's office and it rolls and rolls until it collides into his filing cabinet. She's dropped pens before, thrown pens, thousands of pens, and they haven't rolled like this before. She drops the same pen in the mailroom and has to fish it out from where it's rolled under the photocopy machine. She sets the pen on the floor in the staircase and has to chase it as it rolls and bounds down the steps.

Crawley Hall's grown a tilt.

She throws the pen into her desk drawer. Stares out Leonardo's office window. She raises her arms above her head, stretches, her joints popping, her head throbbing. She would like a drink. Of rum. She misses Angus.

She stands outside his office door, the occasional graduate student walking in and out as they rifle through his bookshelves, the books left behind from the Celebration of Life. Edith pulls out a seventh-edition copy of his edited anthology from one of the shelves. She begins reading the introduction: *This volume is above all a companion to poetry, a form as old as humankind* ... Her eyes start to tear up and distort the words. She shuts the book. Runs her hands over the curling cover. A reproduction of a crack in a wall and a flower growing out of the crack.

She tugs opens his filing cabinet and absconds with a three-quarters-full bottle of Bundaberg.

Angus spoke of a crack in the men's basement washroom. She will find that crack. She buys a scone in the basement cafeteria for fortification and travels the basement floor plan until she hits one of the men's washrooms.

She opens the door. A normal washroom except for a startled art student in paint-splattered clothes at the urinal exclaiming, W*huzzawhit!* while trying to keep his back to her and his whizzing penis out of her sight. Wrong washroom. All the urinals hanging in an orderly row on the wall.

She travels backwards through the labyrinth, dabbing her lips with a napkin to blot away icing. She pops the last of the scone into her mouth, brushes her hands off on her skirt. She circles past the cafeteria again, now closed. Walks down shallow steps, up more shallow steps. A door. Her hand suspended just before the handle. She pushes, and the door gives way. She grits her teeth.

– Angus! she calls down the hallway lined with study carrels. – I'm not scared! Please show yourself! I need to talk to you!

She steps down the hallway, the chairs tucked neatly into their carrels. The whisper of a smell she's smelled before. Dead mouse. Compost.

There's a men's washroom on her right with an Out of Order sign taped to the door. She pushes in. Doors on two of the cubicles wilt off their hinges. A cracked urinal lies on its side on the floor, a yellow CAUTION ribbon strung around it, tiles on the floor fractured. A crack originating from the outline of where the urinal used to hang on the wall. She steps over the yellow tape, touches the crack's beginning with her finger. Her finger following the crack, she steps out of the men's toilet into the corridor, tentatively following the crack around the corner as the hallway bends right again.

She stops. – Angus! she calls.

She pushes forward, tracing the crack, tripping her finger over rows of student lockers in dark hallways she's never seen. Like Crawley Hall's hallways have sprouted new thumbs, extra knees. A bulletin board peeling with audition notices means she's near the Drama rehearsal spaces, the Philosophy, the Linguistics offices, now Music, now Dance. So this is where they moved these departments. The crack widens, she can poke her fingertip in, and she steps past Greek and Roman Studies, Religion, Comparative Literature, Finnish Studies, Slavic Languages. She turns a corner. Another hallway filled with three-legged or backless chairs piled on top of one another, wooden boxes, the crack as wide as three fingers in some parts. In a section where a chunk of wall has fallen out, someone has stood up a troll doll with fiery plasticized hair. A section of crack so wide she could stick her head in if she wanted. Not even a crack anymore so much as a fissure. Another section so wide it's become a ledge. Her eyelid clicks.

A flash of white bounds somewhere inside the crack. She peers into the dark, grasps the ledge with her fingers. She touches on the flashlight on her phone. Shines it inside the fissure.

Nothing. Just crumbling, oddly bulbous rock. Just like the outcropping that grew on the outside of the building. She turns off her flashlight. Peers again into the fissure. Not white, but light. A sliver of sunlight. She must be looking into the sinkhole.

She picks a bit of scone out from between her molars with her tongue.

Her phone chirps. The traitor Bev. Edith sauntered into the Kaffee Klatsch last night, ready to become a fiancée, and who ruined her night? Associate Dean Marian Carson. Drinking a glass of red wine and reading a book at *Edith's* favourite table, the one where she would sometimes sit and grade papers or prep for classes while Bev whipped up her lattes and steamed her flat whites. Edith backtracked and hovered in the doorway. Bev looked up from a metal pitcher of steaming milk and mouthed something unintelligible, but Edith didn't care. She dashed away from the coffee shop and tried to run up the thirty-six floors to her condo, hoping her rage would propel her up the stairs. At the sixth floor she caved in and took the elevator up the remaining floors, glaring at the bald stupidity in the infinity of reflected Edith faces.

Edith stands on her toes so she can see further into the fissure.

To her right, a brown hare squeezes out from the fissure, drops to the floor, hops to the staircase door.

The hare butts the door open with its head, hops into the stairwell. Edith hesitates at the doorway, then follows, her heels clicking.

The brown hare steadily lopes down the stairs, the white on the back of its ears, the brilliant white on its upright tail and rump as its long bony ankles angle up, then descend away from her. She slowly follows the hare downstairs.

Edith thought she was already in the basement. Crawley Hall has more basement? She passes a door marked Sub-Basement. Tries the doorknob, but it's locked. She continues clicking down more steps. The fluorescent lights in the ceiling suddenly stop, which she's sure is against some kind of building code. She taps on the light in her phone. She trips more than once on the stairs' chipped and crumbling edges. The hare's white rump glowing. It halts, looks over its shoulder at her briefly, its eye flaring red in the phone's spotlight, hops downward again.

More eyes glow red in the dark. Lining the walls at the level of her knees, rows and rows of shining jackrabbit eyes survey her as she descends the staircase. Murky darkness beyond the spotlight shining from her phone, the fluorescent lights in the upper floors of the stairwell only a dull, distant smoulder. She descends, step after step.

Murmuring. From down below. She pauses.

– Hello? Edith calls.

The murmuring ceases. She hopes it might be Coral. Dreads it might be Coral.

– *I'm here*, a voice says, right next to her ear.

She falls backwards up the stairs, stumbling, but afraid to turn her back to the pit.

She continues backing up, her breathing jagged, suddenly dripping so much sweat her phone slips a little in her hand, an infernal heat blossoming inside her and setting her limbs on fire. She does not recognize the voice. The hares motionless, shining-eyed puppets awaiting animation.

– *Don't walk away*, gasps the voice. – *I need to talk to you*.

Edith turns, leaping two stairs at a time, slipping and stumbling, clicking and clacking in her idiotic shoes, sweat splashing from her forehead, her chin, drizzling down her arms.

– *What did you* think *you'd find?*

She clambers the stairs three at a time, drops on all fours, phone shoved into her sweat-soaked underpants as she uses her hands, her feet, and gallops up the stairs to the first open door she can find, bursts out of the stairwell. Out.

From: 'Lisa Ives' <lives@uofi.edu.ca>
Subject: Interim Deans
Date: Sat., Dec. 21, 12:09 pm
To: allstaff@postal.uofi.edu.ca

Sent on behalf of Dean Phillip Vermeulen:

Dear Faculty and Staff,

This is to inform you that Dean Vermeulen has decided to step down from his role as Dean of Liberal Arts in order to dedicate his time and energy to his health and wellness. In his place, Associate Dean Carson will serve as interim dean for the next three months. She will then go on to take the well-deserved research leave owed her.

Because of her extensive experience with university upper administration, Dr. Lesley Hughes has agreed to take over as dean after Dr. Carson completes her interim deanship until a search for a permanent dean can take place – most likely in two years. Dr. Hughes will resume her duties as the Leung Endowed Chair when a permanent dean has been installed. Thank you to both Marian Carson and Lesley Hughes for volunteering their administrative experience in this tumultuous time, and Mona Leung and the Leung Foundation for their patience and understanding.

May you all have pleasant and productive holidays.
Lisa Ives
Dean's Office Administrator
lives@uofi.edu.ca

Since the news of the dean's stepping down two days ago, she has slept in her office on the yoga mat because she can't go home. She can't leave Coral and Angus alone and at the mercy of the voice. She can steel herself against the voice, she just needs time. She's swam both mornings in the U of I pool, eaten a scone from the basement cafeteria for breakfast, then other meals she buys and eats at the food court. She tries not to marinate in her fury at Bev and Marian. She takes a few sips of Bundaberg as a nightcap, and a couple of sips first thing in the morning to help her wake up, to dull the anger, the fear. She could do this forever while she waits for Angus and Coral to appear. She patrols the hallways, peeks her head into empty classrooms, open office doors, tries to find the haunted hallway with the disappearing stairs, even if it's just to look at it, but that hallway continues to hide itself. She will try to answer the voice next time, try to extract answers from the voice. She doesn't have to go all the way down to find the voice. The campus will close down soon for the holidays. And the food court and the little basement cafeteria in Crawley Hall will close soon too. She needs to find Angus and Coral. She hunts in the Jungle. She photocopies hundreds of pages, looking for traces of him along the edges, but nothing. Alice Q. tells her to turn out the lights and lock the photocopy room door behind her when she leaves.

– Have a good holiday, says Alice Q., slinging her bag over her shoulder. The nicest thing she's ever said to Edith.

Wing Lau tells her about how, in order to relax, some people do things outside of work. Like watch Netflix, or plays, or wrestling matches.

– *Some* people do these things, he says. – Doesn't have to be anyone in particular. I don't necessarily mean *you*.

She will not travel down to the voice's home, the basement-below-the-basement staircase, but she plods up and down the stairs higher up, first in one staircase, then in other wings of Crawley Hall, trying doors, entering lobbies, bumping into people who look at her curiously, smile nervously. She does not smile back. She calls for Coral and Angus. She shouts out, – Silly rabbits! Tricks are for kids!

Just for kicks, just as a whistle in the dark.

Sunday, December 23, her last day. Her last chance before the holidays. She tries the regular north staircase and climbs down the stairs to the very bottom. Another door with Sub-Basement written on it. Locked. She climbs back up the stairs onto the main floor, travels across and through Crawley Hall's main floor to the south staircase. She plods down the steps. Meets another Sub-Basement door. She tries the doorknob, the last door on the last level, where fluorescent lights still flicker; the stairs are still normal, the steps still sharp and well-maintained. The door bounces open. Success. She opens the door into the sterile fluorescent light of an unknown room, her chest tight with anxiety, anticipation. Grey concrete floors and walls, silver pipes mazing the ceilings. Rows of parked cleaning trolleys line the walls, overflowing with full bags. She doesn't understand why they aren't dumping the bags in the garbage rather than letting them fester here – surely this is some kind of health hazard. The trolleys and their bags are oddly uniform, two bags per trolley, the top bag on every trolley slightly more bulbous than the bottom bag from what she can see. Posed more like stage props. Metal shelf after metal shelf high along the walls are stacked with hundreds of small animal hutches. Cleaners in their blue smocks sit immobile around tables, rest dummylike on benches and lean against the walls. They don't breathe; they don't blink.

A woman in a blue smock appears at her elbow. – You're on the wrong floor, she says.

– I must have pushed the wrong button in the elevator.

The woman frowns.

– I'm looking for Wing Lau, lies Edith.

– You came down the stairs, not out of the elevator. Wing Lau is in a different department.

– I was looking for my friends. An old man with a beard and a hat? A skinny red-haired woman?

– No people like that down here.

– No, said Edith. – But maybe you've seen them?

– Of course not. The woman cocks her head to the right. – Elevator's over *there*, she says.

– I don't ride elevators. I'm afraid of elevators, says Edith, turning to go back up the stairs.

– The elevator's over there.

The woman punches the elevator button and stands with her arms crossed, waiting for Edith. Dust and jackrabbit turds cluster along the baseboard. Clumps of jackrabbit hair.

– Over *here*, says the woman.

Edith glances one more time at the cleaners grouped around their tables, posing here and there in imitation of humans at their coffee break. A department store display of people standing still as trees.

She feels light in the head; she sways once but catches herself. She stands next to the woman, facing the elevator door, her back to the cleaners, and when the door slides open to the elevator's silvered and faux-wood interior, she lingers, then steps forward. The door clangs closed behind her. She stands with her back to the silver doors – she does not want to see her shadowy reflection in the silver doors, she does not want to see the greasy faces, the hands, caught inside the doors. The cleaners. The elevator lurches upward, and she grasps the handrails in the corner, jams her forehead into the hard corner. The elevator whines as it rises. Her eyes widen, her blood falls to her feet.

A bang on the ceiling as the elevator moves, another bang. The banging of fists, hail banging beneath her feet.

– *I* said, *what did you think you'd find*, whispers the voice down from the shaft above.

Edith vomits, her abdomen squeezing and expelling her fear.

She is so embarrassed, hunched in the corner, her back to the door, crouched over her own steaming mess, her own bald terror.

The tiny room jerks to a stop. The doors slide open behind her. She falls onto her bum, onto her own vomit, rights herself, skitters backwards like a crab out the elevator door, the vomit steaming and drooling in the corner of the elevator. She's accidentally kicked off one of her Hangaku shoes. The door closes. She collapses onto her back, spread-eagled, the cool of the peeled floor beneath her, layered with asbestos tiles, her fingers dabbling in grit, the dusty leaves of an ancient and twisted philodendron poised over her right shoulder.

She hobbles a little way, then takes off the other shoe and walks in her stockinged feet.

She's landed on the fourth floor, and no one's home. She slides across the floor as she tries to reach her office. The floor feels like it's on such a tilt that she has to brace herself against the wall to stay properly upright. She should have left with everyone else days ago, squirrelled herself away in her perfect little house in her perfect little tower, away from this diseased concrete block. She was so stupid. Everyone else always knows what to do; she's never known what she's supposed to do.

She will retrieve her purse and her car keys and escape home.

She slides her key into the lock. The office door falls open and bangs against the wall. Freezing fresh air gushes from her office. The furniture has slid to the windowed side of the room, and one of the bookshelves has obviously crashed through the window. It leans out the window frame. The window frame gapes, an open, jagged square. A sharp wind hits her where she stands, still in the doorway. She turtles toward the window, clutches the window frame, and looks down three floors into the sinkhole.

Hundreds of white jackrabbits. Thousands. Nibbling grass, dozing, boxing, their white blob selves peppering the sinkhole, climbing in and out of the hole, meandering the quad, nibbling in the brown, dead grass, snow-dotted expanse.

Edith draws back from the window, the shock of fresh, brittle air pulling out a stuttering cough from her chest.

Her phone tings. A U of I Emergency Bulletin:

Irreparable structural damage has forced a complete evacuation of Crawley Hall. Students and staff will be notified of new classroom locations by January 2nd of the New Year.

Edith wipes her mouth with her fingers. She fishes out her purse, her coat, her laptop under the mess of desks, books, chairs. She throws her purse strap over her shoulder. No classes will be held in this building anymore. A new year in January. A different building. She will start again. Start properly this time. Coral and Angus never really existed. She never had friends. She will write a book with only *her* name on it. When she gets out of here.

She's not sure how to escape Crawley Hall. She doesn't want to hear the voice in its elevator shaft, in its staircase, ever again, its entitled rage. She bursts into tears. She can't leave.

She palms away her tears.

She's supposed to be at her parents' house in Red Deer for Christmas Eve dinner tomorrow. They will be devastated if she's not there, their only daughter. Sometime during the holidays she will begin writing a new book and begin preparing for the courses she'll be teaching in the new January semester.

Could she jump out the window? Crawl down the side of the building? The ledges are too narrow, too 1960s Brutalist modernist mash-up. She clenches her jaw. Licks her lips.

A handful of dust showers her head.

She pulls away a dust chunk lodged in her eyelash. Not dust.

A moist white worm.

She dashes for the door, throws it open. Masses of brown jackrabbits, frozen alert and tall, their eyes focused on her like headlights.

She leaps out, not looking back at the *whump* of ceiling that collapses into Leonardo's office.

She sprints in her stocking feet down the hallway, right then left, then left again, slipping, the hares parting in front of her, leaping, jumping, twisting away, until she reaches the stairway door. The door lolling open the wrong way, like a slackened mouth.

She plunges through the doorway and leaps down the stairs, no sound but her own terrified breaths, then a gradual crumbling, clattering, chattering she refuses to hear, she won't, Crawley Hall murmuring and shouting at her as she runs down flight after flight of stairs, her feet used to the edges, the worn depressions now, her hand on the bannister sure. Maybe Crawley Hall's tongue is chasing her down the stairs, maybe not. Maybe Coral and Angus, consumed by Crawley Hall, are chasing her too, but it doesn't matter. She plunges down the last flight of steps, yanks open the door into the main lobby, skids to the doors in the building's main entrance. She pulls at a door handle – she will escape.

The door sticks.

She pulls and tugs, the door stuck. She runs along the line of doors, every one locked or jammed closed, every one savage and unbelievable; she grunts and strains as she pulls. She punches on the doors with her fists. She screams. She bangs her forehead against a wire-meshed window. She just wants to be on the other side in the snow, in the gravel, in the real air. In a shopping mall. Only an inch of Crawley Hall glass, only a few inches of wood, of metal, trap her.

She thumbs the Campus Security number on her phone.

– I'm Dr. Edith Vane, she says, her voice shaking. – I'm trapped inside Crawley Hall.

– Dr. Vane, says the voice, – you must vacate the building immediately.

– The doors won't open, she says. – Please come let me out.

The voice says nothing.

– Hello? she asks.

The phone struck dumb. She looks at it, the sweat and grease from her face clouding the phone's glass.

Somewhere off in a hallway behind her, an elevator door dings.

She doesn't want to know who's getting off that elevator.

She dashes through the hallways, chases each glowing red EXIT sign to another door, but every door stands adamant, soldiers winning this war.

On the other side of every door handle, her car waits for her, her condo waits for her, her books wait for her.

She slides to a stop on the blistering, disintegrating floor tiles in front of the Jungle. Crawley Hall's lurch has broken the glass door to the Jungle – the door frame sags at a distinct, crushing angle, the broken, spidered glass still grasping at the frame. The door dangles from a single hinge.

Behind her a metal duct crashes, and she flings herself past the door and into the Jungle. The door violently squeaks as she lunges past it but does not fall. The air in here, still moist, oddly sweet, clings to her skin. The walls stand intact. The room an undisturbed bubble in the chaos.

She will wait here for Campus Security to rescue her.

Coral. She will save Coral too.

Water burbles in the concrete fountain.

– Coral! Edith shouts.

She stumbles down the stone steps, screeches a table out of her way with her foot, wrenches apart ferns as she hunts, throws herself into spiky bushes.

– Coral? Angus!

She finds a subtle hollow in the ground among the bushes. She has found Coral's form. She can tell the indent is Coral's form because when she bends down and places her palm in the middle of the form, the earth warms her hand. Fine hair, jackrabbit hair, clings to her fingers.

In the walls around the Jungle, the building grinds its teeth.

She squats, then rests her buttocks in the warm indent. The building makes churning sounds around her, a belly growling with indigestion. Protected by the tree canopy, she will wait here for a glimpse of Coral, she will wait here for her rescue, and she's sure a fruit-bearing plant or bush must grow somewhere in here in case she gets hungry. Her water source nearby still trickles and splashes, unaffected, and there's always the coffee machine.

Soon Security will crash through the broken door, and she'll be home in her condo before she knows it, eating leftover pizza, riffling through library books, photocopied articles, Beulah Crump-Withers's journal as she prepares for next semester.

– I'm here! she shouts, just in case.

She settles into the soil, her left ear suddenly itchy. Perhaps a twig fragment or crumb of dirt.

She scratches her ear with her hind leg.

Waits.

Suzette Mayr is the author of four previous novels: *Monoceros*, *Moon Honey*, *The Widows*, and *Venous Hum*. *The Widows* was shortlisted for the Commonwealth Writers' Prize for Best Book in the Canada-Caribbean region, and has been translated into German. *Moon Honey* was shortlisted for the Writers' Guild of Alberta's Best First Book and Best Novel Awards. *Monoceros* was longlisted for the Giller Prize. Suzette Mayr lives and works in Calgary.

Acknowledgements

Thank you to the many people who helped me write this book: Nicole Markotić, demented genius front-line editor, who so often saved me from myself; Rosemary Nixon for her gentle and persistent brutality; and Anne Brewster, Robyn Read, and Nancy Jo Cullen for always telling it like it is. Thank you to Coach House's Alana Wilcox, one of the most generous and perceptive editors I've ever been lucky enough to work with, who repeatedly pushed me off cliffs and down multitudes of rabbit holes so that I could make this book better. Thank you to everyone else at Coach House too for helping to bring this book into being. Thank you for the essential miscellaneous: Debra Dudek, Friedrich Mayr, Jonathan Ball, Catherine Fargher, Sue Murray, Oscar, Coco, Pat Sheil, Michael Sutjiadi, Jonny Flieger, Graham Livesey, Angie Abdou, Val Warner, Jocelyn Grosse, the rest of the Mayr-Beaver-Gromer family, Tom Wayman, Janice Williamson, Robert Majzels, and the students in Robert Budde's University of Northern British Columbia 2016 Creative Writing ENGL271 class. Lastly, thank you to Tonya Callaghan for her unwavering encouragement, love, and willingness to put up with stacks of paper *everywhere*.

References to dinner with Prince Charles and the Duchess of Cornwall (and the dropping of their names) derive from the article 'This Is What Happens at Dinner with Prince Charles & Camilla' by Mia Freedman (MamaMia online, November 18, 2012).

I would also like to acknowledge the support of UNSW Australia, and a Social Sciences and Humanities Research Council Insight Grant for aiding in the research and writing of this novel.

Typeset in Baskerville Pro.

Printed at the Coach House on bpNichol Lane in Toronto, Ontario, on Zephyr Antique Laid paper, which was manufactured, acid-free, in Saint-Jérôme, Quebec, from second-growth forests. This book was printed with vegetable-based ink on a 1973 Heidelberg KORD offset litho press. Its pages were folded on a Baumfolder, gathered by hand, bound on a Sulby Auto-Minabinda and trimmed on a Polar single-knife cutter.

Edited and designed by Alana Wilcox
Cover design by Ingrid Paulson

Coach House Books
80 bpNichol Lane
Toronto ON M5S 3J4
Canada

416 979 2217
800 367 6360

mail@chbooks.com
www.chbooks.com